PRAISE FOR

SECRETS OF SOUTHERN GIRLS

"A twisting, sensuous novel about first love and innocence lost. As mesmerizing as the Mississippi heat, Haley Harrigan's debut weaves two tales together in time as Julie Portland seeks the truth about her childhood friend's mysterious death—a truth Julie has hidden even from herself. Harrigan delves into Greg Iles territory, navigating racial tensions and the secret (and not-so-secret) history of the Deep South. In the end, like the 'oil streak' river that flows through this story, *Secrets of Southern Girls* reveals a stain we all would be better off examining."

—Jenny Milchman, *USA Today* bestselling author of *Cover of Snow*, *Ruin Falls*, and *As Night Falls*

"Haley Harrigan's *Secrets of Southern Girls* is filled with evocative, poetic imagery, relatable characters, and ingenious plot twists that kept me turning pages long into the night! A beautiful, engaging debut by a delightful and talented new author."

—Susan Crawford, author of *The Pocket Wife* and *The Other Widow*

"Heartachingly beautiful, *Secrets of Southern Girls* is a compelling tale about lost love and childhood regrets. This is masterfully written, shifting from past to present as the story unfolds to expose the haunting truth of one girl's desire to be loved and the dangerous secret she possesses. Harrigan's debut is a captivating read that won't let you go until the very last page."

—Kerry Lonsdale, *Wall Street Journal* bestselling author

"Haley Harrigan takes us on a searing emotional journey to a tragic past in sensual and evocative prose. Holds you to the last word."

—Carol Goodman, author of *The Widow's House*

SECRETS OF
SOUTHERN GIRLS

SECRETS

of

SOUTHERN

GIRLS

A NOVEL

HALEY HARRIGAN

Published by Sourcebooks Landmark, an imprint of Sourcebooks, Inc.
P.O. Box 4410, Naperville, Illinois 60567-4410
(630) 961-3900
Fax: (630) 961-2168
www.sourcebooks.com

Library of Congress Cataloging-in-Publication Data

Names: Harrigan, Haley, 1983- author.
Title: Secrets of southern girls / Haley Harrigan.
Description: Naperville, Illinois : Sourcebooks Landmark, 2017.
Identifiers: LCCN 2016053905 | (pbk. : alk. paper)
Subjects: LCSH: Murder--Investigation--Fiction. | Friends--Fiction. | GSAFD:
   Mystery fiction.
Classification: LCC PS3608.A78145 S43 2017 | DDC 813/.6--dc23 LC record available at https://lccn.loc.gov/2016053905

Printed and bound in the United States of America.
VP 10 9 8 7 6 5 4 3

For my mother, Renee Sterling: best friend, gossip queen, and wine buddy. You are my favorite Southern girl.

PROLOGUE

She only has lovers in wintertime.

In summer, the days stretch long like lazy animals, and the sun's rays reach like warm fingers down between buildings and slide across her face and arms. It's harder, then, to think of dark things. But winter in New York is suffocating, and it is all she can do to breathe, to take in the icy air through her nose and mouth, to taste the cold on her tongue as it slips in and leaves her insides frostbitten and numb. It is all she can do to survive. Even Beck must feel it, or something similar, because those little smiles stretch smaller and fade faster.

Maybe it is the skin in summertime. She can see it, everywhere, when warm weather finally, mercifully, arrives. The skirts swishing and swaying around bare legs like a tribe of dancers, the bright exposed toes peeking jubilant from stylish sandals. Walking to the subway, how easy it might be to brush a hand, light as a kiss, against the arm of another. A common electric accident when so much skin is on parade.

That can't happen in the cold. Bundled tightly in her scarf and parka, she is alone, insulated. In wintertime, she doesn't linger in the streets, doesn't stop to look in windows, rarely tastes the lacy snowflakes that fall feathery against her dry lips. She scurries along to her destination, a sheet of loose-leaf paper propelled forward by the wind.

Or maybe it's the city itself in winter, the way the buildings take on new shapes, imposing and dangerous as dark strangers, the structures climbing upward and leaning down at the same time, peering at her through glass windows like a thousand scrutinizing eyes.

When cold weather ends, she pretends those nights never happened. Those lovers and their bodies and the touch of their hands and the time she spent with them all fade away like bad dreams. The sharp edges blur in her mind as *last night* becomes *last week* and *last month*. When she sees those men afterward, her cheeks tingle with embarrassment, and she makes up excuses when they try to see her again. She knows Brighton sometimes sees the early flirtation, the exchanging of names and numbers; still, she doesn't talk about it with anyone. It's her own secret need, her own secret weakness.

She is careful in the ways that count. It isn't a game, although she has been with men who believe otherwise, men who think she's playing hard to get. Some send flowers; some call the next day just to say hello, as though a simple word can bridge the distance between them. One man spent every night for a month in her bed (January, or she wouldn't have allowed it), until she finally stopped returning his calls, stopped letting him in. He'd thought she was simply a challenge. Conquerable.

The men aren't strangers. She meets them in acting classes, at the yoga studio, through friends of friends. Most of the time, they come to her home, the tiny Grove Street apartment that she and Beck share. She lets them in late, long after she has tucked her daughter into the cushiony pink softness of her comforter, although some nights Beck is with her father and the room sits empty. She makes the men tiptoe past the closed door of Beck's bedroom and leave before sunrise. But Beck has never been the kind of child to come searching for her in the night.

She pours wine. She lights candles in her dark room. Sometimes, she and her guest talk quietly for hours. On those nights, she fills and refills her wineglass until she can talk freely but remember little. She tells lie after lie when he asks her questions. Better, so much better, when things don't get too personal.

Sometimes, there is no talking at all. Those nights are easier. On those nights, she drinks very little. She doesn't need any help taking the comfort her body craves.

The men aren't all the same, but they might as well be. When the season has passed, she can hardly distinguish one experience from another. She makes it a point not to. Certain things she shouldn't have: the soft pleasure of a dinner by candlelight, long phone conversations, fingers intertwined with her own. If there was music, she can't recall the songs.

But while it's happening, he—whomever *he* happens to be—puts his hands on her and becomes *more* than just a man she's brought home. He becomes a part of her, and for those moments, she loves him. For those moments, she can pretend that she isn't alone in that way.

On those nights, she falls asleep with arms wrapped tightly around her, skin pressed against naked skin, the tiniest beads of sweat on her inner thighs. She doesn't dream about a field or a bridge or a dead girl. She doesn't dream at all. She always moves away from him in her sleep, before the sun comes up. And then he is gone and candle wax has formed hard, dark rivers on her nightstand.

It's her own twisted survival tactic, and it is enough.

1

"BUT...I DIDN'T DO IT. I DIDN'T KILL HER," JULIE WHISPERS. "She was my friend. I loved her. Please...please believe me."

Usually, she *wants* to be pulled into the charade, the dazzling drama of the stage. She was born for it, made to tell stories that aren't her own. It's all she's ever needed, isn't it—this spotlight, a bit of recognition? But this ridiculous scene about friendship and betrayal... She wants no part of *this*. It's almost over, though, and there is no way out of it anyway, short of admitting in front of the entire class that this silly soap-opera-style plot (written by the youngest person in the group) has affected her in such a visceral way.

So, she plasters an expression of false innocence on her face and tries to focus on the man in front of her. She doesn't know him, can't even think of his first name. In the scene, he is her lover, but in reality, he can't hold her attention. He is taller than she is and she has to look up to see his face, but she keeps looking over his shoulder instead, her eyes shifting up to the ceiling, where exposed pipes slither, snakelike, across the metal ceiling of the converted warehouse. It's always so cold in here, while those pipes hang idle, strange adornments.

Classical music plays softly in the background, but it seems very far away. Julie's body resists everything about playing this role, so she has to force her behavior: the fast, frantic rhythm of her breathing, hands wringing together in a nervous dance. She is supposed to be nervous, because her character is, after all, guilty.

She tries, fails, to keep the images from springing to her mind: a forest at night, fireflies blinking in the dark, a young girl with golden hair and a big secret. And then it isn't so difficult to connect with the role. She looks at the man in front of her with what she knows are pleading eyes. He isn't as good an actor as she is, but the disdain in his expression feels real enough.

"Love?" he says softly. "Your love is like poison. Your love is death." She gasps, and he turns away from her and stalks off the stage while she sinks to the floor in pretend sorrow.

"And…that's our scene."

Julie rises to her feet and faces the small crowd with a tight smile, a mock curtsy. She sits down and tries to shake off this ominous feeling. It should be over now, but she has let herself fall too far into character, and all she can think about is Reba, her soft laugh, her thoughtful eyes. Julie has always believed what her drama teachers told her, that the best acting comes from forging a connection between her own memories and the role she plays. But sometimes the memories are too vivid—like photographs flashing through her mind—and in the end it isn't worth it, not even for authenticity. She wipes the heel of her palm across one eye and then the other, trying not to smear mascara. She isn't fragile this way.

"Nice job, Julie," says Lila, the instructor. "You too, Jonathan."

"Thank you," Julie murmurs.

Jonathan—that's his name—nods and takes his seat near the back of the room.

"Now, who wrote this scene?" Lila asks as if it isn't obvious, as if everyone doesn't know it was the kid. The overly dramatic tone of the scene and the clichéd dialogue mark it as his as surely as if he'd spilled his own blood onto the pages they all hold in their hands. Still, Lila looks around the room with interest (real, or maybe pretend; she *is* an actress, after all) as she leans against the stage.

The boy, all of eighteen years old, raises his hand tentatively. He is perched on the edge of his folding chair and looks as though he might topple out of it and onto the concrete floor. His hands clench his knees, and his slender face, pockmarked with acne, is flushed with excitement. Or nerves. He rights himself in the seat just in time and settles into an uneasy position.

Julie crosses her arms to warm herself. She's shivering now, and she doesn't know if it's the chill in the room or something else entirely.

"Okay, Robert," Lila says, waving her hand toward the kid. "Tell me what your scene was about."

As he stammers on about the meaning of his scene, Lila reaches into the purse she'd tossed on the edge of the stage at the start of class and pulls out a silvery metal lighter and a pack of cigarettes. She produces one powder-white stick, presses it to her lips, and lights the end, a hot little fire in the chilly room.

Smoking is all but outlawed in New York City, but here she is, lighting up inside the warehouse. Julie leans forward, as though the tiny flame might warm her, might help her to forget. Lila sips from the cigarette, an elegant movement that makes Julie wish for an instant that she were a smoker. She thinks of her cousin, Toby, of the crude way he would suck on the ends of his Camels, cheeks sinking in and puffing out like a fish. Revolting.

Julie wants to listen but can't concentrate. The writing doesn't matter to her anyway. Her job, the only thing she's interested in, is becoming someone else, whatever character is provided for her.

Screenwriters and performers alike attend this workshop. The writers create the scenes, and the actors take them, learn them, and perform them in front of the class for critique and discussion of the scenes themselves and the actors who bring them to life. The mixing together of it all creates near-constant chaos. But from that frenetic energy (according to Lila, at least) comes great inspiration. *Everything is connected*, Lila told them on the first day of the workshop. *You'll see what I mean.*

"Ultimately," a man says from the back, "I think the writing was lackluster. Sorry, dude. But the acting… Julie, is it?"

She sits up taller and looks behind her to where the man is sitting.

He speaks to Lila and then Julie, looking back and forth between them. "The acting was so good that it almost made the whole thing believable. Julie, your guilt was so *real*. You really looked as though you had killed your best friend. I mean, were those tears in your eyes? It was good, really good."

Julie smiles a weak thank-you, nods, and turns back to the front as though his words only affect her in a professional sense.

Lila pulls her iPod from its dock and the classical music stops, the signal that class has reached its end. Julie grabs her bulky tote bag and rushes to the restroom, shutting the door and locking it before she lets her head sink into her hands, breathing in and out deeply and evenly, the way she tells her yoga students to do. She dabs at her eyes with toilet paper and checks her face. She *looks* calmer, at least. She rinses her hands with ice-cold water and faces herself in the mirror.

It's not your fault she's dead. It's the same thing Julie has told herself, over and over, for ten years.

But it's a lie, and she knows it.

2

JULIE IS RUNNING LATE, AGAIN, AND HER TOUR GUIDE UNIFORM IS a wrinkled mess. The so-tacky-it's-almost-cool-again I Heart NY tee (for sale at every street stall in the city), the red thermal she wears underneath, and her dark skinny jeans are in a tangled pile on the floor from the last time she wore them. Julie shakes each garment out and pulls it on anyway. She looks in the mirror and ruffles her hands through her hair to make the shortish strands stick out at odd angles. *Cheesy chic*, she thinks, frowning at her reflection. Her tour groups like her style, at least. They find her believable, authentic, a native New Yorker. No one would believe she's a country girl from backwoods Lawrence Mill, Mississippi. Most of the time, she doesn't believe it herself.

She's run out of deodorant without realizing it, and the oval-shaped plastic tray scrapes against her underarm. *Click, click,* useless. Why didn't she stop at the market on her way home last night? She bends down, rocking on her heels as she rummages through the cramped cabinet beneath the sink in the bathroom that she shares with Beck. Finally, she finds an acceptable substitute and reaches past the towels to the white container in the back. She squeezes the baby powder into her hands with a cloudy, white *poof!* before patting it gingerly under her arms, trying her best to keep the powder from making snowy prints on her jeans. The scent of baby powder always makes her think of Beck as a baby, evoking the familiar, frightening newborn smell of her daughter at her youngest.

Beck is awake already, of course, and Julie finds her in the closet, pulling out her school uniform. Beck is better at mornings than Julie. At five years old, Beck is already better at most things. Her skirt is green and black, with a white button-down shirt and a winter jacket, a deep-green fleecy thing with her school's golden crest on the right pocket. It reminds Julie of the Girl Scout jackets she and Reba wore when they were young.

"Morning, Mom," Beck chirps, bright-eyed.

"Good morning, Rebecca," Julie responds, as she helps Beck into her jacket. Beck rolls her eyes, always does when Julie uses her "grown-up" name. Julie runs the purple-handled brush through Beck's soft, white-blond hair until it lies long like a shiny sheer curtain. "Ouch!" Beck cries each time Julie hits a snag.

Beck's shoes are missing. After ten minutes of searching, Julie finds them, the black patent little-girl delicacies sitting neatly on top of the microwave, as if it is the most natural thing in the world. As though they belong there and not on the carpeted floor of Beck's closet, poised for the invasion of little feet. "Why were my shoes on the microwave? We're going to be late."

"Sorry," Julie says, distracted. "Sorry, let's go." But she's forgotten her purse, and as soon as the door is locked, she has to unlock it all over again. Her phone buzzes in her pocket, but she ignores it for now.

They scurry downstairs and across the street into Brew, the little old-fashioned bell on the door announcing their entrance. It always makes her think of Nell's Flower Shop, where she worked as a teenager. How many businesses still use bells like these?

Beck drinks hot cocoa with a sprinkle of cinnamon on top. She places her order with the woman behind the counter and Julie places hers, adding a banana-nut muffin for Beck. When they first moved into the Grove Street apartment, Julie thought that Brew was a bar, given the name. She had been embarrassingly disappointed to find out that it was a coffee shop, although it comes in handy on mornings like these.

Walking out of the shop, Julie sees their reflections in the window, warped like faces in a stream. Beck is so small beside Julie, but her light hair glistens. Her father's hair. Julie is hardly visible.

Beck attends private kindergarten in the Village, not far from their apartment. Evan, Beck's father, pays for it; Julie would never be able to afford it on her own. It's a fancy school with entitled children and smug mothers who look at Julie strangely when she kisses Beck good-bye in the mornings. She knows they judge her, her age, her clothes: the cheap T-shirts on tour bus days, her skimpy athletic gear on yoga mornings.

Not surprisingly, though, on the rare occasions when Evan can be bothered to attend a PTA meeting or open house, these same women line up to shake his hand, to swoon over him and confess, pink-faced and smiling, how much they love his performance in whatever play or musical he is starring in at the time. When Julie attends meetings without him, which happens more often, the parents and teachers overlook her, as if she is Beck's older sister or her babysitter instead of her mother.

It doesn't matter. If not for the impact it would have on Beck, Julie would go out of her way to show these mothers how little she cares about winning their approval. She would wear the dark-red lipstick that makes her lips look even fuller than they already are, show some cleavage in a low-cut tank, maybe flirt with their husbands just for fun. Ten years ago, she wouldn't have thought twice about doing something so bold, would have flaunted her youth and her looks and *dared* them to say something about it. But she isn't that girl anymore, and these days, she has Beck to think of. She can't jeopardize her daughter's opportunities to form lasting friendships with her classmates because their mothers don't approve of Julie. So she smiles and stays silent.

"Good-bye, Mom," Beck says as Julie kneels and kisses her forehead. Beck smells sweet, like a plump fruit, but Julie can't recall the fragrance of her shampoo. A few strands of hair sweep, wispy as butterfly wings, against Julie's winter-chapped lips. Beck's blue eyes are bright and deep, and she is *so pretty* in the sunlight.

Sometimes when Julie looks at her daughter, so poised and so smart, she can't help but compare Beck to herself at that age. She'd been a lost, confused, tiny little mess. Newly orphaned, an intruder in her aunt's house. She can't help but worry that something might happen, outside of her own control, and that Beck might be left alone the same way, that maybe age five is tainted for their family. But Beck would fare much better than Julie had, no matter what the circumstances.

Julie watches her until she reaches the double doors of the school. Once Beck is safely inside, Julie begins the frantic race to get to the subway. She moves as fast as she can without breaking into a full-out run, slipping between and around and in and out of the bustling crowd, hoping that her train hasn't left already. She rushes down the stairs that lead underground to the Christopher Street station, moving alongside others in suits and heels and ties and briefcases and long coats. Finally, she stops to wait for the train, which, *thank goodness*, has not yet arrived.

Now that she's still, Julie has the eerie feeling that someone is watching her, following her maybe, though God knows how they could keep up. The truth is that she always feels anxious down here, like she is somehow trapped inside an empty swimming pool. She can almost smell the residual chlorine, can sense the darkness she knows lies beyond those white tiles, the natural and terrifying heaviness of earth. Even so, she can't help but turn in an awkward circle to make sure she isn't being watched, but no one's paying a bit of attention to her. She checks her BlackBerry and sees that she has a text message from Brighton: Don't forget about the show tonight.

Julie responds quickly, just as the train pulls up. Looking forward to it! Ever since her best friend, Brighton, started dating the drummer in a local jazz band, he's been dying to take Julie to a show.

The tour bus is waiting for her when she reaches the outside of Penn Station, the bright-red double-decker filled with tourists ready for their morning sightseeing, hands wrapped tightly around digital cameras. Mid-March is chilly in New York, but there are plenty of tourists brave enough to sit out on the uncovered upper level. The bus is crowded, with children yelling and people talking. Car horns are blowing out on the street, and for those first few minutes, Julie feels uneasy again.

She has a dream, more often than she'd like, that Beck is a baby again and her sad, urgent cries echo off every wall, but Julie can't find her. She searches under pillows and tosses the comforter back, desperate. And then Julie is in a field at night, clawing at the ground, her hands dirty with black soil and covered with dewy-wet blades of grass, and the cries are her own.

The sounds of the bus, the yelling, the general exuberance of the city make her think of the dream and evoke the same sense of helplessness. But there's no time to be frightened, so she grabs hold of the metal pole up front and plants her feet firmly as the bus cranks to life and prepares to lurch away from the curb and into a sea of yellow cabs.

"Barely made it today," Marlowe, her driver, says casually, as if it is no matter to him. He smiles, steering the bus into traffic. "Rough morning?" And then he laughs, a low belly chuckle that never fails to make her smile too.

"Like always," she replies. And then she begins her tour.

"Hey, guys!" she says into the microphone. "How's everyone doing this morning? Are you ready to check out New York City?"

Clapping. A few cheers. The growl of the bus engine.

Brighton, a compulsive reader, says that a good story should unwind smoothly, like a spool of silky thread. But Julie's story, if she were to tell it, would be more like a ride on the See NYC! double-decker bus—the rocky start, screeching stops, horns blowing, people yelling. Just waiting for that crash.

She does the downtown loop: Times Square and the Village and Chinatown and Central Park. It's just another performance, and this is just another role. She often lies when fascinated tourists inquire about her life. She has invented this character's entire world. Though Julie is a private person, her tour-guide alter ego is bubbly, chatty, and outgoing. She's herself, only different. Better.

How long now since she gave up on the idea that acting would truly blossom into a career? How long since she stopped believing there would be a callback from one of dozens of auditions, that she would get the part that would change her life and there would be no more of the part-time jobs, sewn together loosely like stitches on a poorly made quilt, to make enough money to support herself? Since Beck was born, probably—since the realization that her life was no longer her own.

Still, those visions haven't dissolved *completely*. She hasn't stopped auditioning, has she? Who knows what might come along? If she would allow Evan to introduce her to the actors and directors in his inner circle, she'd probably be on Broadway already. She has too much pride for that, though, so she gets by—this year, on yoga classes and bus tours.

She actually enjoys the tours. She is always looking for oddball facts about the city. She knows all the basics: the exact size of the Statue of Liberty (151 feet tall from base to torch, 305 if you count the pedestal), the square footage of Macy's (2.2 million), the number of bridges and arches in Central Park (36). She and Beck Google New York City together when there is nothing better to do, and Beck helps decide on unusual facts for Julie to use on her tours. Beck's favorite is the one about pigs on Wall Street, how they were used until the 1920s to eat the garbage that accumulated on the sidewalks. Julie and Beck laughed at the thought of it—pigs dancing and snorting, sweeping down the street like fat, pinkish trash trucks.

On the bus, the sun is bright and the streets are busy. A teenage boy in the second row catches her attention. He has dark hair and dark skin, but those aren't the only things that make Julie think of August. It's the muscular build, and the camera on a thick strap that he wears around his neck. The resemblance is so strong that she finally has to look away.

She is thinking of him again, of the whole damned thing, despite her efforts not to.

Times Square is a glittering, electric jewel even in the daytime, but Julie advises everyone to come back at night, when the giant pulsing ads throw their vibrant colors out against the night sky. Times Square fascinates her like nowhere else in New York. It is always alive, always breathing, always defying the dark.

The lights never go out.

3

"Julie," Brighton says, smiling, as she approaches the entrance to Sax, an oversize wooden door painted with a constellation of scattered golden musical notes. He has already removed his suit jacket and slung it over one arm, already loosened his striped tie.

Brighton is the only one of Julie's college friends who, after her divorce, chose her over her ex-husband. There were others whom she'd believed to be confidantes, but they clung tightly to Evan and forgot about her when it all ended. Not that she blames them, but that makes it all the more touching that Brighton remained true to *her*. He used to be an actor, like her; they met in drama class at NYU. *The classic American cliché*, she used to call him. *Tall, dark, and handsome.* And it's true. He is taller than Julie, with dark hair and eyes and portfolio pictures so dazzling that she can't believe the man doesn't act full time. She can see him so clearly as the well-muscled playboy on some steamy soap opera. He still does commercials, occasionally, but he was a double major in college, degrees in drama and finance, and he seems to genuinely *like* the career he has chosen.

"Hey, Wall Street," she says, glancing over his shoulder when she leans in to give him a hug. There is a short line of people waiting to get into Sax, but Julie follows Brighton right up to the front. His name (plus guest) is on the list. She knows there should be some kind of thrill involved in getting this kind of special treatment, but it makes her a little uncomfortable. She meets the eyes of a man near the back of the line and smiles what she hopes is an apologetic smile. He looks away.

"Should I have worn my business suit too?" she teases Brighton.

"Ha," he says. "As if you even own one. Work late, remember? No time to change."

A bouncer sits on a high-backed metal bar stool, and he speaks to Brighton briefly before stamping their hands and waving the two of them through.

"Oh, the perks of being with the *band*," Julie says.

Sax is a long, narrow space, with the stage set near the back and a row of black leathery booths to the left and right against the exposed brick walls. Round metal tables are scattered in between, leaving a small space for dancing in front of the stage, even though Julie has never seen anyone actually dance at Sax. Mostly, people drink and talk and flirt against the sultry backdrop of live jazz music. Brighton leads her to a table in the center of the room, best for viewing and for listening. As soon as she gets comfortable, he heads to the bar for drinks.

The music is just starting, a female singer fronting the all-male band with a myriad of instruments. The girl (or woman, though she looks so youthful) has long, captivating hair, as fascinating to Julie as the lovely, haunting voice filling the room. Her voice is mesmerizing, deeper than Julie thought it would be. But her hair—it goes far beyond the natural boundaries of her small shoulders to spill around her arms and breasts and nearly reaches her hips. Reddish brown like wheat, and she is barefoot. The resemblance to Reba is powerful, but not obvious. Julie *feels* it more than she sees it. The woman is rustic and sensual, but somehow innocent.

Brighton returns, carrying two pints of Blue Moon, an orange slice snug against the rim of each glass.

"Perfect," Julie says, reaching for hers. She presses the orange between her fingers, letting the juices spill into her glass before dropping the rind in as well. "So, how was work, Wall Street?" she asks.

"Stop calling me that. Work was fine. Busy. So, what do you think of the band, and, more importantly, what do you think of my drummer?"

"They're great, he's great," Julie says, though she's barely looked at the drummer. She can't stop staring at the singer.

Reba would have liked this music, though she always craved softer melodies, songs she could sway to in the free emptiness of her bedroom. Soft sounds. Julie wonders what Reba would think of her here in a jazz club, so different now.

She is thinking of Reba again, can't seem to stop lately, like she's been thinking of August so much. But in truth, there is hardly a day that passes when she doesn't think of them.

Julie sips her beer and tries to drink away the unease that's been with her lately, this idea that someone is hiding in the shadows, just out of her line of sight. She toys with her beer glass, picks it up, sets it down, picks it up, and finally drains it. The beer doesn't help as much as she'd hoped it would. She's starting to feel closed in, stran-gled. Jesus. She's embarrassed by the urge to look around, to stare at each face until she finds the one that's here for her.

She spins around in her seat—she can't help it—but instead of faces, *hands* are what draw her attention. All of these people, all of these palms pressed to cool pint glasses, fingers wrapped around wine stems. It's been a while since she's had a lover... Maybe that's what this is all about. She imagines hands on *her*, gentle touches sweeping away the paranoia crawling along her skin.

She's oddly enchanted by all of this movement: hands gesturing in the air as a woman tells a story, a hand shaking another in greet-ing, hands nervously adjusting suit ties. One pair of hands clenched together tightly, the tension apparent and out of place in such a setting. Intriguing. Her eyes drift along to the rest of him, his elbows propped on the bar, his leather jacket well worn but obviously expen-sive. His face. It's the man from the line, the man who'd turned away from her smile.

He's staring at her. And she knows why.

She can't believe she didn't recognize him right away. Even after all these years, she should have guessed. It's too late for him to look away, to feign nonchalance—she's already caught him.

"August." Julie breathes his name, an invocation apparently, because as she says it, he starts walking toward her.

"What?" Brighton says, looking around. She nods in the direc-tion of the bar. "No way," Brighton says, eyebrows raised, following Julie's eyes to the man crossing the room. "August? *The* August? *Here?*" Brighton is the only one who knows. He's the only one she shares her secrets with.

August is halfway to the table now, and Julie has to get away. "No," she says, mostly to herself. "This isn't happening." Her hand jerks, knocking over her beer glass. The orange rind and the last lingering drops of beer spill out, while the glass itself rolls across the tabletop and over the edge, crashing to the floor and shattering. Heads turn to see the source of the disaster. Julie looks at her mess, horrified, then grabs for her purse as Brighton looks on.

It isn't real. Things like this don't happen. Not in a world this big, in a *city* this big. There's no way he could have found her in real, three-dimensional life.

"Shit," she says. "Shit." Julie looks helplessly from Brighton to August. It's *him*. A walking, talking, tangible fucking reminder of the past. She pushes her chair back and forces her way through the mess of tables and bodies, thinking only that she must *get away*.

She is running down the sidewalk when she hears August calling her name. "Jules! Jules, wait, please!" But she can't stop.

4

IT'S BEEN WEEKS NOW SINCE I MET HIM. BUT I THINK IT'S important to remember how everything started, even if the start is already behind you. Beginnings are the best part of any story, aren't they? Filled with so much expectation that things will only get better and better, when sometimes, the best is already happening and you don't even know it yet.

5

It's the third time August has found Julie now, although he would have no way of knowing it. The most recent contact was the letter, six months ago. She hadn't checked her mail in days, was rushing right past the mailboxes in the lobby of her building when she turned around and went back to the wall of neat metal cubes. She and Brighton were coming back from a movie, and it was after midnight. Brighton stood at the elevators, impatiently tapping the half-broken "up" button while Julie, exhilarated from the cold night and the wine they'd stopped for on the way home, twisted her small copper key into the lock, then bundled her mail together in one arm and scurried into the open elevator.

It was on the bottom of the stack when she set the mail down on the counter. Hard to believe she didn't know, didn't feel it ticking like an impatient clock there in her hand. Surely she should have felt it, heard it? The name no one had called her since she left Lawrence Mill scrawled in ink across the envelope. *Jules*. Seeing it like that was familiar and foreign at the same time—it *is* her name still, and yet it isn't. He'd written the wrong address—the apartment she lived in with Evan years ago. Yellow forwarding stickers made the envelope eye-catching in the sea of bills and catalogs.

She thought of Reba then, of how both girls were fascinated with the postal service when they were young. They wrote letters to each other and stamped them with the most interesting stamps they could find in Aunt Molly's junk drawer. Then they tucked their letters to each other into their side-by-side mailboxes, lifted up the little red flags, and waited until those same letters returned, Reba's letter in Julie's mailbox and vice versa.

It was difficult to convince the postman to take their letters away, instead of simply swapping them on-site. "You're next-door neighbors, ladies," he said, shaking his head when they cornered him at his mail truck one afternoon. "You're with each other every day. Why bother with the letters?"

But they pleaded with him, and he finally agreed. After that, the letters came back with the stamps marked over with mysterious black ink. They spent hours imagining where, exactly, their letters might have traveled before returning to them. Exotic locales, big cities, *at least* across the entire state of Mississippi—surely not just down the street to the Lawrence Mill Post Office and back again.

Through those same mysterious pathways, August made contact with her that night, for the second time in ten years. The letter in her hand felt different than the email that had come before, more real somehow. He knew where she was. More or less. She tore open the envelope and unfolded the letter, read through it quickly, and then ripped it into tiny bits that fell like damaged snowflakes onto the kitchen countertop.

The email, that first tentative contact, had arrived in her inbox three months before the letter came up in the mail. She was heating up frozen pizza while Beck tapped away on the computer at the small desk in the living room. Death Cab was playing on the iPod, and Julie could hardly hear Beck's singsong voice when she said, "Mom, you've got email." She was so small that her feet didn't touch the floor when she sat in the desk chair. Beck is as excited about email these days as Julie and Reba used to be about mail from the post office.

"What?" Julie asked.

"Email! Three messages. Want to know who they're from?"

"Sure," she said, pulling the plastic seal from the edge of the pizza. "Probably spam."

It wasn't, though. Beck read out the return email addresses for Julie one letter at a time. If it was a name or an actual word (and not a random jumble of letters and numbers), Julie asked Beck to sound it out. Extra practice, for school. But when Beck spelled enough letters to make out *his* name, Julie dropped the pizza, the still-icy pie rattling the metal of the old stovetop.

"*Who?*" Julie said. She didn't want to believe it, went to the computer to see it for herself.

And there it was, his name in the sender column, no silly nickname or slew of letters to make her doubt it, only his name, simple and bold. She isn't hard to find in the digital world. She's less comfortable with technology than others her age, but she has a Facebook page with her email address listed on it. Brighton said something about it being helpful for her acting career. But still. August was looking for her.

"Beck, don't you have homework?" Julie asked quietly.

"No, I don't have any."

"Go get it," she said.

"But I—"

"Beck, go."

Beck slid from the desk chair and Julie fell into it, one hand gripping the edge of the wooden desk.

Sorrow drips into your heart through a pinhole, the voice sang from the iPod dock. Haunting, chilling. Julie opened the email, the mouse already damp with sweat from her palms. She read through the message, blinking as the music played.

"Mom, are you okay?" Beck asked.

Your love is gonna drown.

Julie clicked Delete, jumped to turn the song off, and looked at Beck blankly. She felt very far away from her daughter at that moment.

"Mom, who is she?" Julie didn't know if Beck had managed to sound out the name or if Julie had spoken it aloud without realizing. "Who is Reba?"

6

So many nights, Julie dreams of Reba. The dream that comes most often, the one that is most vivid, takes her back to when they were children. Even in the dream, she knows it isn't real. The scene is too perfect, too glossy, like a Photoshopped picture. Ethereal.

They run through the forest, laughing. But then Reba runs ahead, and Julie yells for her to come back. They'll be in trouble if anyone finds them playing here.

The trees hold glittering emerald leaves that sparkle but hang out of her reach. Even the lowest branch is above her head. The trunks of the trees are deep brown and too smooth to be authentic. When Julie stops to run her finger against one, it feels more like the sanded backs of the chairs in Molly's old dining room set.

The sun sits lower in the sky than it should. It's midday, but the sun feels low enough to touch and shines so brightly that when the light falls against the leaves, the leaves reflect it back, jewellike. Green and yellow and white light dances along, everywhere, and Julie is blinded.

In the dream, nothing else moves. The wind doesn't howl or even whisper, the shining leaves hang still, and the sun sits suspended, the blurry orange-white orb never faltering behind clouds. There *are* no clouds, only bright rays of sun.

The sun covers everything.

Julie runs. She calls Reba's name, and it is the only sound in the forest, which normally sings—loud and alive with birds and crickets and the river. Where has the river gone? She looks to the left and sees the riverbank, the riverbed dry and empty, the bridge planks broken and scattered along the bank. And the forest, stretching back farther than she can see. She runs, but her feet make no sound, no crunching of leaves or flattening of wild grass beneath her.

Finally, there is Reba, standing by a growth of honeysuckle bushes, the white of their flowers so pure and sparkling that Reba seems to glow beside them. She plucks the honeysuckle gently from the bushes and strings together a chain of flowers.

She doesn't eat the syrupy liquid from the center, but leaves the thin, milky pistons pointing, surrounded by silky petals. It isn't real, but it is. Honeysuckle aren't daisies and have no stems to tie, but they cling together anyway, the ends of the wild weeds forming something much more elegant than a daisy chain.

"I lost you," Julie says.

Reba doesn't look up. "Isn't it beautiful?" she whispers. She finishes the chain and slips it over her head. And it *is* beautiful, the wreath of wildflowers around her neck shining, the petals iridescent as pearls. She smiles.

But then Julie can't see her face. And slowly, Reba fades away, every bit of her, and the flowery chain falls to the ground.

The necklace glistens, but when Julie picks it up, it wilts too quickly in her hands, as though her fingers are poisonous. *This can't be real,* she always thinks at this part of the dream. *What's wrong with the flowers?*

But she knows the answer already. It isn't the flowers. It's Julie. She kills the things she loves.

Brown petals fall to the ground and curl up until there is no chain at all, only dead flowers at her feet. Her hands are outstretched but empty.

Julie calls for Reba but there is no answer, and she knows then that she is alone.

In the mornings when she wakes, her eyelashes cling, salty, to one another, and it is hard to open her eyes.

Nell told Julie once that thinking about someone often enough will make them appear. They will be in your thoughts, and then suddenly they will be standing behind you at the grocery store or in the car next to you at a traffic light, when you've gone years without seeing them at all. *It happens all the time,* she said.

But then there are all the times Julie has thought of Reba and she's never appeared, not even once. She knows what Nell would say to that: *Honey, that's not how it works. You can do a lot of things, but you can't think somebody back from the dead, no matter how hard you try.*

August isn't dead, though. She should have tried harder not to think of him.

7

Julie is a mess when she leaves Sax, and she knows she can't go home yet. She walks the city blocks near her apartment, trying to calm down, all the while imagining August stepping out from around each corner.

Beck's sitter isn't in the apartment when Julie finally unlocks her front door. It's Brighton she sees instead, sitting on the sofa, sleeves rolled up, a tumbler of whiskey in one hand and his eyes alert with worry.

"Jesus, Julie. Where have you been?"

"Out. Thinking." She walks into the kitchen and pours a glass for herself. She eyes the mostly full bottle. More than one way to forget. How easy it would be to mix the whiskey with a sleeping pill or two, to fall back into old habits. But she knows she can't. She knows how much she scared Brighton years ago, after Evan left. Beck was too young to remember, but Brighton won't forget. He doesn't hold it against her, though.

"I sent the sitter home," Brighton says. "I didn't think you'd mind."

Julie sits next to him on the sofa. "I don't."

"So," Brighton says finally. "That was August."

"Yeah," she says. "Apparently."

"Are you afraid of him? I mean, I know the story and all, but you sort of lost your shit back there."

"I don't know. I mean, not afraid. But he's *here*, Brighton. And he's been following me."

"Yeah, I know."

"What?"

"Yeah. I sort of met him. After you left. I approached him."

Julie wants to be angry, but a certain exhausted numbness has taken over, and all she can do is stare.

Brighton sighs. "I wanted to know what he's doing here. Why he tracked you down."

"And?"

"Turns out he came to the city looking for you, but he didn't know what to say when he actually found you. So he's been hanging around for a few days, trying to get up the nerve to talk to you. I told him the stalker routine wasn't the best way to win points. I don't know why you're so surprised that he'd show up, though, after the email and the letter. He was bound to turn up in person sooner or later."

She's silent.

"I'm no psychologist, Julie, but you've been torturing yourself for years. Now August is here, practically at your doorstep. Would it be so bad to at least listen to the guy? Maybe going back there wouldn't be the worst thing ever."

"You're taking his side."

"I'm on *your* side."

"I can't, Brighton. I can't go back."

He looks at her, clearly trying to figure out the best way to proceed. Finally, he shakes his head. "Jules, huh? I've never heard anyone call you that before."

8

Rain smashes against the single window in Julie's room, pelting the glass with hard little pops as she pulls on her yoga pants. The sound makes her think of Toby. She saw her cousin once, months ago, but it's been years since they've talked.

She doesn't miss him.

On quiet nights when they were teenagers, Toby and his friends would crowd into Toby's car and drive through the neighborhoods in town, throwing eggs at dark houses. Julie was forced along only once. She had no choice, because Toby was her ride home from a late-night play practice at a classmate's house. Two friends were with him, loud and so strung out that they crushed an egg in Toby's car and tried to scrape up the yolk with their hands. They dumped what ooze they could collect out the front window of Toby's Firebird, the slick remains sliding down their wrists and forearms.

The wind caught a bit of it and slung it onto Julie, and she was trying to clean the disgusting egg mess from her long hair when the three boys leaned out the car windows, bodies so far outside of the vehicle that she couldn't believe they didn't all tumble out into the street. The Firebird swerved along the empty road while they hurled the eggs at the windows of an anonymous house. At least, anonymous as far as she knew. Maybe they had a vendetta she didn't know about. She didn't see it, only heard the sound, the *smash, smash, smash* of whole eggs colliding with glass, with vinyl siding, with brick. Pelting like hard rain. She remembers being glad for once that Reba wasn't with her. Reba was too good for Toby and his trashy friends.

Toby. August. Reba. It's all back now, as fresh in her mind as if she were still a teenager and not a grown woman.

All day long, Julie expects August to materialize, from the time she and Beck leave the apartment in the morning through her yoga classes to the second she arrives back home at the end of the day. If she's honest with herself, she's been expecting him for the past ten years. Hasn't she known that one day she would turn a corner and he would be standing there, and he would want to know everything? He'd want to know what happened to Reba that night. He would ask, and she would say the words, would finally admit the horrible, horrible truth.

Strange, now that she's seen him with her own eyes, she can't *feel* him anymore, doesn't have that prickling awareness of being watched. So she manages to be unprepared, standing barefoot in her kitchen, cleaning up the remains of Indian takeout, when he finally knocks.

"Mom," Beck calls. "Someone's at the door. Can I get it?"

"No, sweetie. Go to your room and get ready for bed. I've got it."

Julie takes a deep breath, hands trembling slightly as she unlocks the door. And there he is, standing right in front of her, and she might as well be seventeen years old again.

"Jules," he says. He has a deep, strong voice, similar to the ones she remembers narrating the books on tape that Aunt Molly used to listen to. Molly kept them in the car all the time after Uncle Ted left, as though music was too pleasant for her mood. The books on tape weren't just for road trips, but for ten-minute drives to the grocery store or to the Thomas Pharmacy and Car Care, so that any time Julie went somewhere with Molly, a piece of a story, a few sentences, deposited themselves into her memory. These days, when she hears those same book titles, she recalls not entire plots, but a mishmash of strange sentences. Senseless.

"August." It's the best response she can come up with. August, whose name she has never forgotten. He never became just the boy Reba loved or the boy who changed it all, although he *was* certainly those things. If not for him…

"How did you get in here?" She knows she didn't buzz him up.

"I followed someone in. No one asked any questions. I can't believe it's really you. Finally…" His voice falters, falls away. "I've, um, I've tried so hard to find you." He didn't really expect to find her, though. She can tell. This is unrehearsed.

"What do you want?" she asks, as if she needs to. He looks awkward, hovering in the hallway, and it's too late for her to run. She can't help but step aside and motion for him to come in.

"I don't know, Jules," he says, running one hand over his very short hair. "Did you get my letter?"

She could lie, planned to, but it's the truth that comes out. "Yes."

"The email?"

"Yes."

"You could have, you know, responded. Or something."

"I *could* have."

"You know what I want, then. I want to talk to someone else who *knew* her. Who knows what went down back then, how it all fell apart. I want to go back there, to Lawrence Mill, and I want you to go back with me."

She leads him to the sofa where they both sit, but she doesn't respond.

"You could have saved me a lot of trouble by responding to the damned email," he says, looking down at his hands.

She is suddenly angry. "I don't know who you think you are—"

He holds up a hand, and she snaps her mouth shut without finishing the sentence.

"Please," he says. "You know the truth about what happened that night, don't you? You knew her in a way I never got to. You know so much more than I could have ever hoped to know."

"I don't know what you mean," she says, and the lie sounds weak. She stands, walks to the kitchen, and he follows. "I haven't been back there in… God, who knows? A decade?" she says, pressing her hands flat against the cold surface of the kitchen counter. "I can't do it." The lights in the kitchen seem too bright, the air uncomfortably warm from the dishwasher groaning in the corner.

"Look, I'm sorry for barging in on your life. This all happened a lot differently than I thought it would."

"How did you even find me?"

"Internet." He smiles, a soft, sad smile, and she can see how Reba was drawn to him.

Julie hears a door open, and Beck comes bounding into the kitchen in her purple pajamas. "Mom," she says, stopping in her tracks when she sees August. The intrigue is apparent on her little face.

"Hi," she says to him.

"Hi." August is surprised to see her, but he smiles at the little girl warmly.

"I'm Beck. Who are you?" Beck loves conversation, will talk to anyone. Julie has a certain fear of someone stealing her away—all they would have to do is say hello.

August laughs.

"This is, um…this is August."

"Oh. Hi, August."

"August and I went to high school together."

Beck is very interested in this piece of information. "You knew Mom in high school?"

"Sort of," he says.

"Sort of? Did you know her, or did you not?"

"I did."

"You did? What was she like?"

"She, well…she…"

Julie interrupts, has to at this point, with the fascinated look on Beck's face and the decidedly embarrassed expression that August is wearing. "Beck, August and I need to talk alone, okay? Go get in bed."

"Okay. Nice to meet you, August."

"You too, Beck."

"Yours?" August asks, amused, when Beck has gone back into her bedroom.

"Mine."

"Listen, Jules, will you just not rule anything out yet? Think about it. I'm going to be here in town for a little while. We don't have to figure it all out tonight."

Julie sighs. "How long are you going to be around?"

"Until I talk you into going to Lawrence Mill with me."

"Not funny."

"Not trying to be." He looks down at the floor, then back at her. "Hey, I know about the diary. You have it, right? I mean, I thought that…you know, if I really can't talk you into going to Lawrence Mill, then you might at least give me the diary. Or let me borrow it, maybe."

Julie stares at him, confused. "Diary?"

"You don't have to lie about it. She was bringing it to me that night at the bridge. Reba *wanted* me to have it."

"August, I'm not lying. I didn't know she had a diary. You never mentioned a diary." She stands, stunned, thinking of how dangerous a journal of Reba's could have been in the wrong hands. If it's even true, and not some lie August has cooked up to get her back to Lawrence Mill. It's hard to believe her friend would have been so careless as to document the things that happened that year.

"Yeah, I know. I knew you wouldn't just give it to me. I figure it's probably…you know, sacred to you, or something…but if Lawrence Mill is definitely out of the question, I was hoping you'd let me at least take a look."

"She wrote…about the two of you? In a diary?"

August's dark eyes study her, trying to decide if she knows more than she is telling him.

"You really don't have it?"

"I really don't."

"Reba wrote about *everything* in that journal." His voice has taken on a curiously frantic rhythm, and his hands reach out and clench her arms in a way that feels at once intimate and unfamiliar. "If you don't have it, then who the hell does?"

9

AUGUST HAD THOUGHT HE'D NEVER SEE JULES AGAIN, AND NOW here he is, in her apartment, talking to her like he knows her. He thought he would feel triumphant, thought that something unsettled inside him would finally quiet. Did he expect her to make him feel whole again? Jules had never belonged to him. She isn't his lover, never was, although maybe she could have been. If it had been her, and not Reba, alone in the field that day. But he knows that isn't true. It was always Reba, for him. It always *had* to be Reba. Not that it matters now.

He remembers Jules well from high school, her cold, hard edges and tough attitude. She just didn't give a damn. Such a contrast to Reba's welcoming softness. It was a beautiful picture, though, the two of them, always together, Jules's long dark hair and dark eyes and sexy mouth, dangerously appealing. And Reba, small and blond, all sweetness and innocence. You couldn't help wanting to touch them and to stay away at the same time.

It's not like he showed up on a whim. How long has he been

trying to get in touch now? A year or so, at least. Thinking about her
for so much longer than that, but figuring he was probably better
off not knowing everything. He's changed his mind about that as he
has gotten older. Now, he needs to know it all, has given up on ever
moving on until he does. Lately, he feels like he's sinking, like his heart
isn't in the present anymore, like the past could swallow him up.

So, he gave in and came to New York to try to find Jules. She's the
only one who has the answers. He feared having to search through
the whole damned city, but finding her had been easy. He didn't know
her address, but a simple Google search of her name brought up the
website for the bus tours, her photo right there under the Meet Your
Tour Guides tab. If he believed in those kinds of things, he would say
it was fate. Only, once he saw her leaving work, he didn't know how
to approach her, what to say after all this time. He knew he was being
sketchy and borderline criminal, but he started following her, thinking
that the words would come. It was a messed-up way to start things.

His instinct had been to follow her last night, when she ran out
of the club, but common sense had won out for a change. Chasing
her down the street would only make it worse. He needs to explain
himself, but here he is, coming apart in her kitchen instead. He's got
to pull himself together.

She's different now, he can tell. It's more than the hair. She was
so reckless back in high school, radiating all that sensuality and confi-
dence. Now she's poised, controlled. She has grown into herself.
It isn't his place to say so, but she is even sexier now. There is still
something…aloof about her, but she has lost those hard edges, that
coldness. He can tell that if the right person touched her these days,
she might feel something.

But she is uncertain, not at all the carelessly confident girl from his recollection. Though maybe it is his presence that's done that. And she doesn't have the diary, which is a shock. That changes things.

He remembers that day at Reba's locker so clearly that it might have been only yesterday. The last time he spoke to Reba. She seemed so wary of him, and she talked about giving him the diary. She said they needed to meet somewhere later, that there were things he needed to know.

But they never did have that talk, and he never did read the diary.

Someone out there must have it, though, the lavender book he gave Reba for her birthday. He has always imagined it with Jules and isn't pleased to think that someone else might know Reba better than either of them did. He *needs* to know what's inside the diary, and Jules is his only connection to that awful Mississippi town. He has to convince her to go there with him, because the only place they'll find that book, if it can even be found, is in Lawrence Mill.

10

SOMETIMES I THINK ABOUT WHAT WOULD HAPPEN IF JULES AND August ever met—like, really met, outside of school. If I ever got the nerve to tell Jules that August is more than some boy in one of our classes. That he's special to me.

I can't imagine them as friends; they have nothing in common besides me. But, maybe that would be enough. I wonder. I see us all together, chatting peacefully by the river or outside Nell's.

It's hypothetical, a scene born entirely from my imagination. They'll never know each other that way, because I'll probably never be able to tell Jules the truth.

And anyway, I meant to start at the beginning.

11

JULIE CAN'T SLEEP.

Thinking about the meeting with August keeps her awake for hours, wandering the apartment without purpose. She curls herself into a ball on the living room sofa and tries to watch the infomercials on TV. Then she is up again, in the kitchen, opening the refrigerator door and eyeing its meager contents, listening to that soft, regular hum. Back to the sofa. She can't close her eyes, not when the things she doesn't want to remember are waiting behind her eyelids. But it is night, and things are still and quiet, at least inside the apartment, and she can't help but think, even with her eyes open wide.

Diary…

Knowing such a thing might exist makes her *yearn* to hold it in her hands.

Forget it, she whispers to herself in the darkness. (Does she whisper it, or is it only a thought?) Maybe there is no diary. Maybe it is only a fabrication, put together by August to convince her to go to Lawrence Mill. How could she go back? But how could she not, if Reba's diary *is* there, somewhere, waiting for her to find it?

You have to forget. But she can imagine Reba's face in her mind, the almost-parted lips, water swirling the blond strands of her hair. Her wide-open eyes, staring.

"You think you know what you want," Lila says, taking a long drag on her cigarette and breathing an elegant smoky curl into the air. "We all think we know, because that's the easiest way, isn't it?" She wears a white button-down shirt, top three buttons undone. The pointy-nailed fingers of her right hand toy with the pearly buttons. "You think you want to be an award-winning actress, a famed playwright or screenwriter. Am I right?" No one speaks. Julie sits, arms crossed, alert.

"But before you can know what you really want, before you can *get* it, you have to know yourself. *Really* know. And how many of you can say that you really, truly know yourself? One of the most difficult things for artists is to do what's necessary to fully understand who they are, to realize their own unique fears, to know *why* they feel the things they feel. The best, most authentic way to become someone else, or to write something life-changing, is to know yourself. What I suggest to all of you is this: to truly understand yourself as an artist, you have to understand where you come from. You don't have to embrace it, but you can't deny it, either. Sometimes that means going away from what you know. But sometimes it means going back."

Julie stares at Lila, those long fingernails red as a ripe apple against the white of her shirt. She can't do it—no matter what Lila says, no matter what August says. She can't return as though she was there only yesterday, as though she belongs there. As though she has any right to be there, when Reba isn't.

But the words echo in her ears. *Go back.*

"I can't just leave," she says to August, the second he opens his hotel room door. "I've got responsibilities here—my daughter, work. I can't just pack up and go." She's never thought of how hard it would be to turn him down if he was standing right in front of her, and not on the imagined other end of a letter.

"Jules, I'm not talking about a permanent move. A few days, a long weekend, maybe. I'll take care of the plane tickets. We'll both leave from here."

"Why now? We could meet there later—during the summer, maybe."

"You think I'm lying about the diary. I'm not. If it's there, don't you want to find it? How can you wait here and wonder? Besides, if I leave here without you now, I'll probably never hear from you again. You think I'm going to take that risk?"

"What about you? Don't you have a job? How can you be here indefinitely? How can you have time for this?"

"My work is freelance. I own my business. I make my schedule. I planned for this when I came here."

Julie feels a surge of jealousy at his freedom. But also, standing here with him, she feels guilty, like she owes him the answers he wants, because she is the one who took away the thing he wanted most. Even if he doesn't know it. If he knew everything, he wouldn't be so determined to keep her close, wouldn't want to be near her ever again.

So it is guilt that does it, but she also can't deny the allure of Reba's journal, a chance to read her best friend's thoughts. It would be so painful to read it all, but an opportunity to get close to Reba again in the only way that's left. Julie can't turn her back on the possibility.

"I'll talk to Beck's dad about keeping her," she says quickly, before she changes her mind. "See what I can work out. I'll keep you posted."

12

CALLING EVAN SHOULDN'T BE SO HARD, BUT GOD, JULIE HATES it. He is almost always the one to call to schedule his visits with Beck. His work makes his time with his daughter erratic—sometimes he has her for two weeks straight, other times he goes months without seeing her.

To have to call him at all, even this once, is a form of giving in. But if Julie is going to consider taking this trip, she'd like to know that he'll be around. If he won't be, she'll have to schedule Tara, the sitter, for the long weekend. But maybe Evan is performing in New York or on a break right now.

Her call goes to voice mail. She hates him for forcing her to leave a message—such evidence that she needs him. When he calls her back ten minutes later (was he screening her call?), she learns that he *is* in New York for the next month, until shooting begins on an independent movie he's committed to.

Hearing his voice makes her chest hurt, a tiny, unnatural pain, like moth wings flapping against her heart. It used to be such an immobilizing ache, but now it's only a flutter, a handicap she has learned to live with.

She walks home from the subway station with the cell phone pressed against her ear. "I need you to meet me somewhere, when it's convenient for you."

"Julie…" He mumbles her name. She can hear his ambivalence, can almost *feel* it sizzling through the phone. Simple phone conversations are strange enough.

"It's about Beck, of course."

"Oh. Everything okay?" His normal, confident voice returns. *Father* is a role he can play. She's only thrown him off for an instant.

❧

They meet at Brew the next day. *I'll be in the neighborhood*, he said, but she didn't ask why. She sits at a table in the back, sipping black coffee and watching for him through the wide front windows. The shop is bathed in afternoon sunlight. It almost convinces her that when she walks out the door, she won't feel the chill.

There are only two other patrons in Brew at this time of day, a man and a girl, at separate tables. The man is wearing a business suit and reading *On the Road*. Evan used to love Kerouac. He had the same book tucked in his messenger bag on the day she met him. The girl, the other patron, is dark-haired, with earphones tucked into the curls of her ears. She is bent over a notebook, pen in hand. Julie wonders if it's a journal.

Evan wears a dark wool coat and blue jeans and has such a confident walk that, in the instant before he opens the door and she sees his face, Julie has already recognized his silhouette through the window. She realizes, belatedly, that she could have had this conversation with Evan over the phone. Maybe she'd wanted this excuse to see him.

Evan. Confidante, lover. Husband, for a moment. Enemy. Stranger. His eyes stand out on his face, blue like the cerulean crayon in Beck's craft box, or like that paint sample Julie found in the hardware store when she and Evan painted the old apartment. They never even used that color, but she kept the sample—a reminder. It lives in her night-stand, taking up residence with other small mementos. Night Sky, the sample is called. But Julie has never seen a night sky as deep, as intense, as Evan's eyes. Now they are her daughter's eyes too.

His other features are sharp but boyish: pinky cheeks and small, pink lips on a body that is slim, slightly muscular. His hair hangs longer than the last time she saw him, dark blond and windswept. When they first met, Julie was taking a Greek mythology class, and Evan reminded her powerfully of the boy god Eros, youthful and yet somehow overwhelmingly sensual.

Touching him seemed so natural once, but she doesn't do it when he finally approaches, removes his coat, and tucks it around the back of his chair before taking a seat at the small table.

"Julie."

"Evan." He wears a brown T-shirt, with a long-sleeved thermal underneath. She's seen him wear this combination before.

She knows his entire body. As he sits across from her fully clothed, she can see him in her mind, wearing nothing. She remembers it all—the feel of his skin beneath her palms, the inexplicable roughness of his hands, the mole on his pelvis. Sandy-colored leg hair, the curve of his calf, thigh. The moon and star tattoo on his back, and how she used to trace it with her fingertips while he slept. She has a matching star on her hip.

"I need to go out of town," she finally says. "Soon. Maybe next week, even. Just for a few days. Can you keep Beck?"

He glances down at the table, his eyelashes a full curtain against the blue-stained irises of his eyes, and she thinks of how he looks while sleeping, lashes sealing the pale, peaceful half-moons of his eyelids. "Where are you going?"

She isn't sure it's any of his business, but she answers anyway. "Mississippi."

"Home?"

"Not home. New York is home."

"Is everything okay? You aren't thinking of moving, are you?" It pleases her a little to see the quick panic on his face, even though she knows it has more to do with Beck than with her.

"No, of course not." Even Evan knows she has never been back.

"Okay, sure. I'll be happy to keep Beck. But, Julie... I mean, you're going to come back, aren't you?"

It stings. She remembers when she gave birth to Beck. After they were discharged from the hospital, she'd thrust the baby into his arms and begged him to take her. *You have to*, she'd said.

"Of course I'm coming back. You think I'd just leave her with you? I know better. Full-time parenting isn't exactly something you have the time for."

She doesn't even *mean* to be so harsh. Call it self-sabotage, a way to protect herself from the possibility of them ever growing close again.

"Jesus, Julie. Don't start."

There was a time when she loved the way he looked at her. She can't stand it now. So she focuses instead on the chalkboard menu behind the counter.

"So, you can do it?"

"Yes. Absolutely."

"Okay." She stands up, too quickly. Her chair tips—she catches it just before it clatters to the ground. "Okay, well, thank you. We'll talk again when I know more." She blinks, swallows. It always seems to end this way.

"Hey, Julie, wait," he calls as she is leaving, but she pretends not to hear.

"Okay, let's do it. Let's, um…let's go to Lawrence Mill." She says it cautiously, like she might still change her mind.

But August is at her apartment, and before she knows it, they are on her computer, booking plane tickets. He finds a flight straight through to Mississippi and books it, puts the tickets on his credit card. When Julie calls her bosses, they give her the time off without too much of a fuss. It's done, just like that.

"Jules," August says. "I really want to find that diary."

"Me too." She feels ashamed, though of what it might say about her. She is embarrassed about many of the things she did back then, and she would rather that August not read about them. But someone else is out there, knowing about all of those things. And that thought is unbearable.

13

It's like a strange dream, sitting next to August on the airplane, like they mean something to each other. Like they aren't strangers.

Once, when Julie and Reba were teenagers, Reba had asked her this question: *If you were a bird, what would you do?* Reba's strange musings were sometimes random and sometimes not, but they always felt like riddles. Julie had given a thoughtless response. *I don't know…just fly around birdlike, I guess. Why? What would you do?*

Reba's answer was insightful and lovely. *I would see everything. The whole world. But from far away, like a blurry painting. One of those that looks beautiful and simple until you get close enough to see all of the imperfections.* Julie thinks of that now as the plane ascends and she looks out into the sky, at the distorted world below. Deceptively simple.

"So…what's the plan now?" Julie asks August once they are in the air. They were quiet on the cab ride, uneasy alone together and unsure of what was to come. Then there was the bustling airport, the baggage check, the moving, the waiting. Now there is nothing else to distract them.

"I don't actually have one," he confesses. "I didn't know things would really get this far, this fast."

"Me neither."

"Well, first thing. We know we need to find the diary, but how are we going to figure out who has it?"

Julie wants that book so badly. It's tangible proof that Reba existed, that she was there, on the earth, even for a little while. More than that, Julie can't help but harbor an ambivalent hope that Reba's diary will give some clue of what really led up to the events of that last night. *Why* it all happened the way it did.

Even if she can't get at those answers, there are the details of August and Reba's love affair, all of those things Julie can never ask August. How they met, how they fell for each other. She wants to know *everything* there is to know about Reba's last year. It's a tantalizing vision, Julie holding the diary in her hands and *knowing* Reba the way she always had when they were younger, before August came along. When they shared their secrets freely.

"Okay…" Julie says. "You said Reba was giving the diary to you?"

"Yeah, the night at the river. I was supposed to meet her there, but, well…"

"I know," Julie says. "I know why you weren't there."

"So the diary should have been found with or near her…her…"

"It should have been near the river," Julie finishes when August can't complete his own sentence. *With her body.*

"But I know she wrote all about the two of us," August continues.

"And if the police or investigators or someone else found it, then it would have been news. They would have come for me, probably."

"Maybe she didn't use your name," Julie says, thinking. "And Reba's daddy was friends with the police chief, so maybe they didn't release it, or something. I don't know. Maybe it washed away...in the river. What made you think I would have it to begin with?"

August narrows his eyes, studying her. "Because you were there that night. When she jumped. When she...killed herself. I thought you must have ended up with it."

"I wasn't there." She can tell that he doesn't believe her.

"I think you were. I think you followed her again, like the night you caught us together."

"August...there wasn't anyone else at the bridge that night," she says carefully.

"I think there was," he says quickly, too quickly. "I don't think she was alone."

She studies him. "If I were there, wouldn't I have stopped her?" She can see—in his face, in his eyes—this fervent *need* to believe that Reba wasn't on her own out there, in the dark, in the night.

They are silent for a moment, before August speaks again. "Her boss at the flower shop found her, right?"

"Yes. Nell."

"I don't think the diary washed away. Reba wanted me to see it. She would have left it for me, when she... Well, you know. Do you think that Nell might have picked up the diary, before the paramedics got there? I don't really know how it went, exactly."

"Maybe. She could have done that, if she thought she was protecting Reba."

"Okay. So, what do we do?"

Julie sighs. "Sounds like we're going to see Nell."

14

Lawrence Mill doesn't have its own hotel, even after all of these years, so August and Julie booked rooms at The Inn in Opal, the somewhat charming city that serves as a miniature getaway for the tiny, less charming neighboring towns. From the heart of Opal, it's a ten-minute drive, off the highway onto country roads and right into Lawrence Mill. Compared to Lawrence Mill and those other nearby towns, Opal is a thriving metropolis, with a movie theater and a string of chain restaurants lining each side of the main road like gaudy jewels on a necklace, and even an old-fashioned downtown square in the heart of the city. Three hotels, but The Inn was Julie's suggestion. Fitting, she thought, since as teenagers, she and Reba spent so much time there—or rather, at the adjoining bar.

The Inn is a stucco three-level box that sits off the main road. The parking lot is nearly empty when they pull in, August behind the wheel of the rental car. Black Honda, though Julie wasn't really paying attention when they picked it up. Being back in Mississippi makes her feel off-balance, wrong. She is already fighting the urge to run.

"Well, here we are," August says.

Fickle rain poured and then drizzled and then poured again during the hour-long drive from Jackson, but it has finally stopped, at least for the moment. It is evening, but the four oversize street-lights make the parking lot as bright as daytime. Julie expected the Mississippi weather to be warm and springlike, but it is cool here too, only slightly warmer than when they were standing outside JFK before they left the city. She hasn't bothered to button her jacket, but now she pulls it together tightly at her waist with one hand while she grabs her overnight bag with the other.

"Let me," August offers, reaching for the bag, but she shakes her head.

"I've got it."

The glass doors of The Inn don't open automatically, even though for some reason Julie expects them to. She has to release her grip on her jacket, and the left side blows away from her body like a page turning in the wind. She grabs on to the fabric as soon as she is inside, even though once the door is closed, she can no longer feel the chill.

Julie looks around. When she left Lawrence Mill, the renovations on The Inn had just been completed, but viewed with fresh eyes, the decor looks dated—or maybe this look was already out of style when they chose it. Then she realizes she hasn't set foot in this place for ten years, or even eleven. These renovations *are* dated now. The walls are papered, covered with forest-green vines sprouting burgundy roses perpetually in bloom.

August lingers out by the car. Does he know, somehow, that she needs to take in this scene on her own? The reception desk is to her left. To her right is a long hallway that she knows connects to Southern Saddle, the country version of a hotel bar—a run-down place with mediocre food and drinks, and sometimes a honky-tonk band playing in a corner.

"Hi," Julie says to the receptionist, a young woman with alert brown eyes that are shiny behind thick glasses. "I have a reservation."

"Your name, ma'am?" the receptionist asks with the same Southern drawl that Julie has worked so hard to suppress. College drama classes taught her how. The receptionist's fingers hover above a keyboard as she awaits an answer.

"Portland," she says. "Jules. Julie." She's been back for only moments, and her childhood nickname is already on her lips. Is it so simple, then? Does being here cause to her to automatically revert back to Jules? *Jules*, who seems like a separate person now. She glances toward the door. It's raining again. August finally walks through, carrying his bag. Stray raindrops dampen his shirt.

"Hmm...Julie Portland...Julie Portland..." The reception-ist's fingers move across the keyboard. Then she stops, looks up. "Jules Portland?"

"That's what I said."

"Jules Portland!" An exclamation this time. "From Lawrence High School? No, it can't be!"

Julie looks at the woman again, carefully.

"Um, no," she mumbles. "I think you've got me confused with someone else."

In the moment before the woman speaks again, Julie hopes fiercely that she won't speak at all, will simply accept Julie's lie, give her the keys, and send her on her way.

"No, it's got to be! I'm Maggie Harris." The woman smiles, a huge smile with two front teeth that slip inward toward each other, left tooth tucked slightly beneath the right. Her smile is too big, too happy. "You dated my brother in high school! Jake, he went to Woodbrooke, remember? Probably not. I guess you dated a lot of boys. Well, you know what I mean. It was a long time ago, about the time your friend... That *was* your friend, right? So tragic. Suicide is so rare around here, you know. I don't think we've had another one since."

She clasps a hand to her mouth and then lets it fall. "I'm sorry, that was just *so* rude of me," she says in a voice that doesn't sound sorry at all. "Anyway, Jake used to sneak out to meet you, used to get into some big trouble with our parents." She laughs, then notices August. "Hi, sir," she says. "I'll be right with you." It's clear that she doesn't realize Julie and August are there together. Which they really aren't. *Together* is a word that grossly misrepresents the relationship Julie has with the man behind her. She barely knows him.

"I really think you've got the wrong person," she says to Maggie Harris. "Can I please get my key? I'm in a hurry." The woman stands there, still looking at her with that big smile. Julie has to fight the urge to slap her. "The key," she says again.

The girl's smile retreats as she finally, slowly, reaches under the counter. "Well, yes, your room key..." She trails off. "But Jake, he sure talked a lot about you, well, back then... You sure did a number on his heart. He's a doctor now, you know, graduated med school and all that." She hands Julie the key. "I'll be sure to tell him you said hello!"

"Hey there, you have a reservation?" Julie hears Maggie Harris say as she finally turns her attention to August. Julie walks down the hall, around the corner near the elevators, where she knows the woman can't see her anymore.

"Sorry," Julie says to August, when he finally rounds the corner himself, key in hand. "I had to get away."

He shakes his head. "I can't believe the first person we ran into knew who you were. This really is a small town."

"Now you know why I never visit."

August reaches out to touch her arm, but pulls it back before his skin actually makes contact. "Do you want to…I don't know…get dinner?" he asks as they step off the elevator.

Julie shakes her head. "Later, okay?" She's upset about the interaction with Maggie Harris, and there's not much he can do to comfort her.

He nods. "Okay. Dinner down here in maybe an hour? Does that sound good?"

"I'll meet you at Southern Saddle."

Her room is dark and cold, but she doesn't turn on lights or shut off the air conditioner. Instead, she abandons her small bag by the door and falls into the too-firm coils of the double bed, feeling the wash of anger that always comes when someone mentions Reba's death in an offhand way, or as a way of telling time. She hasn't been around anyone else who knew Reba in so long that she'd forgotten the feeling. "You know, it was the winter that the girl…" Always an unfinished statement.

"I want to go home," she says aloud, the words sinking into the thin comforter, where she lies, facedown. The pain is real, but her voice, even muffled, sounds pouty. She sounds less like a grown-up and more like her daughter.

Julie has been away from Beck before, of course—but she never likes it. Evan is a good father, though, and when he's around, he'll have Tara around to help out. Beck *adores* her sitter. The woman is twenty-three, four years younger than Julie, and yet she holds Julie's child as a grandmother might. She is a friend of Evan's family, which is how they found her in the first place. Or, how Evan found her, because he didn't actually consult Julie. Though she is grateful now to have Tara around.

Julie often wonders idly if Evan has slept with Tara. They don't spend an unreasonable amount of time together—not that Julie knows of, at least—but enough, when Evan has Beck on weekends or vacations. It isn't impossible. Evan is a beautiful man, even without the New York notoriety he now possesses. Julie should know. And Tara is young and lovely. Julie tries not to think about it. She doesn't want Evan for herself anyway, not anymore. Still, it stings to think of him with anyone else, and she can't help but resent the younger woman for the possibility. For the *maybe*.

When Julie finally moves from the bed, the comforter, with its ugly green pattern, has rumpled and one pillow is turned sideways. She doesn't fix it. Who really cares?

She showers with the hot water faucet turned on all the way, but only lukewarm water comes out of the sputtering showerhead. She reaches, dripping wet and freezing, for a stiff hotel towel from the rack above the toilet, avoiding her reflection in the bathroom mirror. She knows well enough what she looks like. Not so different from when she was in high school, physically, still tall for a woman. Mostly legs. She towered over the boys when she was younger. Skinny, small-breasted. Her dark hair was long once, but now it is cropped into a stylish, choppy bob that stops just below her chin. Eyes the same brown. Boring brown, she said more than once, when she was young and comparing her features to Reba's. "No," Reba would say. "They are yummy eyes, like chocolate!" and they'd dissolve into a fit of giggles.

The photos in her portfolio are striking. A dark beauty, someone once said at an audition. But Reba was angelic.

Julie doesn't want to leave the room, but there is only one thing she wants more than to stay hidden in this freezing-cold, heavy-curtained cave until she can get back to New York. That diary. She has decided she isn't leaving Mississippi without it, so she might as well have dinner.

She dresses in a black sweater and jeans, and even though she wants to leave her face bare, she forces herself to swipe on mascara and blush before leaving the room. Is it for August? She doesn't know, doesn't want to think too hard about it.

There's no one behind the reception desk when Julie exits the elevator and rounds the corner into the lobby, so she makes her way unhindered down the hallway to Southern Saddle. When she pushes open the thick wooden doors, the dim light and the shock of memories are so overwhelming that she steps backward, afraid.

The hostess, a young girl with brassy red hair, leads her to a small booth in the back corner of the restaurant and sets down two menus. Tonight, there is a man in a cowboy hat and boots playing a guitar on the makeshift stage. When the waitress comes, Julie orders whiskey, then waits impatiently for it to arrive while she tries to take it all in.

15

THERE WAS THIS ONE NIGHT, BACK WHEN SUMMER HAD JUST started, when I remember thinking that nothing exciting would ever happen to me. It was my own fault if it didn't, but still.

The day was turning into night as we walked into Southern Saddle. It was crowded inside, and hazy. There's hardly anywhere else to go for people who crave that kind of rowdy nightlife. Smoke formed these wispy halos over the heads of the patrons around the bar, and the air was heated and heavy.

Before I met August, this was the kind of "fun" I'd get up to most weekends.

Jules gets restless in the summer, says that things need to happen. That things are *begging* to happen. It's enough, she says, to make a teenaged girl go crazy. (I get bored sometimes too, but I'm usually happy enough at home with a book.)

So, we lie to my parents and Aunt Molly, and plead for a ride to the mall (where the good kids go to hang around outside the movie theater or in the food court). Occasionally, we *do* go inside to buy some small trinket—a new CD or a pair of earrings, something to provide as proof that we were just where we promised we'd be. As if we need it. Most nights we just stand there, waving good-bye and waiting and watching until the car pulls out of sight, and then we cross the street to The Inn and its adjoining bar.

Of course it's Jules's idea. The dangerous plans always are. The only one who knows the truth is Jules's cousin, Toby, who hates us both and doesn't give a damn what we do anyway (his words, not mine). He only threatens to tell Jules's aunt Molly when he gets sent to pick us up and we dare to keep him waiting.

We got there early, but on Friday nights, the bar fills up quickly. Men and women spilled through the door in groups, businesspeople fresh out of school with jobs in insurance or banking or one of the few other white-collar options in this area, wearing button-down shirts with the sleeves rolled clumsily to their elbows. Or else they were students from the Baptist college down the road, working themselves up for a good sin. The rest were locals, old widowers or middle-aged divorcées.

Happy hour always started the same way. A group of men—younger ones, or else Jules and I would ignore them entirely—would call us to their table or join us at ours. *What's your drink, baby?* one of them would ask, and Jules would wink. *Just Cokes, for both of us,* she'd say in this voice that sounded like it should be saying all manner of illicit things, and the man would be too intrigued by the sound of her voice to question it. But the bartender, our Bryant, would keep his eyes on us. He would wait until we got up together, pretending to go to the restroom, our red-tinted plastic glasses in hand.

The bar is a raised platform in the middle of the restaurant (no secret what's most important at Southern Saddle, and it isn't the food), with a set of small steps in the back for the servers to get in and out. On the top step, Bryant would "leave" a bottle of whatever cheap liquor was handy. Vodka, rum, or tequila, whatever wasn't being used at the moment. I would keep watch while Jules spiked our drinks.

She never knows exactly how much to mix. (Bryant won't do it for us, is too afraid of getting caught and ending up in jail or something.) So, sometimes the drinks taste strong and hot and bitter, and we gag on every sip until we finally get used to the taste, or until the backs of our throats are too numb for us to notice the taste at all. Those are the times when Bryant has the patrons around the bar distracted with noisy conversation.

But sometimes there are only seconds before I'm hissing that *Someone's coming!* and Jules can somehow always hear me, even over all of the voices and clinks and clanks of pint glasses and loud music blaring through the speakers. Those times, Jules replaces the bottle quickly and we duck into the bathroom. Bryant never bothers asking our true ages; he's a friend of Toby's, so of course he knows. But he's never told anyone else. Some nights I catch him watching Jules with a sweet hunger in his eyes, but he rarely speaks to us at all.

That night, Jules chose a table for us in the center of the room, in front of the bar. I would be more comfortable in a cozy corner, but she knows that.

Jules took long sips of her already-spiked drink, but I hardly looked at mine. It's lame, I know, but I'm always afraid of getting into trouble. I looked at the door and imagined my daddy bursting in, his face ugly-crimson red and his booming voice drawing the attention of everyone in the bar. Jules worries about that too, but she'd never admit it. We *should* be safe, though. No one who knows my parents or Aunt Molly is likely to show up at a place like Southern Saddle. Well, no one besides Toby.

We watched the band set up, rough-looking men lugging speakers and guitars. Before the music started, two boys had already joined us at our table. Jules playfully called them boys, even though the very youngest was three years older than us and using a fake ID.

Jules says boys are drawn to me, but I don't know if that's really true. She says I'm delicate as a flower, or something. But I don't know what to do with boys like that, boys who aren't boys but are actually grown men already.

So I was quiet, while Jules said something witty and provocative so the boys didn't leave. The brown-eyed one, probably twenty-two or twenty-three, asked Jules to dance when the music started, and even though we spend nights in her room listening to Pearl Jam and Better Than Ezra, she looked excited as she took his hand. I even saw her singing along to the same country cover songs we heard there every weekend.

How old are you? the boy probably asked her, and she probably lied, and then she probably let him cover her lie with his drunken mouth. His body pressed against hers, and she likely felt the usual thrill, and then she probably hinted about seeing him later, after I made curfew.

The boy beside me kept asking me to dance, but I shook my head and smiled a smile that I hoped he realized was polite, not flirty. He must have gotten the hint, because he finally got up to move on, maybe to some other underage conquest.

And then I put the smile away, crossed my arms and watched the reflection of the dancers in the front window.

It's funny how you can be in a room full of people and still feel alone.

16

Food seems repulsive. Too many memories in this place. Julie pretends to read the menu, the laminated paper with the lasso border advertising cheap bar food: grilled cheese sandwiches and burgers and wings. She finishes the last of her drink, the liquid filling her body with warmth so soothing that she leans her head back against the cracked vinyl of the booth. She doesn't make a face—she knows how to drink whiskey like a man, learned right here in this bar. When the waitress returns, she orders another. Julie hadn't really planned on drinking tonight, but how else would she have stopped her hands from shaking, stopped the chills dancing along her skin?

She waits for August, desperate for the distraction. She breathes a sigh of relief when the door opens and he steps into the bar. It feels like she's been waiting forever, but he's right on time. The tension in his shoulders is evident, as though he hates being back in Mississippi as much as she does. He must. All of the noises in the sparse room seem to blend into one quiet, dull murmur. It's the first time she's been able to see him like this, to really *look* at him. At Sax, she'd been so close to panic, and every time she's been around him since then has been filled with plans, with negotiations.

He stops briefly to look for her, eyes going immediately to the back, as if he knew she would hide. He's changed clothes as well, into a striped shirt tucked neatly into khaki slacks, all perfectly tailored to his tall, muscular frame. Did he dress for her? His shoes make a *click-clacking* sound on the old hardwood floors when he walks.

The few patrons in the wooden booths look up as he passes, curiosity in their eyes, easy to read as words in a book. The eyes of the waitstaff are on him as well, even after all of these years. Apparently, things haven't changed too much around here. August is the only black man in the bar.

Julie can feel her pulse twitching against the naked flesh of her wrists as he comes nearer, and she doesn't know why her response to him, here, is so *visceral*, as though this is their first meeting. She licks her chapped lips.

"Hey, Jules," he says in his deep voice, taking a seat across from her in the booth, and she can tell that she's not the only one on edge.

She opens her mouth to speak, then closes it again and watches him instead. Has she noticed, before, the small outline of a dimple on the left side of his mouth? It seems ready to form a happy indention in his cheek if he should grin, laugh. But his dark eyes are haunted, and she wonders if hers are the same. Reba saw something in this man, something beautiful, and, looking at him now, Julie sees it too.

17

THIS PLACE IS A DIVE. IF HE'D KNOWN IT WAS LIKE THIS, August would have suggested they go somewhere else. He never came here as a teenager, though he remembers hearing occasional talk of kids who did. He cracks his knuckles and tries not to fidget under Jules's obvious scrutiny. Fails. "You're kind of staring," he says finally.

"Sorry." And then nothing. The burden of conversation seems to fall to him; wasn't this whole thing his idea, after all? But he has no idea what to say. He studies Jules like she's been studying him. She's pretty in a provocative way, runway-model pretty, and if he were a normal, well-adjusted man, he'd feel lucky just to be sitting across from her. Men glance in her direction every few minutes, admiring her like an expensive antique. They appreciate her beauty, but they know she's not for them. She's outgrown this town.

August can't ignore the glances he's getting, either. It hasn't escaped his notice that this place isn't exactly packed with diverse patrons. The waitress shows up, and August looks at Jules's empty whiskey glass and the half-drained one beside it before ordering one for himself.

"You know, you've changed some," he says, grasping for a conversation starter when the waitress is gone. "Since then."

"You never knew me." Julie pulls her silverware from its paper napkin and begins toying with the spoon, tapping it against her palm. "We weren't friends."

It's a cold thing to say to him after all of these plans they've made together, and he looks at her cautiously. "No," he agrees. "I guess we weren't."

Silence again. The bad lighting in this dump makes her look closed off and far away, and he has an urge to reach out and touch her to make sure that she's really here. But her hands are occupied, and after the whole stalking debacle, he knows he needs to tread lightly.

"Ever been married, August?" she asks.

"No," he says quietly. "I've never been serious about anyone...since her." He sounds pathetic, and he knows it, still carrying a torch for his high school girlfriend after more than a decade. It's the truth, though.

"Oh."

"What about you?"

"Once. Beck's dad."

"Beck," he says. "It's Rebecca, isn't it?" The spoon she'd been tapping against her palm falls hard to the table with a loud clatter. "You did that, named her after Reba?"

"Yes."

"It's nice."

"You hungry?"

"No."

"Me neither."

August sighs. "What is it about this place that makes everything feel so *heavy?*"

"Memories," Jules says.

"God, I feel like a teenager again, and not in a good way."

She nods.

"Well, we're here. Let's talk, get to know each other or something." He rubs his chin with his thumb and forefinger in an effort to appear more relaxed. "You're an actress."

"Sort of."

"Interesting job, pretending to be other people."

"I guess." She doesn't elaborate. He hopes it's being in this bar that has her treating him like they're on two completely different planets. Hell, maybe it *is* the memories. He knows they're getting to him already.

To fill the silence, he talks a bit about himself. The details are one-dimensional; his life feels flat as cardboard, and he can't work up the enthusiasm to fake it. He owns a real estate photography business in Virginia. It's a one-man operation, making yuppy homeowners' houses look good enough to drive up the selling price or catching the best angles of high-rise apartments for website photos. He could do more, maybe; he'd gotten his MBA after undergrad at his dad's insistence. But it's nice, mostly solitary work, and he always did love photography. So, there's that.

"You know," he says after a while, "I haven't been here since my family left, after everything…" He trails off. "I thought I would be able to *feel* her here, in Opal, in Lawrence Mill. Almost like I thought she'd still be here somewhere, living and breathing. Almost like she didn't die. Like she didn't jump off that bridge, even though I know she did."

Something breaks through that closed-off expression Jules has been wearing, and her lips part. He thinks she's going to say something important and he leans forward in anticipation of her words, but then she closes her mouth again.

"What?" he asks.

She shakes her head and looks down. "Nothing." But she bites her lip, and it's clear she's hiding something. He wants to pry, but he has his own secrets too, and God knows he isn't ready to share them. Still, he wonders what she's keeping from him.

"She's not here, you know," Jules says.

"She is," he says quickly, determined.

"No, I mean here, in this place. She hated it here. I used to make her come, on weekends, when we were young." The phrase hangs in the air, unwelcome, because when wasn't Reba young?

"Then let's get out of here, call it a night," he says, waving a hand to get the waitress's attention. It's going to take time with Jules, to get her to warm up. He can see that now. "Do you have a plan for tomorrow? To find the diary?"

"I think so," she says. Nell is their only lead in finding it. Nell *has* to have that book.

18

SUMMER BREAK WAS HALFWAY OVER WHEN LIFE, SLEEPY UP until that point, became something else. Something wide awake. I didn't ask for it, but maybe I needed it anyway.

In July, the air in Nell's Flower Shop smells like wilting roses. Jules and I sat on wooden stools behind the small counter and listened, half attentive, as the woman buying an arrangement of daisies gave us the details of her niece's recent tonsil operation.

"Oh, she's all right now," the woman said, her eyes large and open wide, acting for all the world as if a tonsillectomy is the most dangerous thing a person can encounter. "Lucky's what she is, though. Never know what can happen with those kinds of things. Never had surgery myself. Nope, healthy as a horse all my life." She smiled slightly, smug despite her best intentions.

I smiled back. "I'm glad she's okay."

We've worked at Nell's every summer since we turned fourteen. To an outsider, the shop might look like a roadside stand, a curious wooden shack where fruits and boiled peanuts are sold in plastic grocery bags to travelers seeking out the biggest tomato, the ripest cantaloupe. But the residents here know better. With cheery white walls covered with old-fashioned tin signs advertising everything from ladies' lingerie to the *Saturday Evening Post*, shabby, well-worn hardwood floors, and the most unusual mix of flowers found for miles around, Nell's place is something special. Flowers crowd the entire store: blooms blossom in coolers and on tables and wilt slowly on countertops, and flower petals lie sullen on the floor before they are swept up in the afternoon.

My mama got us the job the summer she grew tired of watching us sit out in the garden or on Aunt Molly's front porch, restless, feeling the day trickle away like the sweat from our foreheads in the lazy Southern heat. Mama and Nell have been friends since they were girls themselves. On Sundays after church, Mama and Nell sit at our kitchen table, drinking mimosas and knitting or sewing or discussing recipes they've found in their women's magazines. They used to invite Molly too, but they gave up after a certain amount of rejection.

Nell is round and full of smiles, and she is the most outspoken woman I've ever known. *Go to Nell if you want an honest answer,* people say. *Lord knows, she'll tell you the truth.* But the thing is, people rarely want the truth, no matter how much they pretend otherwise. So these days, Nell stays in the back as often as possible, surrounded by her flowers, while we take orders and I chat politely with the customers, and Jules pretends to care.

The woman continued to talk about her niece's hospital stay in minute detail and was delighted when we discovered that the girl is a classmate of ours. Jules rolled her eyes.

"Oh! I'll tell her you said hello! What were your names again? Her mother is at the hospital with her now, but I'm headed right over. It's such a small world, isn't it?"

"It is," I said. "The world is so small. You'll have to send her our very best wishes."

Jules covered a snort with her hand, disguising it as a cough.

The bell on the door tinkled as the woman left, and we were alone at the counter. I rose from my stool and headed out to the back porch with Jules at my heels, the screen door slamming shut behind us.

We settled into the green plastic lawn chairs anchored in the gravel behind the shop. The gray pebbles sparkled like glass in the sunlight.

I don't mind working at Nell's, but my favorite part is when the shop is empty, and Jules and I can sit out back and chat and watch the tall weeds glinting golden instead of green, on their way to a crisp death beneath the hot sun. It's exactly the type of thing Mama was trying to keep us from, idling this way, but *she* was the one who wanted to keep us busy. We didn't come up with the idea on our own.

If you were to sprint through the weeds (which we did in the evenings, on our way home), you'd come to the edge of a forest, tall trees and dark Mississippi soil that parts only for the river that runs lazily through Lawrence Mill and Opal. We can hear it from the back of Nell's shop.

Jules and I kicked our feet back and forth in the plastic chairs, trying to work up some kind of breeze. "I had a date last night," Jules said, as if I didn't know already. I'd watched from my bedroom window as the light from an unfamiliar car swung into her driveway, two shiny spotlights illuminating Jules's face as she hurried out the front door, laughing like it was all a riot, and threw herself into the passenger seat. It's still sneaking out, even if Aunt Molly isn't home to see it. With her job as the night receptionist at the hospital, Molly doesn't see the things that go on around here after dark. But I worried for Jules anyway. Rumors spread fast in a town like ours, and God knows Molly (who isn't exactly the most understanding woman) believes every rumor she hears.

"I know," I said. Sweat sneaked like teardrops down my chin and neck.

In our summer stupor, we both jumped a little when the shop bell jingled, and the hardwood floors creaked beneath the weight of footsteps. Jules groaned but pulled herself up from her seat, and I watched the glistening sweat slide from the backs of her knees when she stood. "I've got this one," she said, and disappeared inside.

I turned Julie's empty chair toward me and propped up my feet. I was concerned about the things Jules did after dark. Concerned, but undeniably curious. I was afraid that she would end up in some kind of trouble sooner or later. But I can't deny that I was lonely then, and secretly envious of the mysterious (and potentially wondrous) mischief Jules got herself into.

A silver flash in the field caught my attention, and I turned my head to find the source of the sudden light. It is a testament to all the fairy tales I've read in my life that my first thought was of magical things, especially when the light quickly vanished. But then it returned, shimmering like a diamond in the field before disappearing again.

It looked like there was an animal crouching out there, but then I realized it was a person, squatting low in the weeds and holding a camera in front of his face. A camera pointed at *me*. I used one hand to shade my eyes as I jumped from the chair, the cotton of my skirt swaying around my calves with the motion. I took a step.

"It was Mr. Breyer," Jules said, rattling the screen door as she reappeared. She said something about it being Mrs. Breyer's birthday, and Mr. Breyer waiting until the last minute. *Men*, she said with a laugh, like they're all exactly that way. And I guess she's been around enough of them by now to know.

"I saw someone," I said.

"Where?"

"Out there. A man. With a camera." I scanned the length of the field and found it empty. He'd been there one second and gone the next, evaporating like water turned to steam in the heat.

"Weird." Jules shrugged. If she thought I was hallucinating, she at least had the good grace not to say so.

Funny how a beginning can sneak up on you.

19

THE HOTEL CURTAINS HANG SO THICK AGAINST THE WINDOWS that Julie can't see any light at all, and for a moment, she doesn't know where she is. She rubs her eyes, pressing harder than she means to against the tender skin of her eyelids so that fuzzy, dark stars dance in front of her eyes before slowly fading away. She crawls from the stiff hotel sheets and pushes one floor-length curtain back to reveal sunlight so bright that she promptly drops the curtain again and stumbles backward. The air conditioner was humming all night, and now it's freezing in her room.

Next is just a transition from one point to another, Lila said in last week's class. Of course, she was talking to the writers about changing the scene, manipulating the action. Julie thinks about what she is going to do next, about what Nell will say when Julie walks through the door of her shop after all of these years.

Her overnight bag sits on the threadbare carpet at the foot of the bed, its dark contents—skirts, shirts, pants—reaching outward like arms in all directions. She trips over it on the way to the bathroom.

She dresses in jeans and a light sweater. The absence of a menu confirms that The Inn still doesn't offer room service, so she locks up the room and heads to the elevator in search of food. In the lobby, she nibbles a bagel and drinks a cup of black coffee from the continental breakfast. The coffee sizzles against her tongue, singeing her taste buds so that she can barely taste the bagel when she bites into it. She eats quickly, willing Maggie Harris not to materialize. August rounds the corner as Julie is tossing half of her bagel into the trash.

"Morning," he says.

"Morning."

Coffee cups in hand, they leave the hotel and climb into the rental car. The sun is so warm that it is hard to believe that only last night she'd huddled inside her coat, shielding herself from the rain. Still, the steering wheel is cool against her palm. She turns the key and sits, thinking of where to go.

"I don't mind driving," August says.

"It's okay. I know the way." She slips the car into Reverse and accidentally peels out of the hotel parking lot. "I don't actually drive a lot in New York," she says apologetically.

The Opal Mall was right across the street from The Inn, back when Julie lived in Lawrence Mill, but now there is an elaborate strip mall with a Barnes & Noble, a T. J. Maxx, and a Target where the mall used to be. The whole thing feels strange, familiar and foreign at the same time.

She heads away from Opal, driving on the two-lane highway that will take them into Lawrence Mill. Julie leans forward to twist the plastic radio dials, but Opal only has two local stations, country and soft rock.

"Do you mind Elton John?" she asks, and August shakes his head.

Along the highway, small trees are blooming with pink-and-white dogwood blossoms, planted and tended by the Opal Women Gardeners Association. Julie remembers riding into Opal in the backseat of Aunt Molly's car, watching dogwood petals drift onto the windshield like delicate pink snow. But Molly doesn't live here anymore. (Thank goodness, or Julie would have had to make time for a visit or be guilt-ridden for avoiding it.) She retired and moved to a condo community on the Gulf Coast last year.

Julie veers off the highway, leaving the dogwoods behind and pressing her foot against the brake pedal as she approaches an aging stop sign. The red of the sign is faded, the white a dirty brown, soiled. Something now indecipherable has been spray-painted across the sign, and curly smears of blue paint cover the word *STOP*. If she turned right here, she would see the rows and rows of narrow, dusty brick apartment buildings with rusted screen doors and dirty sidewalks. Government housing. She doesn't have to actually make the turn to see that those buildings are still standing.

Past that old housing project are huge, once-lovely houses that were falling apart even when Julie still lived there. She can't imagine the shape they're in now. Decaying bones of homes that were once considered stately, they had the misfortune of being located in what eventually became the worst part of town. The last time Julie saw them, the houses were painted too-bright pinks and yellows and teals, the paint peeling away in wide jagged strips, the original white paint or raw wood exposed in places, somehow jubilant. Aunt Molly made Julie and Toby roll up the car windows and lock the doors when they drove past.

"I think you're supposed to actually turn here, Jules," August says, when a car horn blares behind them. She makes a quick left onto Magnolia Street, the narrow road that snakes all the way in and then quickly out of Lawrence Mill, as though even the road is in a hurry to get the hell out. The kids who lived in the city and went to Opal High School used to refer to Lawrence Mill as *Opal's Outhouse.*

Tiny homes line this part of the street, dressed in old, white wood siding with dark-gray roofs like jaunty, ragged hats. Narrow concrete pathways lead from front porches to tin mailboxes. Julie remembers these as cute, happy little homes, but now these too have paint peeling and shutters dangling helplessly against glass panes. The lawns are overgrown, with old signs pressed into the ground, peeking over the tall grass like faded flowers and advertising various political candidates and religious activities: *Sonny for Mayor* and *Lawrence Mill First Baptist Homecoming, September 22nd.*

She passes a speed limit sign for thirty miles an hour and presses the brakes again. One night when she and Reba were sixteen, they'd asked Toby for a ride home from Southern Saddle and then spent an hour in the car with him, trying to evade the police. Toby was driving seventy down Magnolia when the police car made a U-turn in the road and the blue and red lights started to flash, illuminating the dark road. Toby maneuvered the car into a neighborhood, where he took a left and then a right, trying to find a hiding place on the dark streets.

He finally stopped in a cul-de-sac, where he snapped off the headlights and threw a tiny plastic bag at Julie, barking at her to hide it under the seat. The white substance inside was like soft powder beneath her fingers as she tucked it away. They waited, all three of them, while Toby cursed and mumbled things they couldn't hear, and Julie and Reba watched, expecting the cops to find them at any moment. But incredibly, it never happened. Julie shouldn't have been so surprised—Toby managed to escape punishment for every bad thing he ever did.

August and Julie pass the mill houses next, the two-story structures fragile and wilting. When Julie was in high school, it became trendy to buy and renovate the mill houses, but that trend seems to have come and gone. Erected by necessity, just before the Lawrence Mill opened in 1901, the thirty or forty homes are laid out in a neat grid, as though the construction had been planned for months in advance, as though housing the millworkers wasn't an afterthought.

"We were in that one," August says, pointing. "You know, when my family lived here."

The now-unused train tracks are still so rough that the Honda bounces up off the road as they cross over. And beyond the tracks, there it is: the Lawrence Mill.

"I thought they tore this down," Julie says. And they have, some of it. She remembers the facade as being dark brick and sprawling, grand. But now most of those bricks lie in heaps, those once-imposing walls half demolished. Windows, long boarded like closed eyelids, line what remains of the exterior. Through the holes and missing walls, Julie can see the exposed brick interior and overturned tables—all that is left of what was once an empire, a castle. They're breathtaking, these ruins, and Julie and August are quiet in the car as they pass. She'd expected bulldozers or cranes, or else a completely flattened landscape, not this abandoned in-between. Aunt Molly sent her the newspaper article about the mill closing and about the petition to preserve the building as some sort of historic landmark, but that was years ago. Julie thought that a decision would have been reached by this point.

She sighs and forces her eyes back to the road. The Lawrence Memory Gardens are a mile from the mill, past the old Thomas Pharmacy and Car Care, and that's where she leaves August. It's better for her to visit Nell on her own, and the memory gardens are where August tells her he wants to go. Still, she doesn't feel good about leaving him alone in a cemetery.

"It's okay, Jules," he says. "I've never been here. I need to do this. You know where to find me when you finish up. Good luck." He shuts the car door and starts to walk up the shaded hillside, and Julie backs out and heads toward Nell's Flower Shop.

20

THE LITTLE SHOP HASN'T CHANGED AT ALL. JULIE USED TO LOVE this place: the white, wooden sign announcing *Nell's!* in pretty cursive, the small gravel parking lot leading up to the homey front-porch entrance, the weeds and wildflowers filling in the places where the gravel had worn to dirt. It's all straight out of a memory.

But when Julie looks beyond the shop, she sees that some things *are* different. Drastically so. She bites her lip, hard, and sits for a moment, staring. Then she takes a deep breath and slowly opens the car door.

The gravel makes a jarring *crunch, crunch* beneath her feet as she walks, and she thinks of Beck chewing cold cereal on a quiet morning. The shop bell tinkles when Julie pushes the door open.

"One minute!" She hears the voice from the back, too distinctive to belong to anyone but Nell. Julie looks around, wondering what she's going to say. What will Nell think, when all these years have passed and Julie has never even called to say hello? In the cooler to her left, she can see fresh lilies in the first stages of soft bloom. All of the scents must be mingling together and confusing her, because she can see that the lilies are sealed away, but she can smell them, she swears, the heavy perfumy scent of lilies and something like honeysuckle forcing its way into her nose, her lungs. *It's not air*, she thinks. *It's too sweet.* She opens her mouth to breathe but the scent gets in, and now she can taste it too. She touches her fingers to her throat and gasps, but that doesn't help, and for a moment, she knows she will surely suffocate.

"What can I do for you?" Nell asks, stepping out from the back room and breaking whatever hold these memories have on Julie. For a second, Nell looks at her like she is a stranger, and Julie stands still and speechless. She has come unannounced, and she wonders again if maybe that was a mistake.

She can feel it when Nell recognizes her. "Well, well!" she says. "Good Lord, Jules, get over here and give me a hug!" Her friendly, frosty-pink-lipsticked smile is so familiar, so comforting, that Julie feels like crying. Finally, she can breathe again. She crosses the room and throws her arms, childlike, around Nell's neck.

"Jules," Nell says, her arms patting Julie's back as they hug. "Girl, it's been a long, long time."

"Nell, the field is gone," Julie whispers.

"My God, so you *can* talk. Sit down, sit!" Nell points to a stool behind the counter and perches herself on the one beside it. Nell's hair is the same orangey shade Julie loved so much—no gray, even though it's been ten years.

"Honey, what are you doing here? Not that I'm not thrilled to see you, because I am. But things are okay with Molly, right?"

"What?"

"Sweetie, is everyone okay? Molly's all right? I haven't seen her lately, but if anything was wrong, surely I'd have heard."

Julie blinks. "No. No, not Molly at all. It's nothing like that."

"Then what brings you back? I haven't seen hide nor hair of you around these parts in years. But I'm glad you're here," Nell reiterates, patting the top of Julie's hand.

Julie must look overwhelmed. She certainly *feels* overwhelmed. "Well, I actually came here with someone. To Lawrence Mill."

"Oh." Nell raises an eyebrow. "Boyfriend? I wouldn't have thought you'd want to bring a special someone around here."

"Not my...special someone." She takes a deep breath. "I...um... Actually, I came here with August. August Elliott."

"Come again?" Nell shakes her head quickly in disbelief, as though her ears have betrayed her and she hopes to jostle them back into working order.

"You heard me," Julie says. "August."

"*Reba's* August?"

Julie nods.

"Thought my ears had stopped working on me," Nell says. "Well, spill, then. You'd better tell me everything."

21

THE DAY I FIRST SAW THAT STRANGE, SHIMMERY LIGHT IN THE field, Jules and I took our usual shortcut home. We go to my house most of the time, even though Molly's house is right next door and we could just as easily go there. Except that Molly's house never feels like home to Jules, and she doesn't like to be there any more than she has to. I would tell Jules it's all in her imagination, if that was really the case. But I'm not comfortable there either. People say that there is a difference between a house and a home, and Molly's house is... well, a house. Even Toby, who is Molly's child outright and not there because of circumstances, is always locked away in his room, if he's around at all.

When we were kids, Jules and I spent almost all of our time on the banks of the river or playing on the thin, rickety bridge that connects the banks, even after Mama chased us down the time we left the front yard without permission. Oops. That didn't keep us from the river for long—*our* river, we decided. Even now that we're older, we like to think that it belongs to us.

So we walked along the river on the way home, and dipped our toes into the shallow water and shivered. How can the water be so cold when the air is so hot? I followed Jules over the wooden bridge, jumping over the sagging seventh plank (four, five, six, jump!). I was bare-armed in a tank top, and Jules was bare-legged in jean shorts. We let the tall, crisp grasses whip against our skin as we ran through the field—until my skirt got caught on a stray twig, and then we walked the rest of the way, with me holding up the ends of my long skirt until we reached the clearing that led to David Nickel's property.

David, a friend of my daddy's, used to live with his family, but then his wife left him and took their little boy. It was the talk of the town for a while. Just across the street is my house.

It's bright white and perfectly symmetrical, except for the garage on the left. Jules says it's nauseatingly pretty, and I think she would have hated this house on principle, if not for the fact that I live in it. The only thing missing is the picket fence. Molly's house next door is larger, but it's painted a sickly green, with black shutters (Ted painted them before he left—Jules and I watched him up there on the ladder with the paintbrush) and closed blinds covering every window.

Jules tells me that Molly could afford to live in something even larger, not that she needs it, but something more inviting, maybe. Jules knows more than Molly thinks. She knows, for instance, about the insurance money from Jules's parents, and she's seen the checks of varying amounts that Ted sends in envelopes with different return addresses each month (as though he is afraid Molly might track him down and drag him back here against his will).

Jules followed me up the wooden steps, onto the porch that stretches across the front of my house, and to the blue-painted front door. I could hear the clatter of pots and pans as we walked inside. We followed the sound and saw Mama at the kitchen counter, measuring out flour into a coffee mug. A plate of cookies, oatmeal raisin, sat on the countertop.

Mama greeted us with a shy, nervous smile. Always as if she is surprised to see us. I can never tell if the surprise is a pleasant one.

"I made cookies for you girls," she said, as though this was a new phenomenon. "Dinner will be ready in an hour. I'll set a place for you too, Jules." She smiled. "Harold had a big meeting at work today. I have a feeling we'll be celebrating soon." My daddy was up for a promotion at the mill, and everyone expected him to get it. I just couldn't wait until we didn't have to hear about it all the time.

Mama pushed her hair behind her ears, then immediately spun to the sink to wash her hands. She has a habit of doing this—touching her hair or face while she is cooking and then washing up quickly, like her germs might ruin the meal.

My mama isn't pretty, not the way she used to be. Her hair, the color of straws on a broom, is shapeless against her chin. She's short like me, but her body is thin and straight, no curves to speak of. The only remarkable thing about her is her eyes. They're huge, like mine, the color of pool water. Jules says my eyes are my best feature, but on Mama, those eyes are strange, hovering over her tiny nose and thin-lipped mouth. Her eyes make her look innocent in a way that she shouldn't, at her age. I hope that's not what I have to look forward to.

"Thanks for the cookies," I said, picking up the plate and heading to my room with Jules following behind.

Jules and I sat cross-legged on my bedroom floor, the soft carpet fibers rubbing against my legs in that way that is both scratchy and soothing. The room is covered in white, with pearly-white walls and puffy, white cotton-ball pillows on my white eyelet bedspread. It's too girlie, and I dream of a room painted the color of the ocean. The white was Mama's doing; this was her idea of what having a daughter would be like. It's probably not worth the effort (or the argument with Mama that would surely come) to change it all, anyway.

"Finally, the meeting," I said. "Maybe now we'll stop hearing him go on and on about the damned promotion." I slid a CD into the stereo, and Fiona Apple's velvety voice sang to us. Mama would lose her mind if she knew I owned this CD—so sensual. "Slow Like Honey" played through the speakers. I moved my lips, without sound, to the words of the song.

"Tell me about your date," I said.

Jules was quiet for a moment, mentally editing the story for my ears, I'm sure. "It was with the boy I met on the Fourth of July, at the fireworks. Do you remember?"

"Which one?" I laughed.

"Jake. He's our age. Goes to Woodbrooke."

"Well, what's he like? What did you talk about? Where did you go?"

But I could guess the answer. They went to the park, I bet. I imagined the wet heat of Jules's mouth pressed against her date's as she straddled him in his car, under the moon, in the middle of the night.

"He's…nice," Jules said. When I raised an eyebrow, she elaborated. "Boring, kind of. He only wants to talk about school. He wants to be a doctor. And he was annoyingly afraid of getting caught, kept talking about his friend so-and-so who was nearly arrested when the cops found him at the park with his girlfriend a few months before. He's nice to look at, though—dark hair and eyes and a great smile. He plays football."

"Hmm…good kisser?" I teased.

"Yes," Jules admitted. "That part wasn't as boring as the rest."

I'm not allowed to date. But, technically, neither is Jules. It's just that there's no one around to stop her.

The slamming of the front door made us both jump. I can't help but tense up when my daddy comes home. Like I'm doing something wrong, even though the worst I could be accused of then was listening to improper music.

Jules is as used to my daddy by now as I am: his size (tall, wide), his booming voice, his cheeks, red-tinted and mottled as though he's just finished running a mile or two. But that day he was louder than normal, letting out a yell that seemed to shake the house. Even Jules sat up straighter.

We started to hear other things—cabinets slamming or maybe a fist crashing down on a table. "Uh-oh," I said.

We couldn't hear what he was going on about. His normal "Hello, ladies!" was certainly missing, but the sound of his voice wasn't getting closer to my room, which meant, at least, that whatever had gotten him all worked up, it wasn't us.

It didn't take long for it to click. "Oh no," I whispered. "The promotion." Curious and terrified as I've always been when Daddy is angry, I eased open my bedroom door and tiptoed into the hallway. We crept along past the wood-framed photos lining the walls, family portraits of Mama and Daddy and me in dress clothes, smiling stupid forced smiles. At the end of the hallway, we could see my parents in the kitchen. Daddy stomped back and forth across the room, rattling the place settings on the dining table.

"I can't believe it! *My* job! *My* job!"

"Harold, calm down," Mama said, her voice quavering as she smoothed her hair. "The girls are home."

Daddy's hands were clenched, white and visible against his otherwise red body. "*How* could this happen?"

"I don't know," Mama said, looking down and shaking her head. "Harold, I don't understand." Instead of going to him, she shrank against the wall, as though she could disappear into the country-themed kitchen wallpaper.

"That was *my* promotion! Everyone knew it! Everyone knew it belonged to me, damn it! Every day for twenty-five years, Libby, twenty-five years I have gone to work every day at that dirty, smelly, blistering-hot hell, and all for nothing! *Nothing!*"

Jules looked at me, and I nodded. Definitely the promotion, then. The fury on his face made me feel light-headed and panicky, but I couldn't turn away from it.

"I'll quit! That's what I'll do!" he shouted, hurling a set of perfectly wrapped silverware across the room. We flinched, and so did Mama, as spoon, fork, and knife crashed against the wall and clattered noisily to the floor. "Enough! I've had enough! And the worst part, Libby? Oh hell, I haven't even gotten to the worst part! Libby, do you know who took *my* job? Do you know?"

Mama shook her head again, silent.

Impossibly, my daddy's face turned an even deeper shade of red, making him look like a demon when he opened his mouth and let out a trembling roar. "A *nigger*, Libby!"

I could hear Jules gasp. *Oh no. Here we go again.*

Three months ago, before the end of school, a white girl, Penny Decker, was caught under the bleachers with James Edgemont, a black boy. Everyone knew they were dating, and that was scandal enough throughout the school, especially among the teachers. But when the principal caught them together half-naked and told Penny's parents, they insisted it was rape, and James was arrested. Penny didn't say he forced her, but she didn't say they were a couple, either. She got scared and didn't say anything at all.

The KKK held a protest right outside the high school. I guess I was the only one naive enough to be surprised that the KKK existed in Lawrence Mill in 1997. They wore awful white robes, carried signs, and accepted donations. The Jackson Channel 12 news crew was out with their cameras and caught the whole humiliating scene. A prominent civil rights lawyer from Massachusetts got wind of it and came to town to take on the case. Once he got everyone talking—Penny's friends, the teachers, even the high school janitor—it became pretty clear that what happened between the two teenagers was consensual. The charges were dropped, and James walked away with a big settlement. And Lawrence Mill's racial divide—hard-edged and ugly and not as buried in the past as folks liked to believe—was exposed to the entire country.

Now James is doing the talk show circuit and is practically famous (and good for him, after what he went through) and Penny Decker is a high school dropout, shunned by all of her friends and living at home with her parents in their trailer that the bank's about to seize. Needless to say, Penny and James aren't a couple anymore. Jules says that Penny got what she deserved, for letting James take the fall like that. I guess I never really understood what was so wrong with them being together to begin with, but enough people around here thought it was shameful.

The racial issues have just started to die down. All this tiny town needs is something to stir them up again, and if anybody would do some stirring, it would be my daddy.

"Oh, *Harold*," Mama said. "Surely that's not what happened."

"And not even one from around here! Oh no, a town nigger could never steal my job, wouldn't have the nerve to, even if it were offered! They sent someone in—*sent someone*! A Yankee at that, though they act like he's Southern enough, sent from corporate in Richmond. And those…those two-faced, backstabbing assholes in management knew it was happening. They moved him to Lawrence Mill a week ago! He starts *tomorrow*! I'm going to be the laughingstock of this whole goddamned town! A laughingstock! I've had it!"

(He was right. I don't know if they were laughing, but by the very next day, most of the older folks in town were talking up a storm about Daddy's promotion going to a black man.)

"But, Harold, why?" Mama asked. "Why didn't the promotion go to you?"

"How the hell should I know? Goddamn it, why does everyone expect me to understand everything? That's what they said today when they told me about it, right before they called a company-wide meeting to introduce my new boss! 'We've got to get some diversity in these upper-level positions, Harold,'" Daddy mimicked, his tone high-pitched. "'We know you understand.' Understand! I do *not* understand! I won't have it!"

Jules looked uneasily at me. *I should go*, she mouthed, gesturing to the front door. *Want to come with me?*

I shook my head. It would only make things worse if Mama and Daddy went to my room later and didn't find me there. So, while my daddy continued to shout and throw things every which way, I watched Jules slip quietly out the front door, and the overwhelming desire to escape nearly made me run right after her, no matter the consequences.

22

"Yep, old Harold losing the promotion had everyone talking for a while," Nell says. In one hand she holds a short glass filled a quarter of the way with bourbon, pink fingernails pressed against transparent crystal. To Julie's surprise, Nell had put the CLOSED sign on the door of the shop once they began catching up. *Lord only knows when you'll come my way again*, she'd said.

"He said he would be the laughingstock of the town."

"Well, he damn near was, for a time. You know how people are around these parts. That was juicy gossip, but only until the next thing came along. Most people had forgotten about it by the time he pulled his little stunt, got his revenge."

"I guess I still don't understand it all." Julie's hands tremble against her will, the bourbon in her own glass shaking with the movement. "I mean, everyone must have known it was Mr. McLeod who set fire to August's house, so why didn't they keep him in jail?"

Nell is quiet for a moment before she speaks again. "Well, according to the police, there wasn't any proof. Was that true? Who knows.

But with what happened to Reba right after that—well, you know, I guess people felt more sympathy for him than anything else."

"I didn't," I say, and I realize it's true. I'd felt more pity for myself back then.

"Well, Harold always was a mean old bastard. Never cared much for him myself." Nell shook her head. "But losing a child can break almost anyone."

Julie doesn't want to talk about Harold. It's too late to feel sorry for him. She looks around, the vibrant colors in the shop and the familiar smells soothing after the initial shock. And Nell—so much the same that it is hard to believe any time has passed.

"Nell, what happened to the field?"

"Oh, honey, I sold my land five years back. It was a slow season, and the county wanted the land for a park, and I didn't have much of a choice. So they came in and dug up the field and the little forest, and now it's some kind of recreational park. Right after it was finished, the mill closed, and folks started leaving this town in droves, so a new community park turned out to be a pretty dumb idea. Glad I got my money when I did. I don't go down there much, nor does anyone else. Named after the old school principal, Leonard Hobart. I hear there is a walking track there now, and a playground and a tennis court. I don't even know who takes care of it anymore, if they do it all." She shrugs. "What's done is done."

"And the river? The bridge?"

Nell laughs. "Well, it'd be difficult to move a river, wouldn't it? At least with this town's budget. Of course it's still there. But I believe they tore out that old bridge and put something new and sturdy in its place."

Julie sighs. "I can't believe the field is gone."

"Neither can I. But tell me about *you*, Jules. Tell me about your life in New York. You famous up there yet? I haven't even gotten a Christmas card since you went away, you know. And what on earth are you doing here with August?"

"I'm sorry, Nell," Julie says, smiling sadly. "I guess I thought I needed to leave all of this behind."

Nell sets her drink down and pats Julie on the knee. "I know how it is. I'm not holding any grudges. Now, go on."

Julie tells Nell a short version of her life, a cold summary of her marriage and divorce. She tells her about Beck, about acting, about how she is still trying to make a name for herself in the acting world.

"You've got a daughter!" Nell exclaims, her brown eyes twinkling. "Where is she? I want to meet the little devil!" Julie explains that Beck hadn't come along. "Well, a picture then. I've got to see her. I bet she's as pretty as you are."

"She doesn't look a thing like me." It comes out flat. "She looks just like her father."

"Show me a picture and let me see for myself," Nell urges with a hearty laugh.

"Hang on," Julie says. She pulls her cell phone from her purse and displays a pixelated photo of Beck from last year with a smiling face and chubby pink cheeks.

"My Jules with a little girl," Nell says, shaking her head. "Gorgeous. I can't believe it. Your own little family. Speaking of family, what about Toby? Will you see him while you're here? He's still around these parts, you know. Opened Opal's first art gallery downtown, lives in a nice little loft above it. I thought he was crazy when he came up with the idea, but I guess he does well enough. Online sales are good, and those tourists that come out to Opal now on the weekends seem to like his stuff. Not my taste, though. Did you see him when he was in up in New York City for that art show?"

Julie thinks about the flyer she received in her mailbox months back for the show, how he purposefully sent her an invite. She went alone to the gallery and was surprised and horrified to see the huge canvases leaning against the walls, Toby's name scrawled at the bottom of each one. Elaborate, detailed paintings of wooden bridges, with small, confused faces depicted in the curves of the wood. Julie's face. Reba's face, fading against the dark of the splintered planks. And there was Toby, long hair pulled back, stubble on his face, dressed in torn jeans and a button-down shirt, shaking hands and accepting praise for his work, the art he'd made from tragedy. He smirked when he saw Julie, and she ran from the gallery without speaking. She hadn't seen or heard from him since.

She wonders why Nell seems to know—or care—so much about Toby. "No," she says, shaking her head. "No, I didn't see him."

"And August?" Nell asks. "How did you two end up here together?"

"He sort of...found me. In New York. It's an odd story. We're looking for something here, actually. A diary. It belonged to Reba, and this may sound strange, but I was wondering...well, I was wondering if you know anything about it. If you *have* it, maybe?"

She can't miss the nervous expression that settles on Nell's face, the quick side glance into the back room. "What in the world would make you think that I would have something like that?"

Julie is caught off guard, wondering if Nell will really lie to her. Because it is clear that she knows about the diary. She used to think that Nell didn't lie. What a naive thing to think of anyone! "I-I don't know. Something August said made me think that you might have found it...that day. At the river."

Nell shakes her head. "I can't help you, honey. I wish I could."

"Oh." Julie doesn't know what to do next, what to say. She hadn't considered a scenario in which Nell might have the diary but would be unwilling to turn it over, that it might be right here in this shop and Julie wouldn't be able to get her hands on it.

"Maybe there's something else, some other way you two could find closure," Nell says. And Julie nods like this could be true, but she knows it isn't.

23

It was early August, and school hadn't started back yet, but play practice *had*, and Jules was all wrapped up in it, like always. The new drama teacher was holding tryouts, even though school didn't officially start until the next week.

A fan of the classics, Ms. Madrie had decided on *Romeo and Juliet*, which Jules was furious about, because she is one of the few people on the planet who hates Shakespeare. Honestly, who else *hates* Shakespeare? All those gorgeous words. Still, Jules was the obvious choice for the lead.

"It's kind of sweet, isn't it?" I said to her, back when she first got the letter about tryouts. "And your names are so similar—Jules, Juliet. It's like you're meant for the role." But Jules rolled her eyes. She isn't one to buy into starstruck romance.

They won't even perform the play until January, but these things take preparation, I guess. Jules was already practicing lines at night in her bedroom mirror, watching her facial expressions as she spoke. Even though Jules hates Ms. Madrie's choice of play, she would have been so angry if anyone else got the role.

So, Jules was busy with tryouts, and I was at Nell's, working alone at the counter, the next time I saw him.

It was a Tuesday, and the shop was empty except for Nell and me. With no customers and the shop tidy, I went outside and flopped into one of the plastic chairs. I propped up my legs, tugging the long, lightweight skirt I was wearing so that instead of draping around my ankles, it pooled at my knees. Gypsy skirts, Nell calls them. I guess it's a silly fashion choice, especially in this kind of heat. I can't explain why I like them. My hair felt like it weighed a hundred pounds, and I held it up with both hands, using it to fan my neck.

I knew well enough that I could have been indoors, cooling down. The air conditioner in Nell's shop worked fine. (At least, it did then.) But there is something…*exciting* about this kind of Southern heat. Anything can happen. It's what keeps us outside, Jules and me (when Jules is around), even when sweat covers our bodies like an extra layer of dewy skin.

Nell had just hired Jules's cousin, Toby, to drive the delivery van. I'd tried my best to talk her out of the idea, but she didn't want to hear it. A favor to Molly, most likely, but Nell knows how volatile Toby can be. He and Jules can hardly stand to be in the same room together, and he makes me feel uneasy too, in a way I don't really understand. Something about the way he looks at people, like he can *see* their secrets. He's flat-out gorgeous, but he can't be trusted. Jules had no idea that Nell had hired him, and I knew she would be absolutely livid when she found out.

I couldn't wait to go back to school. I love it all: the learning, the structure, the feeling of being surrounded by knowledge and teachers and people who know things, and books that tell me how the world is supposed to be. Feeling like I know something today that I didn't know yesterday.

I was hoping that once school started back, Jules wouldn't want to spend every weekend at Southern Saddle, but it was likely that she'd want to keep it up, even though it's no secret that I don't like to go. The noise, the alcohol, all of the insincere men showering us with attention because they want things from us. Is it so terrible to hold out for something genuine? Outside of the fact that my daddy would kill me if he found out I was there. I should have told Jules I wasn't going back, but have I ever told her no? Most of my life, she's been pulling me along, and I've never really minded. I'm grateful for it, even. And play practice meant that she might not even have time for Southern Saddle. Jules would get the part, of course. Is there anything Jules wants that she doesn't get?

When I saw him, finally, I had the feeling that he had been there for a while. I stood up, and he was closer than last time, crouched again in the tall grass, camera to his face.

I didn't think about what I was doing. I just starting running toward him, skirt held up around my knees so it wouldn't catch in the weeds. Maybe I should have been afraid, but my curiosity won out. I knew the moment he realized I was coming after him, because he stood up straight. He was taller than me (but everyone is), and his skin was deep brown, which was much more alarming than his height, if I am the girl my father raised. He turned to run.

I thought of all the things my daddy has tried to teach me, all of his warnings. I should have turned back around, gone inside like a good girl, probably called the police to alert them that a black man was doing suspicious things behind Nell's shop. I know I should have. But I thought of Jules, of what she would do, and I knew she wouldn't have thought twice about confronting this stranger. And so I kept going.

"Stop!" I called after him, when I knew he could hear me. But he kept running toward the thick trees.

"Wait!" I yelled again.

I don't know what finally made him stop, but he did, just before he reached the trees. He looked at me, and I kept running and running, still calling out for him to stop even though he very clearly *had* stopped already.

"Hi," he said, when I stopped in front of him, gasping for air. I looked down at the ground and back up slowly, my eyes pausing at the big camera, silver and black and hanging on a long strap around his neck.

Finally, I took in his face. "You," I said, because I didn't know what else to say and the silence felt elastic, like it could stretch on indefinitely.

"Um…me," he said. He was young, probably around my age. His hair was dark and cropped close to his head with a hint of a curl forming at the ends, and his eyes were like the night without a moon, mysterious and intriguing. I was at eye level with his throat, and I watched his Adam's apple slide up and down, pressing against the tender skin there when he swallowed. I could feel myself blush.

"You're taking pictures of me," I said. "Why?" I took in the rest of him, the muscles of his arms exposed beneath the sleeves of his T-shirt. I put one hand on my hip and tried to look intimidating.

"You caught me," he said, a slow smile spreading across his face.

He had a dimple in his left cheek. "It was the flash last time, right? That's what gave me away."

"What?" I wiped a hand across my forehead.

"The flash. On the camera. The flash in the middle of the day. It was an accident. I know better."

"Why are you taking pictures of me?" I asked him again.

"Because the ones from last time didn't turn out," he said. "That's what I'm trying to tell you. The flash."

"Who are you?"

He was silent, looking at me with that same lazy smile.

"Fine. Maybe I'll go call the police and let them know that some crazy...boy is trespassing and taking strange pictures." I turned around without any real intention of calling anyone. Was I flirting? Is this how it's done?

"Hey," he said. "Hey, come on. Look, I'm into photography. It's what I do."

"Why me?" I asked.

"Not just you. It was that shop at first. Flowers, right? The way it looks from back here. So interesting. And then I saw you. It's harmless, okay? They're just pictures." He studied me. "I'm August." He held out his hand for me to shake, and I looked at it a long time before taking it, my hand small inside his.

"Hi." That first touch, his hand warm and soft, gave me a tiny thrill, and I felt excited and sad at the same time.

"Hi..." He trailed off, and it took me a moment to realize that he was waiting for me to introduce myself.

"Reba," I said. I saw that our hands were still linked, so I dropped mine quickly.

"Reba," August repeated. "Interesting name. Nice to meet you, Reba."

"Short for Rebecca," I said. "Why don't I know you?" I couldn't believe how rude I sounded, but Lawrence Mill is so small, and he seemed close to my age. Even if we wouldn't naturally spend time in the same groups, I should still know his face.

"Do you know everybody?" he asked, and I couldn't tell if he was being sarcastic, or if maybe he was flirting with me too.

I shrugged. "Sort of."

"Well," he said. "I just moved here. I'll be starting at Lawrence High School next week."

"Oh."

His eyes were so dark and mine so light, and I couldn't help but think of how funny it was that we were looking at each other and seeing someone so opposite, right down to the eyes.

"I have to go," I said. "I'm working. Nell will be looking for me." Silly thing to say, like he knew who Nell was.

"Well, nice to meet you," he said. "Maybe I'll see you around. I'd like to."

"Maybe." I started walking away.

"Hey!" he called after me. "Do you want to see them? The photos of you and the shop? I could stop by your house or something...show you, if you want."

I thought about my parents, and what they would do, my daddy in particular, if this black boy who was very nearly a man showed up on our doorstep, looking for me. Especially these days, when he is holding a grudge against what seems to be the entire black population of Lawrence Mill. A teensy, tiny part of me found the idea of

August even more appealing because my daddy would lose his mind if he ever found out, but having him come to my house would be reckless, even by Jules's standards.

"I don't think so," I said. "But, maybe I *will* see you around." It sounded more like a promise than I intended it to, and I was running back to the shop before he could respond.

I heard the soft whisper of my name before I'd gotten very far away, and I don't know if he was really saying it, or if it was only the sound of his voice, lodged already in my head.

That's how I remember it all happening, at least.

24

THE BELL TINKLES BEHIND JULIE AS SHE LEAVES THE FLOWER shop, and fresh, grassy air fills her lungs. After adjusting to the perfumy smells inside, the light, clean air tastes toxic, makes her feel light-headed. Or maybe her own confusion has her feeling that way.

She has to fight the urge to run back inside and confront Nell, to find a way to force her to produce the diary. Because Julie would bet any amount of money that Nell has it. If she didn't, the news that there was a diary would have been as shocking to Nell as it had been to Julie when she first heard about it. A bombshell. A revelation.

Why doesn't Nell want her to have it? If Julie were still a headstrong teenager, she wouldn't have been able to sit there and play along while the woman who'd been like a mother to her told her the biggest lie Julie had ever heard. She tells herself that she's smarter now, that she's calculating her next move, and that's the reason she didn't demand that Nell hand over the diary. But the truth is that she was *stunned*, too surprised to even speak.

She was stupid to have thought that Nell would welcome her

back after so long, that Nell would have *wanted* her to have the book. That Nell would still be the same person after all this time.

When Julie and Reba worked at the flower shop as teenagers, Nell kept a small safe tucked on a shelf in the back room. She kept the cash from each day's purchases locked away there until she could get to the bank, but the safe also housed an array of items of sentimental value that Nell would pull out and look over from time to time: a decades-old newspaper clipping of her when she was crowned Cotton Queen in high school, a black-and-white photo of her parents, the first dollar (in a ziplock bag) she'd ever made at the flower shop.

If Nell had Reba's diary, would she keep it locked away with her other treasures? The way Nell had glanced in that direction, like she couldn't help but give herself away, makes Julie think maybe she would. Does that safe even *exist* anymore? When Julie was sitting in that shop, she'd felt certain that the diary was there, *right* there, just out of reach. Would it be valuable enough to Nell that she'd keep it hidden in her safe?

Or, were those words simply so shocking, so scandalous, that they had to be locked away?

Julie is driving away from Nell's shop, her mind on that book when she sees, down the street, the entrance to the subdivision where she and Reba grew up. Despite her desperation for the journal, the impulse to visit her old neighborhood is too much to ignore when she is so close, and she swings the car onto the narrow, sidewalk-lined street. But then finds herself intentionally slowing down, forcing a fascination with trees on the front lawns. The thin twists of branches, the frail light-green of new leaves. Ten, maybe twenty more yards, and there it is: Reba's old house, like something lived in by dolls, the paint on the wood siding still white as a wedding cake. Children play in the yard, little girls, one barefoot in a white dress.

Reba's family is long gone from this place.

Aunt Molly's old house is right next door, green like a dark, mossy pond, the house still somber and solitary compared to the cheerful home next door. Julie steers her car to the curb and idles, looking to every window, thinking of what was beyond those glass panes, how it used to be—the confinement of her room in the upstairs corner. Toby's room right next to it, where his music was always thumping, and Molly's room on the opposite end of the house, as far away from both of them as she could get while still under the same roof, on the same floor.

Julie never dared explore Molly's room, even while her aunt was away. Not even the indulgence of sneaking, with some boy, between the stiff sheets of Molly's tightly made bed. No. Julie's lovers, if you could really call them that, young and inexperienced as they were, never even stepped through the doors of Molly's house, and the woman's bedroom remained not so much a mystery (because mystery implied intrigue, wonder) as a sealed-off place existing on another plane entirely.

The living room was where Molly spent most of her time. After her night shifts at the hospital, she changed into sweats and wrapped herself in a blanket on the sofa. She would fall asleep there instead of in her bed, the new morning sunlight streaming in through the closed slats of the blinds and the TV humming without volume, its bright pictures flashing colors onto Molly's face as she snored. Julie saw her that way on a hundred different mornings, would stop briefly in the doorway of the living room on her way out for school and watch her aunt, her breathing heavy but even, and the expression on her face peaceful. Julie was almost able to imagine Molly as a different person, the person Julie's mother had loved, had been close to. But only then. Only when Molly was sleeping.

Julie fights the urge to spin the steering wheel and drive away. Home is a question mark, confusing. Is Lawrence Mill home? It never felt that way, back then. Still, she idles, the car in Park, and stares at those two houses for a very long time.

Julie was five years old when her parents died, and Aunt Molly and Uncle Ted came to New York to claim her like a stray piece of luggage. It's hard to remember her parents now, but she has never forgotten the car ride from the airport with those strangers, her aunt and uncle. Uncle Ted, still around then, loaded Julie's small suitcase into the trunk, and she crawled into the backseat. When he cranked the car, Molly turned the radio off, and they traveled in silence for the hour that it took to get to Lawrence Mill from the airport.

She stared out the back window at the lush emerald trees racing past. In Mississippi for the first time in her life, she couldn't shake the uncomfortable feeling of being stranded in the middle of nothing but forests and land.

A car accident had killed her parents, though they didn't even own a car. Their rental had gotten bashed and beaten when an eighteen-wheeler hit them.

Years later, Julie stumbled upon photos of the wreckage, photos that Molly kept hidden in the attic—for insurance purposes, maybe. The car was so battered that Julie couldn't tell the make or model. She looked at those photos and thought that she should *feel* something. But there was nothing except the strangest, softest sorrow for the broken shell of a vehicle, the craters in the metal like bruises.

That same day, Julie found the black-and-white photo of Uncle Ted and her mother as teenagers, embracing with carefree smiles on their faces. It had to have been before Molly and Ted ever dated, certainly before they married. Julie understood then why Uncle Ted had always been so soft and caring to her, and Aunt Molly mostly hard and reserved.

The irony was that Julie and her parents had been on the way to Lawrence Mill the day of the crash, to visit Molly and Ted and Julie's cousin, Toby. She had never met any of them; her mother hadn't seen Molly in years. So, they rented a car for a road trip. Julie thinks that her father was particularly excited about it, although maybe she made that part up. It isn't as if there is anyone around to contradict her. The accident happened before they even made it out of New York State. Killed instantly, her mother and father both. But Julie was in the backseat, and so small, and tucked against the floorboard behind her mother's seat. She thinks that she remembers the scratchy, felt-like curls of fabric from the back of the passenger seat rubbing against her face and arms when the EMTs pulled her from the car.

Julie's mother, Margo, had left Lawrence Mill two days after her high school graduation. Her parents and her older sister, Molly, were so infuriated with her decision to leave that they refused to drive her to the airport, as though refusing her a ride might stop her from leaving altogether. A friend drove her instead. Julie often imagines her mother waving an exuberant good-bye to Molly, who would have stood in the driveway with her arms crossed and her mouth a firm, straight line.

In New York City, her mother was a dancer. Before she married Julie's father, she'd actually been a Rockette. (This was more impressive to Julie once she moved back to New York as an adult and saw the Rockettes for herself.) Aunt Molly had photos of Julie's mother dancing, and these Julie took with her. In the pictures, her mother wears a big, red-lipsticked smile and glamorous sequined outfits with elaborate headdresses. In some of the photos, she is alone, but in others, she has her arms wrapped around other women who wear identical costumes. They must have been her friends. Julie's father was an entertainment reporter for the *New York Times*. She would never know how they met, but she imagines her mother—long, dark hair, heavily lashed eyes, plump lips—seducing her father. In the only photos she has seen of them together, he is wearing button-down shirts and ties, but her mother's arms are thrown passionately around his neck, her face nuzzled against his. They look blissfully happy.

Aunt Molly and Uncle Ted were their only family, the only people to call when Julie became an orphan.

Riding into Lawrence Mill, five-year-old Julie saw the old buildings, the mill, Nell's Flower Shop, observed things as any outsider might. Ted drove the speed limit. They turned into the neighborhood where Ted and Molly lived and drove past houses, some of which were still being constructed. The driveway they turned into led to a two-story house, pea-green with gray shutters, a mailbox enclosed with decorative bricks.

Julie started to cry.

Uncle Ted opened the car door and scooped her out of the

backseat, but when he put her on her feet, she sat down right there in the driveway, her face stinging with tears. Through her blurred vision, she saw a little girl playing in the yard next door, in front of a white house with a blue-painted door. The little girl had long, light curly hair and wore a white dress with streaks of grass stains across the front. She played alone, skipping and singing and seemingly lost inside a world of her own creation. When she saw Julie, she stopped, and they looked right at each other across the expanse of yard between them. The girl had a sunny, yellow dandelion in her hand.

"Come on now, Julie," Ted urged. "It's going to be all right." He saw her watching the little girl next door. "Hey," he said. "See that girl? That's Reba. She's your new neighbor. I bet you guys are going to be best friends. Come on, let's go inside now, and then you can meet her really soon." He bent down to Julie's level and waved to Reba. Reba waved back. "See? It's going to be okay."

He held out his hand and Julie took it, following him into her new life.

25

IT'S HARD TO BELIEVE, NOW—IMPOSSIBLE, EVEN—BUT OF THE two of us, Jules used to be the shy one. I remember the first time my mama took her along with us to a Girl Scout meeting. I'd known all of the other Daisies since forever, or at least for as long as I could remember. Jules was the first person I'd ever met who was *new* to our town, and that made her fascinating. Every little girl wanted to meet her, but when I tried to introduce her, Jules stood behind me and wouldn't say a word.

For the longest time, I was the only one our age that she would speak to. Which was fine with me, actually, because I preferred her company to any of the other Daisies. To anyone at all, really.

I wanted her to have a nickname, like me. So I renamed her, made her new. We *were* Rebecca and Julie; we became Reba and Jules.

I was terrified that my new friend, Julie-turned-Jules, would go away again, as quickly as she'd come, so I tried to make sure that she loved Lawrence Mill, that she loved me. I didn't know then that she didn't have anywhere else to go. I kept her busy with books I liked, and Barbie dolls, and showing her the field and the forest and the woods. I told her everything there was to know about the town, about how you could get a scoop of ice cream for only fifty cents (I didn't know if fifty cents was a bargain for ice cream—it was before I understood money—but I knew that the price pleased my parents) at the old-fashioned soda counter at the Thomas Pharmacy and Car Care, how during the summer the Opal Library hosted a summer reading program (we'd just finished it when she arrived in town that year) and you got free pizza if you finished every book on the list, how Lawrence Elementary School was in walking distance from our houses and how when we were a little older we'd probably be able to walk to school instead of riding the bus. I saw the older kids walking all the time.

Those were the things I found important, then. Isn't that funny? We still get those fifty-cent ice-cream cones sometimes.

26

JULIE WONDERS IF ANYONE SHE KNOWS FROM HER CHILDHOOD still lives in this neighborhood. Not that she's going to find out. Reba's and Aunt Molly's houses both have different occupants now with different stories. Aunt Molly went to the coast, but who knows where Reba's mother ended up?

Julie thinks of the day that she, herself, left Lawrence Mill. It was a month after graduation, and she can't believe she lasted that long. She packed one suitcase and left everything else behind. Toby didn't need persuading to drive her to the airport, a cigarette smashed into the fingers of his left hand as his right hand tapped against the steering wheel. When they arrived, he took Julie's suitcase from the trunk of the car, set it on the sidewalk, slapped his hand against her shoulder, and muttered "Good riddance" before driving away, his car coughing out gray clouds of smoke from the exhaust pipe. She looked back, only once, toward the highway.

"Good riddance," she whispered.

And when she boarded that airplane, she really believed that she was leaving the past behind. She thought then that her feet would never again touch Mississippi soil.

Julie looks at the clock. *Shit*. She thinks of August at the cemetery, how she has left him there alone for what *must* be too long now. With one last look at those two houses, she turns the car around and drives.

It's afternoon now, and she's forgotten how bad traffic gets when school lets out for the day, even in this tiny little dot-on-a-map town. If people *have* moved away in droves, like Nell said, you wouldn't know it by looking at this mess. The elementary school, middle school, and high school all sit side by side at the end of one short driveway. Buses pull in, and cars drive out in a slow stream. Julie sits, stuck, in the line of traffic on the two-lane road.

Lawrence High School is on her left as she idles. Students emerge from various doors of the building and pile into cars in the small parking lot or start the walk home to one of the nearby neighborhoods. Some wait for the yellow buses lining up at the curb. Other students have already made it to their cars and have joined the exit line. A blue Volkswagen Beetle—the old kind, beaten all to hell—creeps along, part of the outgoing traffic. Two teenage girls sit in the front seat, windows down, singing along to music that's blaring from their speakers. Julie doesn't know the song.

Even from a distance, these students all look so much younger than Julie felt at that age, when things seemed so innocent and even sex was new and simple and uncomplicated, at least for her. She thinks of all of the times that she and Reba walked together. Reba held her secrets so close, and not once did she part her lips to set them free.

27

SCHOOL STARTED BACK ON A BLAZING-HOT SUMMERY DAY, THE kind of day that *usually* taunts me with images of sipping lemonade or swimming lazy laps in the pool at the Millworkers Association. But not that day. That day, I was excited, buzzing like a bright-yellow bee on a flower as Jules and I walked through the doors of LHS to begin our senior year of high school. Seniors!

I remember giggling at something Jules was saying about Jake, the boy she was sneaking out to see almost regularly. Giggling, but I was nervous all the same, because the minutes were ticking by and we were late *on the first day of school.*

Jules hadn't been able to find her perfect first-day shoes, and she had proceeded to wreck her room looking for them. No other shoes would do, and she was convinced that Toby had hidden them on purpose. She'd found them eventually (in her closet), and the leather-strapped sandals *did* look perfect on her tanned feet. But...we were late.

It's no secret that Jules doesn't care much about school except for drama club, and she certainly isn't ever going to be hurried for anything as mundane as class. When we finally reached the classroom for first period, Jules waved me ahead and pointed toward the restroom across the hall. "Go ahead," she said. "I want to check my hair. I'll be right behind you." I nodded without arguing, because how could I stand being any later?

The other students, most of them at least, were already seated, giants in the tiny desks that seem made for first-graders. They all looked up at me as I walked in. All of those eyes made me feel instantly self-conscious, and I could feel my cheeks growing hot. If I wasn't careful, they'd end up all pink and mottled, the way my daddy's cheeks look when he gets angry. Stupid unwanted trait. I glanced around the room, desperate to find a seat and get myself in it. I recognized all of the faces in the classroom, every single one.

My eyes were pulled, though, to the warm, dark eyes of the boy I'd met most recently. August sat close to the front, with no one in the seat in front or beside him. He nodded to me, a nod so slight that no one else could possibly catch it. I felt my lips part as though I might speak only to him, even in the crowded room. When I realized that I was just standing there, staring, I quickly chose a desk one row away from him. I didn't look at August again, didn't speak a word.

But still, there were unspoken things.

28

Finally, Julie reaches the cemetery. She drives past the ornate sign, through the open metal gate, and along the narrow lane that winds through the memory gardens. She knows where to stop the car, because if there is one thing that time hasn't dulled in the least, it's her own memories of the time she spent in this place. She doesn't want to be here now, empty-handed, without the thing that was supposed to make her feel close to Reba again. Seeing that grave is as fresh and painful as it was a decade ago.

August is sitting on the ground, leaning against Reba's gravestone with his eyes closed.

"Hey," Julie says carefully, aware that this is August's first visit here, that he will feel the weight of it in the way that she does and also in a way that is unique to him, unique to his feelings for Reba. She has an unwelcome urge to touch him, put her arms around him maybe, to offer comfort, but she keeps her hands to herself.

"Hey," he responds, opening his eyes slowly. She isn't surprised to see that they are red-rimmed.

"You ready to get out of here?"

"Yeah," he says, climbing to his feet. Julie eyes the carved marble of the gravestone. *Mary Rebecca McLeod*. Her father is buried next to her now, a matching gravestone. Heart attack. Julie isn't sure how Reba would feel about being so close to a man she regarded as half stranger, half adversary.

Julie spent so much time here in the past that she doesn't feel the need to dwell now, and she is grateful that August is ready to go. She said her good-bye to Reba here, before she had left Lawrence Mill. To be back now, to see it all unchanged—when Reba *should* have changed, should have grown into an adult the way that Julie had, the way that August had—well, it's enough to bring back the darkness that Julie has fought for so long. She's got to get away.

"So…did she have it?" August asks as he slides into the passenger seat, and Julie can tell by his voice that he is both eager and afraid of the answer.

"She did."

He takes a surprised breath. "So, you've got it? Just like that? You've got the diary?"

"No."

"What? Why not?"

"I don't know. I mean, she has it. I'm ninety-nine percent sure of that. But she told me she didn't." She steers the car out of the cemetery gates.

"So she *doesn't* have the diary?"

"You're not listening. She has it. I could tell by the look on her face. She wasn't surprised when I mentioned it. She knew about the diary already."

"So maybe she knows about it, but she's not the one who has it."

"No. She *does*. I think she has it, and I think it's right there in her shop."

August looks confused. "Then why wouldn't she give it to you? I thought you trusted her. I thought she trusted *you*."

"Me too," Julie says. "She used to. I think there's something in that book she doesn't want us to read."

"I don't care," he says, shaking his head. "I don't care what it says. I *need* that diary, Jules."

Julie nods. "I know. Me too."

"What do we do, then? How do we convince her to give it to us?"

She shrugs. "I'm not sure yet."

They pass the old Thomas Pharmacy and Car Care, which closed for good in the time Julie has been away. The pharmacy's big windows are boarded up, and the garage on the side is open, gaping wide like a mouth. Toby worked there for a while after he stopped doing deliveries for Nell.

The old mill is next on Magnolia, and on a whim, Julie swerves into the giant parking lot across the street. The mill and the Baptist church used to share the stretch of asphalt; these days, she assumes only the church crowd uses the space.

August looks up in surprise but doesn't say anything.

"I know it's random. I just want to see something… You can wait here, if you want."

But August opens the car door and follows her. A tall, silvery chain-link fence surrounds what is left of the Lawrence Mill, presumably to keep people out. Julie has never been inside the mill, although now there no longer seems to be a proper "inside." She had her picture taken in front of it once, along with her entire fourth-grade class when they went on the History of Lawrence Mill field trip. In the photo, she and Reba stand side by side, matching little-girl grins on their faces. They're as far from the rest of the group as they can get, while still being part of the same photograph. Julie left that photo at Molly's when she moved away, crammed into some shoe box or packing crate where the mementos of her childhood had been abandoned, at least until Molly moved away, and then her aunt probably tossed it all.

The Lawrence Mill opened in 1901. On the day it closed its doors for good, the mill was one hundred and three years old. That was nearly four full years ago—Molly had mailed Julie the newspaper clipping. *Monumental*, the attached sticky note had said. *The end of the town as we know it.* In its prime, the mill and the Opal Lumberyard were the largest employers in a fifty-mile radius. Thirty-two hundred people once worked within the mill's dark-brick walls, amid the heat and the noise, in the mornings and through the afternoons and on through the night. Like Times Square, the mill never closed.

Until it did.

Most of the buildings are still standing, at least partially, but with walls missing so that Julie can see the overturned tables and chairs. The heavy machinery is gone, maybe moved out when the mill first closed. But there are metal scraps and shards all over, left-behind parts to unfamiliar machines.

Even in the graduating class of 1998, she had classmates with jobs waiting at the mill, mostly men (although many women had worked there too, especially during the wars and then again during the seventies and eighties), lured by a paying job instead of the supposed rigors of college. They'd bought bright, shiny new cars before Julie had even left for New York, but she imagined that they were still working in that mill until the day it shut its doors, stuck like so many of the men who'd started working at the Lawrence Mill when they were young (like Mr. McLeod) and had grown old, their bodies betraying them in the heat of the building, with the physical nature of the job.

Julie walks around the perimeter of the fence until she isn't visible from the street. She is dimly aware of August behind her. She slides her hand along the cool metal of the fence and wraps her fingers through the diamond patchwork of the links. Then she hoists herself up and up, her black sandals pressing against the metal, and finally over the fence.

"Jules, what the… What are you doing?"

"I want to take a look," she says. August doesn't follow her over the fence, just waits and watches as she drops lightly to her feet. The view isn't much different from inside, but Julie moves around anyway, glancing frequently at the ground to avoid debris. She'd always been curious about what went on behind these walls, back when the walls were intact. Now, staring at the skeleton of what was once such an imposing structure, she finds herself thinking of things that end, of the way things fall apart.

With the trees surrounding the mill turned prematurely green and the weeds growing through broken concrete beneath the cloud-crowded sky, she finds herself thinking of Evan.

Evan was a colossal accident. She didn't mean to fall in love with him, hadn't meant to fall in love with *anyone*. She actually believed herself incapable of it then.

She met him in college, on the first day of the spring semester. It was her second year, the first having spun by in what seemed to be a strange blur of motion. She was late for a drama class, and she was walking as fast as she could without actually breaking into a run.

It wasn't that she intentionally sabotaged herself in college—or at least, that's what she told herself. She knew how lucky she was. Her most desperate wish had been to leave Lawrence Mill, and that wish had come true. There had been stacks of paperwork for scholarships and loans and a whirlwind of favors called in by Ms. Madrie to her friends at NYU, her alma mater. Julie loved it there, truly, loved to look out her tiny dorm window as snow wandered down from the sky and into fluffy wet layers on the ground in wintertime. She could remember snow falling only once in Mississippi (real snow, at least, and not the gentle tease of flurries), and even then it had been cold and icy and rock hard. She and Reba had managed snow angels, but it had been too difficult and the cold too piercing for snowmen.

As for academics, Julie turned out to be fairly intelligent, despite what she thought back in high school. But she still felt so restless, so haunted. She didn't belong there, in New York, while Reba was in some hole in the ground, and if Julie wasn't such a coward, she would have confessed to everyone that it was all her fault. She couldn't sleep at night. While her roommate snored softly, Julie would sit in the dark room, not even bothering to lie down.

She tortured herself by replaying everything in her head. Everything she could remember, at least. When her eyes finally closed, she dreamed of bridges and heard screaming. When she opened her eyes again, her alarm clock was screeching and her roommate had a pillow covering her head and was shouting at Julie to *turn the damned thing off*. And Julie would slowly climb from the bed and dress, all the while watching the clock. The hands seemed to tick faster and faster until she knew that class would be starting, but she couldn't make herself leave the room.

By the time she finally forced herself out of the door, class had usually already begun. Even when she walked as fast as she could, she was rarely less than fifteen minutes late.

That day, it was twenty. The hallways were almost empty, and the closed door to Room 242 seemed menacing. She looked through the glass panel of the door to see the group of attentive faces, and that door felt like a divide between her own world—her sullen, solitary place—and the happy, ordinary world of others.

Evan was sitting in the front row, but she could tell by looking that he wasn't really listening, wasn't attentive like the others. She wondered where it was he would rather be. His hair was blond, messy, and his eyes were so blue that she could see them clearly from where she stood. She watched him, fascinated, her face too close to the glass window.

It took her a moment to realize that he was looking back, not lost in his own thoughts anymore, but staring directly at her. She stepped back, hand still pressed to the cool metal of the doorknob. She turned around to leave, but then thought of her English class the previous semester, how she'd missed the first day. The teacher, old and strict and unnervingly overeducated, had very nearly refused to let her join the class at all. *It's a rigorous course*, he told her. *There's no room here for slackers.* And she'd had to plead with him, beg, right there in front of the entire class.

She twisted the knob and walked in, the creak of the opening door such an interruption that the teacher paused in the middle of speaking. Julie gave her what she hoped was a shy, apologetic smile. The teacher was short, with short, brown, childlike ringlets framing her thick, happy cheeks. And she only stared at Julie for the moment it took her to move quickly into the nearest seat. Which was right behind the lovely boy.

"Big decision?" he whispered, half turning in his desk to face her. His eyes were vivid and hypnotic. She looked straight into them, and for the longest time, she couldn't think of the right words to respond.

"Everything is," she finally said softly.

"I was talking about you, coming to class."

"I know."

Later, Evan told her that when he looked at *her* that first time, her eyes were like dark caverns. Places most people wouldn't dare to explore, but he was brave enough to try.

It's a brick ghost town, Julie decides, finally rising to leave. She wonders why she'd needed to see this place at all, if she'd thought the decaying remains of the factory would mean something to her. The trees shake gently overhead, and she can hear the river, faintly, behind the mill. The sun is setting as she climbs back over the fence, its silver links swaying back and forth with her weight.

29

AUGUST SITS ON THE YELLOW CURB IN THE ALMOST-EMPTY parking lot. He's thinking about the diary. Ever since that day in high school when Reba told him he needed to see it, he's wondered what could possibly be written inside, what could have been so important.

All through college he thought about that book, through grad school, through his adult years after that. If he hadn't been so haunted after losing Reba, if he hadn't felt so guilty, maybe he would have sought out Jules sooner. If he had, they might have found the diary ages ago, and he would have spared himself so many nights of sleepless speculation. He didn't expect any bombshells. He knew that he, himself, was Reba's secret. But, there *was* a certain expectation that reading her words would quiet something inside him that had been screaming ever since the night he lost her.

He watches Jules cross the street back to the parking lot. He doesn't know why she'd wanted to stop here at this crumbling wreck, but why argue? He's along for the ride at this point.

"Sorry," she says. "You probably think I'm crazy."

He doesn't respond, because there's some truth to her words. They climb back into the car, and this time, Jules seems at a loss about where to go next.

"What do we do now?" he asks. "We've got to find a way to get the book."

"Yeah, *I know that*," she says. "I just need to think about how, okay?"

August nods, and they pull out of the lot, past the Lawrence Mill First Baptist Church with its dingy white siding and over the railroad tracks. He assumes they are on their way back to the hotel, unless Julie has another surprise detour planned. She drives with the radio turned off and the windows rolled down so that when they pull up to a stop sign, he can hear the crickets calling in the twilight. And then the sun is disappearing. The dim streetlights and the flickering fireflies create a soft glow, so different from the lively lights of Richmond. On the other side of the windshield, stars are scattered like sparkling confetti against the dark expanse of sky. They end up on back roads August doesn't remember, with Jules steering the car around unfamiliar twists and turns. He doesn't know where they're going, and he's not sure she does, either.

It takes a long time to get back to The Inn, but August doesn't mention it. He doesn't mind, anyway.

30

It's been a hell of a day already, and when Nell walks into the gallery, she has a wary expression on her face that makes Toby think his day is about to get even worse. Out the big glass windows, the sun is setting, and shadows are crawling up the paintings. Creepy, but creepy is how he's made a living all these years, so he can't exactly complain about it.

"Hey, Nell," he says, turning down the angry music he likes to blast. Background noise. Adds to the ambience, or something like that. With the big, black chandeliers and the dark feel of his paintings, it's not your typical art gallery. But hey, the shit sells.

"Toby." Nell smiles at him and hefts a six-pack of beer and a bag of produce onto the counter. She thinks he doesn't eat well enough. That's why she's always stopping in with leafy fucking greens and the like from the farmers market in the square, usually with some kind of craft beer to sweeten the deal. Balance things out. If she brings him something he *does* like, there's more of a chance that he'll eat the rest.

She's right, though; he doesn't eat. He hasn't had an appetite in years, can't remember the last time he *craved* something. Not food, anyway. He knows Nell is trying to look after him, so he can't bring himself to be annoyed with her. It's more than his own mother does for him these days. He's a grown-ass man, she'd say, and he doesn't need her to take care of him. He doesn't need Nell either, but he can't seem to make her go away.

Anyway, it's nice when Nell stops in. But today, he can see that she's got something to tell him, and he's antsy to hear it. She looks around the gallery and winces, the way she always does, even after all these years. She's not a fan of the subject matter he paints, and he can't blame her. But he doesn't choose his art; it chooses him. Over and over again, it chooses him. When he picks up his brush, it's always the same thing. No point in fighting it now. Maybe one day, when he's painted Reba enough times, he'll be able to move on. He doubts it, though.

Toby reaches into a drawer and pulls out a bottle opener. He opens a beer for himself and slides one across the counter to Nell. The gallery's closed already, so he leads her to a couple of chairs in one corner of the room.

Nell settles in and takes a swig of the beer. "She's here."

He doesn't have a clue who she's talking about, and he tells her so.

"Jules," she says. "Here in town, with August, of all people."

Shit. Jules is one thing, but the boy? "Why?" Toby asks. "They a thing?"

Nell shakes her head. "No. But they're looking for some answers. Don't be surprised if she turns up here."

He shrugs like it doesn't matter. "There's no way she'll find out the truth." But there is a way. Nell knows. She's the only one who does, besides him, and she cared for Jules back then the same way she cares for Toby now. He couldn't blame Nell if she told.

But the look on her face has him unsettled, anyway. "Don't be so sure," she says, patting his hand with her own.

He doesn't ask. If she's going to tell, he doesn't want to know.

31

My daddy was avoiding everybody in town since he lost the promotion, but after several weeks of nothing but work and home, work and home, Mama finally dragged him out to church. Which meant we all went, even Jules.

Ever since Jules moved in next door and we became fast friends, Mama has insisted that Jules accompany us to church. Jules isn't religious, not even a little bit, but if she tries to sleep in on Sunday, it never fails that Mama will send me next door to wake her up. It's like Jules is our little orphan sinner, and Mama is determined to save her soul. They don't know the half of it.

That day, the sign out front of Lawrence Mill First Baptist proclaimed, in thick black letters, that *Jesus Is Lord*—or it would have, if the *r* hadn't fallen sideways, making it read more like *Jesus Is Loud*.

We climbed out from the back of Mama's sedan, taking care

not to show thighs or undergarments. "*Be ladylike,*" she whispered. Jules's dress was dark gray and knee-length, sleeveless but modest, a dress she wore only to church. She wouldn't be caught dead in it anywhere else.

David Nickel, who lives across the street from us, stood among the churchgoers on the wide steps leading into the church, chatting comfortably with Joseph Evans, a local attorney and one of Daddy's closest friends.

"Harold," Joseph said as we approached. He wore a dark suit, a white button-down shirt, and a blue tie. He looked like you'd expect a lawyer to look, right down to the fancy pen tucked into the front pocket of his suit. He held out his hand to my daddy. "We've been waiting for you."

David looked at the three of us women, then put his hand on Daddy's shoulder and turned him away, lowering his voice. But I could still hear him. "Listen, Harold, I know we're supposed to pretend like nothing's happened. But nobody, and I mean nobody, can believe what is happening at the mill."

Joseph shook his head. "I don't know what they're thinking. It'll be the downfall of the mill, I'll tell you that."

"Libby! Oh, Libby!" Nell called to Mama, and Mama moved away to gossip. Jules and I wandered, drifting toward the open doors of the air-conditioned church. I strained to hear the rest of the conversation between my daddy and his friends.

"I mean, Harold, we can't have...well, you know...one of *them* come in and take your job out from under you." It was David talking. "It isn't right. We've been speaking with some others that work over at the mill, and they are none too happy about it either."

"Well, what am I supposed to do about it?"

"Now, I'm not trying to offend you, Harold. You know that. Maybe I'm overstepping here. But if you feel like you need to, I don't know, *do* something about it…well, you wouldn't hear any objection from us. That's all I'm saying. And you know you can count on Joe here…if you find yourself in need of any legal counsel."

I looked back, my stomach uneasy. *Something like what?* I wanted to ask, but I was too far away and wasn't supposed to be listening in at all. Besides, a small group had gathered around my daddy, shaking his hand, and those low voices were now indistinguishable from one another.

I can't even remember the sermon from that day, but I remember the sweet Southern lilt of our preacher's voice, the awkwardness of watching Jules shaking (during the meet and greet) the hand of the boy I know she fooled around with the weekend before, and the pleased and determined set of my daddy's jaw as one by one, his friends approached to offer him support. It gave me a chill to watch; even an outsider could see the dirty seeds being planted and something taking root.

32

JULIE SITS ON THE HOTEL BED, RESTLESS. TO CALM HERSELF, she checks in with Beck—or rather, she attempts to check in with her by leaving Evan a voice-mail message. She chews her fingernails and waits for thirty minutes until she gets a call back. And then it is Evan's voice, not Beck's, that she hears on the other end of the line.

"How are things?" he asks, an unexpected inquiry into her life, so rare and casual, that she doesn't know the correct response. "Your trip... Are things going okay?"

"I don't know. I'll be glad to get back."

There is a short pause before he speaks again. "Julie, I know there has to be a reason you decided to go back there. I hope you find what you're looking for." She hears the static sound as he passes the phone, and then Beck's voice is in her ear, tinkling like a little bell.

"Hi, Mom."

"Hi," Julie says. And then Beck is chatting, telling her about school and about how Evan has promised to take her to a concert in the park on Saturday. Julie can't ignore the feeling of being somehow in limbo, not a part of the New York world of Evan and Beck and art and music, but not a part of Lawrence Mill either, not nearly.

After drama class, on the day Evan and Julie first met, he looked at her with a small, flirtatious smile and asked her out to coffee. They went to the nearest coffee shop, which happened to be a Starbucks. He grumbled about it, since as promising New York actors, he felt that they should have been frequenting one of the many interesting local joints. *These silly chains*, Evan mused. *So mainstream.*

But they never did go anywhere else. Call it convenience, but that Starbucks was *theirs*. Even though there was a Starbucks on every corner in the city, that one belonged to them as surely as if they owned it, belonged to that time when, miraculously, Evan forced her to leave her past behind. At least for a little while.

On cold days, they would unravel their scarves and sit, legs touching beneath the small tables, and talk about everything, anything. Except for Reba. Julie couldn't talk about Reba. The thoughts in her head couldn't be translated into words, couldn't come out in the form of sound. But still, in those first months, conversation flowed between them, a river of words, endless. He was from New York, originally upstate, but he'd spent a lot of time in the city growing up. This Julie had guessed, even before he told her. Evan wore the city like a trendy accessory, as natural on him as the woven beanie that covered his longish hair in the cold, with blond pieces of hair sticking out and curling upward into the air.

With a native New Yorker by her side, it didn't take Julie long to feel as though she'd acquired the hint of mystery, of sophistication that separated New Yorkers from the rest, although it did take months for her to fully rid herself of the Southern accent. But even back then, she wore dark colors, black mostly—an artsy cliché that made Evan smile. He joked that Julie always managed to look like she was in mourning.

When the weather was warm (which she'd hated in her first year in the city, the pureness of the sunlight reminding her of Lawrence Mill, of Mississippi summers, even though this new heat wasn't quite the humid, heavy-blanket warmth she was used to), she and Evan sat by the windows or outside, and she watched the light dance across his face. Sometimes, they played a game—an idea Evan had gotten from the words to his favorite song. Sitting with their cardboard coffee cups, they would choose a color, and then they'd count the cars of that color that passed by. The first time, the color was blue, like in the song, but then they did red, and then black. Once, for fun, they tried yellow. The total, before they grew exasperated with counting, was 157. All in a half hour. All taxicabs.

In all of the years with all of the boys that she had secretly dated, Julie had never gone on a date with a man in the daytime. Yet for a month, all of her dates with Evan were during the day. It was weeks before they even kissed (another first). But there was never a moment when she thought, sadly, that they were only friends. That first day, he paid for her coffee, and when the wind tossed her long, dark hair across her face, he pushed the strands back behind her ear with the pad of his thumb, brushing his finger against her cheekbone, and she trembled, hoped he didn't notice. She felt the heat between them even then, even in that tiny moment, felt that he had branded her with his fingerprint, and that she was his.

From that point on, they were always touching, her arm linked boldly through his on their second coffee date, his hand covering hers when he leaned across the table to tell her something important, something meant only for her. He would be so close that she could feel his breath, hot, against her cheek, her ear, her neck. But their romance stretched, slowly, across days, weeks.

They both took their coffee black. Julie liked that about him, liked to imagine things about him based solely on the way he ordered his coffee. Bold, sensitive. He liked life the way it was, not sweetened with fantasies, not watered down with distractions. Those things she pretended to know. As for her, she'd only discovered coffee when she moved to the city and needed it. Because she could hardly sleep at night, she was always cloudy-eyed and confused in the mornings.

She never bothered with sugar or cream, or any of the more interesting, innovative coffee additions. Secretly, her taste buds recoiled, stung with the strong, bitter bite of the dark liquid. And yet it seemed fitting. Even when Evan let her forget, even when her guilt wasn't the first thing she thought of each morning, even then, she made sure to indulge in those tiny punishments.

The time they spent together progressed from drinking coffee and counting cars to long walks around the city to museum visits. One day, Evan took Julie to the Empire State Building, and they pretended to be tourists, taking cheesy pictures and giggling all the way up in the elevator. But despite the silly pretenses, she'd never actually been to the top of the building, and she was thrilled with the view, and fascinated, and terrified, by the world below. She told Evan that she felt like she was in the clouds.

There, in the biting wind, Evan took hold of her arms and drew her close and kissed her, his lips touching first the outer corner of hers and then moving inward until his mouth covered hers completely. It wasn't gentle, and it wasn't rough either, that first kiss, his mouth hot and her, melting.

"I can't believe this is real," she whispered.

"God, I've wanted to kiss you for so long," he murmured into her ear.

"Then why'd you wait?"

"This waiting," he said, his voice low and hungry, "makes it so much sweeter."

She was able to change his mind about that, though.

33

I ALWAYS FEEL A LITTLE LOPSIDED WITHOUT JULES AROUND, LIKE a part of me is missing. Nothing major, not enough to handicap me completely. I'm just...less. We've spent so much time together over the years that it's actually strange to be alone.

And I hadn't seen Jules, outside of school, for a few weeks. It felt like longer. If it would have made a difference, I might have tried to talk her out of the play. *Might.* I probably wouldn't have been very convincing. Knowing she wanted it so much made me want it for her. Jules has carried the lead in the school play every year since we started high school. I doubt she could stay away, no matter what.

It was late August then, and Jules was spending every afternoon rehearsing. She'd stopped working at Nell's as soon as school started back, and it had been ages since she'd been over to my house for dinner. Not that I blame her, with everything so volatile. God, could my daddy *be* any more embarrassing? I don't know if Nell was taking pity on me, but she asked me to stay on part time at the shop, working after school and on weekends. Nell said things were busier than normal, but I can't tell if that is actually true. It doesn't matter, either way. I was only too happy to have an excuse to stay away from home.

It was late afternoon, and I was pushing a broom around the shop, getting ready to close up. Toby had taken a sick day already, so Nell had been forced to load up the white van and make the day's deliveries herself.

I'd cut the lights, save for one lone glowing bulb near the counter, enough to illuminate my path. I watched the floor intently, sweeping up the dying petals with the concentration Jules uses when memorizing lines.

I heard a door open, and I looked immediately to the front door, which I thought I'd locked ten minutes before. But there was no happy jangling of the attached bell, so I spun, expecting to see Nell coming through the back. I remember thinking that she must have forgotten something.

It wasn't Nell, though.

"Hey," August said softly, probably because he expected me to be frightened. And I was, a little. Mostly I was intrigued.

"You," I said.

"Yes." Even though the entire store was between us, I took a step back. I couldn't help it. What do girls do in situations like these, anyway?

"You know me, remember?" He smiled, hesitant. I *did* know him, sort of, but things were different here, more intimate somehow.

"August," I said. "What are you doing here?"

"I wanted you to see something. Is this okay?" He stepped toward me, a daring move. Closer. A pile of forgotten petals lay at my feet.

"I…" I didn't know if I liked being interrupted in my solitude before I was prepared to see him again. I felt as though someone had pulled open the shower curtain in my bathroom to find me naked, exposed.

He came closer, slowly, as if he thought I might actually try to run away. "It's the pictures, from that day. I thought you might want to take a look. I thought…" I watched the dimple in his cheek deepen.

We both looked down to see petals scattering around his feet. He'd walked right through them.

"Sorry," he said, still smiling. His face resembled a child's, one who has made an accidental mess and hopes to somehow escape punishment. "I'll sweep it all up for you again. Here, let me borrow the broom."

"No, that's okay." I tightened my grip on the broom handle.

"Come on, let me help you," he insisted.

"No."

"Why not?" he asked. "Come on…" That disarming smile.

"No," I said again. "Thank you, but, well, I don't mind it. I actually kind of like it."

"Like it? Sweeping?"

I know he was thinking about how weird I am. Of course he was. "This," I say. I don't even want to think about how red and spotted my cheeks must have been at that moment. "I like doing this, gathering the pieces."

He looked surprised and completely skeptical. He laughed, quietly, but I heard him just the same.

"You're laughing at me?"

"You're a strange girl, Reba."

"You don't understand." I turned away from him.

"Okay…so, tell me. Make me understand."

I was quiet for a moment before I resigned myself to this, to sharing my own peculiar ideas with him. "Okay, look," I said finally. I moved to the glass door of the refrigerator and pressed my finger against it. "See those flowers, the lilies?"

He followed my pointed finger with his eyes. "Lilies," he said aloud, as though he had never put a word to them before. Maybe he had seen them, but before that moment, they were only flowers, like all the rest. And then they were lilies. Some had bloomed already, coral petals springing outward toward life, but most were still pulled in tightly, the only visible part the delicate white underside of the yet-to-bloom petals.

I couldn't believe I was still talking, but I also couldn't seem to stop. "Before they bloom, see these?" I asked. "They're white. Pure and innocent, but only white. Common. And then they bloom, and there's this unfolding—they become loud and bright." He laughed at my description, and I pretended not to hear him that time, though I could feel the heat still blossoming on my cheeks.

"But look down here," I said, and kneeled down in the floor by the ruined altar of petals. "See this?" I pointed to the scattered mess, pressed my fingers to the floor, and began gathering the pieces, dark purple with brown creeping into the edges. They were curled up like a rich velvet robe, discarded. Luxurious in their own right. Light, loose bits of orange dust clung to my fingers.

"What are those?" August asked.

"Lilies too. Aren't they lovely?" He seemed to know that I meant the flowers on the floor, and not the ones in the fridge. And he seemed surprised, I guess, to find himself drawn into this strange lesson.

"They are perfect," I said, not waiting for his response. "They are perfect and lonely and beautiful, each little petal. They are what they were meant to be. They have fulfilled their destiny."

"Well, they're kind of…dead." August looked at me, dark eyes searching mine like I was some kind of puzzle he was trying to solve. "But maybe you're right." His voice was deep, a man's voice. He picked up a single petal and held it gingerly in his palm as if waiting for it to crumble. In his other hand was a large yellow envelope.

He let the petal fall onto the pile I'd made with my fingertips. And when he moved his hand back to the floor, it was so close to mine that our fingers collided.

"Are lilies your favorite flower?"

"No." I jerked my hand back, the way I do when I am down by the river with Jules and can't resist dipping my fingers into the icy water. I didn't tell him (because I'm sure he thought I was strange enough already) that my favorite flowers aren't in a flower shop, that my favorites grow wild on the edge of the forest. Others might pluck them to keep things neat, to cultivate tulips or pansies or something similarly domesticated. Others would call them weeds. But I don't care. Wildflowers have always been my favorites.

"The pictures," he said, jolted by my movement. "Do you want to see them? You don't have to. I can show you some other time, if, you know, you're in a hurry."

"No," I said. "Show me."

He pulled the prints from the envelope and handed them to me, one by one. The photographs were black and white, and larger than I expected. Did I say *expected*? I don't mean it. I didn't expect anything at all, expectation implying too much room for error, too many opportunities to be let down. But if I *had been* expecting something, these were more. These were breathtaking.

The first ones were of the shop, seen from the back, its ramshackle exterior pretty and nostalgic through the camera lens. The small wooden building stood determined against the field, the two plastic chairs empty on the short, rickety porch. It was just a shop, and it was more than that too, some sort of sweet magic covering the entire scene.

"Wow," I said. And I wasn't simply being polite. His photos were lovely. Even those simple scenes held a kind of presence. Those photos *said* something, even if I didn't know exactly what. They seemed perfectly uncluttered, stripped free of the complexities of humans, and so much better for it.

Then, I found myself looking into familiar light liquid eyes. I didn't realize, right away, that they were *my* eyes, that it was my hand held up against my forehead (a feeble attempt to block out the sun), my own small mouth slightly parted. I wiped my dusty fingers against my shirt and then gently touched the surface of the glossy paper. "Oh," I whispered.

"Careful," he said. "I like that one."

I liked it too, even though I feel vain admitting it. "It's me," I said, and then felt silly for stating the obvious.

"Yeah."

"But, it's beautiful."

"You are," he said, and before I could respond, "I'm going to visit you here again. Is that okay?"

I nodded. He'd called me beautiful. How could I say no?

34

JULIE PULLS ON A GRAY TUNIC SWEATER AND DARK LEGGINGS. She's nervous about seeing August again, about what he's going to think of the plan she's come up with. Her high black boots don't seem right for the unseasonable warmth, so she tries ballet flats instead. She frowns in the hotel mirror. Her hair hangs in short, loose waves, and she looks young suddenly, so she works with bobby pins and clips and pulls her hair into a sort of messy updo.

But with her hair up, her neck is bare—a surprise of pale skin surrounded by dark fabric. It seems grotesque, this odd elongation of her neck, giraffe-like. This transparency of skin. The bobby pins come out of her hair one by one until her hair is loose again, and when she still feels *wrong*, she tries on every top in her overnight bag before settling back into the original one with her hair down and the boots zipped up around her calves.

She leaves the hotel room early because she can't stand to be alone in there any longer. The elevator seems too small, even though she is the only one in it. It moves slowly downward, giving her plenty of time to worry about whether Maggie Harris will be at the reception desk again, her eyes so observant, so intent. But when Julie leaves the elevator, a different girl is behind the desk.

Southern Saddle is crowded tonight—it's the weekend, after all. Families pack into cozy booths and around tables, and single men and women are settled at the bar in comfortable positions, as though they are planning to stay all night. Julie looks for August immediately, and finds him already seated in the same booth from the night before. He looks tense, but the tight line of his mouth relaxes when he sees her.

"We really need to get out of here," she says as she slides into the booth.

"Hello to you too," he says, taking a long, slow drink of his beer. She watches his Adam's apple rise and fall, the movement somehow elegant and unexpectedly erotic. She wonders how much he's had to drink already.

"I have an idea," she says. "I mean, it's kind of obvious…what we have to do."

"What?"

"That diary is in Nell's shop," Julie says. "I know exactly where it would be. How do you feel about breaking in and taking it?"

"I can't believe this is your solution," August says. But he's in the passenger seat of the Honda anyway, headed to Lawrence Mill. "Can't you just call Nell and have a heart-to-heart with her? Tell her how much the diary means? I'm sure she'll understand."

"*You* don't understand," Julie says. "She told me a lie, August. Nell, the woman who never lies. That means she's serious about not giving it up. This is the only way."

"So, we're going to break into the woman's business? Going to jail isn't going to give us any answers. In fact, I don't know about you, but going to jail would cause a whole lot of problems for me."

"She's not going to know, August. Not until we have the diary, and then we'll apologize. We'll have what we came for, and she'll have to be okay with it."

"Or, she isn't okay with it, and she presses charges, and we're in serious shit. Jules, this is stupid."

"It's not *that* stupid."

"I can't believe I'm doing this," he says, gesturing to his khaki slacks and his teal golf shirt. "You could have at least let me change into something more suited to breaking and entering."

"You don't need it. This is *not* a big deal. I've been in Nell's shop after hours before."

"Yeah, when you were a teenaged employee. You were allowed to be there."

"Look," Jules says, exasperated. "*You're* the one who talked me into coming back here, who clued me in to this whole diary mess to begin with. *You're* the one who wanted my help."

August sighs. "This is insane." She steers the car off the highway and onto Magnolia. A stillness settles over them.

"Do you have family left around here?" he asks finally.

"No. Yes. Sort of, depending on what you consider family. My aunt, Molly, moved away. But Toby, my cousin, is still around."

"Is he the one that worked at the flower shop?"

"Yeah," Julie says, surprised, because Toby and August never came into contact with each other—that she knew of. "For a little while, at least. Did you ever meet him?"

"No. I just…saw him around sometimes, when he didn't know I was there. I was waiting for Reba, you know. No offense, but I always had a bad feeling about him."

"No kidding," Julie says. "I think *everyone* had a bad feeling about him."

"It's hard to explain, but…well, I didn't like the way he looked at her."

"Hmm…" And suddenly Julie is thinking of Toby, his wolfish, cocky grin and evil eyes. Thinking of how much she *hates* him.

When they were teenagers, Toby sold drugs, without stealth or pretense, from his bedroom in Molly's house. It wasn't his real job; he worked part time and halfheartedly for Nell, making deliveries, and he was a full-time art student at the Baptist college. But still. God knows why Molly would ever have been concerned with what Julie did, when her own son was dealing out of her house.

With Molly gone most nights, friends (and non-friends with habits) showed up at the house at all hours. That, or Toby would go out without a word to some secret meeting for some illicit transaction. Julie didn't know much about his so-called business. She actively tried *not* to know. She got used to the faces of the regulars, those who came to Molly's house without shame or fear and left with their drug of choice. Toby hinted that she'd be surprised at the sheer number of upstanding drug users in Lawrence Mill.

She didn't want to understand the things he did. Better if she didn't, in the event that one day cops showed up and raided the place. It never happened, but the possibility kept her away. She never entered his room when he was out, rarely entered even when he was home. She didn't search for his stash, didn't inquire about where and how he got his merchandise. She had no idea then (still doesn't, truth be told) of how these things work.

Back then, she'd never taken a drug in her life, had only seen the tiny packages, plastic bags wrapped around white powder or little white pills or greenish tufts like dead flowers. Toby made no effort to hide his hobby from her. He took it for granted that she would never tell, knowing, as he did, about her own hobbies. Still, with so much activity in the house, she knew enough to keep her bedroom door locked at night.

Toby had been a lanky kid, with long arms and legs jerking awkwardly when he walked, as though he were a puppet whose strings were held by some invisible master. He grew out of it, though, and by college, he was slim but sculpted. Julie never saw him work out, but he must have gone to a gym somewhere. His hair was brown and long and messy, nearly to his shoulders, though he kept it pulled back in an elastic band most of the time. For all of his faults—and there were plenty of them—he wasn't unattractive. His eyes, though hard and uncaring most of the time, were dark and intelligent. His face was angular—strong jaw, strong nose, thick brows.

Julie had once heard, God knows where, that a drug dealer can't (or maybe shouldn't) also be a drug user—something about not getting high on your own supply. Toby was, though. He was unquestionably a user, but he never struck her as an addict. He got high alone (mostly) and only in the evenings or late at night, and then he painted. Murals were his thing, then, and his bedroom walls made up his canvas.

If she had a reason to knock on his bedroom door, and if he said *come in* and not *go the fuck away*, then she might find him painting, face pressed almost to the wall itself, sitting on the floor or standing on a step stool. Paintbrushes, not unlike the ones she and Reba used for watercolors as children, would be littered around the room, with little jars of paint spread out before him. Toby had a friend who worked at Sherwin Williams and brought him free samples from the paint department.

In the glow of the black light, his face would be illuminated, sinister, and his music would blast so loudly that it hurt her ears to stand there and watch. Toby focused on small sections at a time, creating carefully detailed and intricate scenes of surprisingly whimsical things: twisting waterfalls, bridges arching like rainbows. It was his obsession. When he'd painted his entire room, he would cover part of the wall with fresh white paint and start again. Each time he started over, the project took months to complete. But when he was finished, the scenes covered every square inch, and the whole thing felt like being immersed in a fairy tale. Its intricacy was maddening and stifling.

Which was to say that she found it all disturbingly beautiful.

Fuck off, Toby said whenever she told him so.

35

"Oh," August says, as they turn into the gravel lot of Nell's Flower Shop, and Julie can feel his sudden disorientation. Nell's shop stands stark and wooden in the darkness. But behind that is the clearing—the expanse of unruly grass upon which, farther back, sits the brick recreation center. On one side of the building is a playground; on the other is a tennis court. And even though she can't see it, Julie knows from Nell that there is a large asphalt oval behind the building, a man-made track for walking or jogging.

"Hobart Park," she says. "I think it's been here for a while now."

"God, what a stupid name. What happened to the field?"

"Nell sold her land. The field is gone."

"Gone," August repeats.

She doesn't pull into the flower shop's gravel parking lot (too obvious); instead, she turns onto the paved road that leads to the new park, the road that hadn't even existed when the town was theirs.

She pulls close to the curb and stops the car. The Honda's headlights illuminate the new facility.

"You should have told me," August says, looking straight ahead.

"What would I have said?"

"You brought me here. You could have mentioned it."

She nods, but she knows he can't see her in the darkness. "It's so different," she says.

"*Everything* is different."

August opens his door and steps out, uncertain. She follows him. "I can't believe it," he says. "I can't believe that this is where it all happened, and now it's *gone*. It's nothing."

"Yeah," Julie says uneasily. "So…about that burglary…" She nods toward Nell's shop.

"I was here once," August blurts out. "At night," he says. "Late. With Reba."

"In the *shop*?" Julie asks. She shakes her head, surprised that Reba would have brought August here. She knew they'd met at the river, beyond the field, but this is a surprise.

"It was raining."

She waits for him to say more, but his memories belong to him, and he's not sharing.

"Okay, we should obviously try to go through the back door, so we're not visible from the street." She looks around in the darkness. "Not that anyone would be driving through here at this time of night, anyway." Lawrence Mill has no bars, no restaurants—you have to drive into Opal for that kind of thing. This place has always been a ghost town after dark, everything shuttered until morning light.

"Lead the way."

The gravel crunches beneath her feet as they leave the paved drive and make their way to Nell's shop. The back porch sags beneath Julie's feet as she approaches the door. She can see through the windows that there's no one inside. She'd known there wouldn't be. Crickets chirp in the distance. She opens the screen door; it groans in protest, too loud. She puts her hand on the cool knob of the back door, tries to twist it. Fails.

"Okay, it's locked."

August makes a noise behind her that could be a laugh. "Shit, Jules, *of course* it's locked. Did you really expect to just turn the knob and walk in?"

She spins to face him, and he's closer than she'd realized. They're almost chest to chest in the shadows. "I didn't expect it," she whispers. She can feel his breath, hot on her cheek. "But it would have made things easier. Try the windows."

Together, they check the windows lining the back of the shop and find them all locked.

"What now, criminal mastermind?" August says, as if the whole thing is starting to amuse him.

"Do you have a credit card?" she asks. He raises his eyebrows, and she points to the doorknob. No dead bolt, only a simple cylinder.

He shakes his head as he pulls his wallet from his back pocket and hands her a plastic card. His room key to The Inn.

"You know they'll charge you for this, if I break it," she says as she slides it into the space between the door and the frame.

"So don't break it."

She leans down and pulls out a tiny flashlight she brought along.

She keeps it in her purse for emergencies. Not emergencies like this one, but it will work. "Hold this."

August shines the light on the doorknob. "Jules, let's just break the window," he says, aiming the light at the square window that makes up the top part of the door.

"What? We can't just break a window."

"Yeah, we can. We can pay to fix it, after."

"We can't break the window. Give me a minute. I think I'm getting somewhere." When she worked at Nell's, she'd often reach the shop, only to realize she'd left her keys at home. Instead of going back to retrieve them, she'd figured out how to use her learner's license to catch the lock and open the door.

Same lock, same door. She can do this.

She can feel August behind her, feel his warmth. Feel him watching.

The key card catches on something, and she pushes the door open.

"Holy shit, you did it," August murmurs.

"I did it. Follow me." She takes his hand without thinking and leads him into the shop. The wooden floors creak beneath their weight, and something, somewhere, starts to beep. A box on the wall to their right is blinking. They freeze.

"Shit!" Julie says. "Nell never had an alarm when I worked here!"

"Well, things change," August hisses. "How did you not notice it when you were here earlier?"

"I don't know. I wasn't thinking about breaking in, then."

"Do you know what her code would be?"

Julie steps up to the panel and types in numbers. The code on the safe (Nell's birthday). No luck. It's the only code she can think of, though she starts to try all manner of random combinations. Until the box starts screaming a deafening, earsplitting melody. Lights hidden in each corner of the room begin to flash.

"Shit, Jules!" August says. "We've got to get out of here, now!"

She ignores him and heads for the back room. It's not ideal, but they're here now. She's got to get the book. It won't be long before the police show up, but she *should* have a few minutes. The station is at least five minutes away. The safe is exactly where she remembers. With the pulsing white glow, she doesn't even need the flashlight to see the numbers. She twists left, twists right, left again, right again. The safe clicks open easily. Julie opens the door and grabs everything she can feel inside. Cash, attached to a deposit slip, the ancient newspaper clipping of Nell as Cotton Queen. Julie pauses for a second when she sees a more recent newspaper article announcing the opening of Toby's gallery. But there's no diary in the safe. Nothing even resembling a book.

It isn't here.

"Jules!" August shouts over the shrieking of the alarm. "We've got to go!"

But she stands there, staring into the safe, where she was so sure they would find the diary. She's failed. This whole stupid plan was for nothing.

August strides into the tiny back room and grabs her arm. She slams the safe door, spins the lock, and they rush out of the flower shop. They're on the porch, the back door standing wide open behind them, when Julie's cell phone starts to ring from her back pocket. She checks the number. After all this time, she still recognizes it: Nell's home phone. "Shit," Julie says. Nell knows. She thinks of ignoring it, but she can't bring herself to do it.

"Nell. Hi."

"Jules Portland," Nell says, her voice stern but barely audible over the pulsing alarm. "Where exactly are you, right now?"

"Now?" Julie asks. She has to walk closer to the car to hear her own voice.

"I know you broke into my shop. I have security cameras. Does it even mean anything if I say I'm disappointed in you?" It does, actually, stings a little. Not the way it would have, ten years ago. "You've been in town all of, what, twenty-four hours, and you're breaking into my place of business?"

"Are you going to have us arrested?

"I should."

"We didn't take anything. And I'm disappointed in you too," Julie says. "I know you have the diary. Why not just give it to us?"

"You don't want it, Jules."

"So you *do* have it. Where?" Julie looks around, waiting for the police sirens. "Nell, are the cops coming?"

"*Of course not.* I saw you and August on my laptop, and I told the police it was all a misunderstanding, that I'd set the damned thing off myself. God knows why." Julie breathes a sigh of relief. "The diary is at my house. It's *always* been at my house. You think I'd keep something like that in a public place? But I saw that look on your face today, and something told me you might try to come on in the shop and see for yourself. There's a reason I never told you about it. Like I said, you don't want it."

"Yes, I do," Julie says, an edge to her voice. All of this time, for all of these years, Nell has had a part of Reba that Julie has been without, and that seems unforgivable now.

"It would only hurt you, sweetie," Nell says, her voice suddenly soft. "It would hurt August too. You both are better off without it."

The warnings only make Julie want it more. "Nell, you can't... keep this from me. I loved her. She was my best friend."

"I'm sorry. It was for the best then, and it's for the best now. There are...things you didn't know about Reba. Things she didn't *want* you to know. You and August need to shake this town off your boots and leave the past where it belongs—in the past. Move on, the both of you."

"We *can't*," Julie says firmly. "We can't move on, not when neither one of us has the whole story. We *need* that book. We *need* to know. I'm not a child, Nell. You can't protect me anymore. Please. Please, give me the book." August is beside the car now, watching her, waiting to see how this all turns out. His fingers tap an anxious rhythm against the passenger-side window.

"Jules, you're not going to like what you read. And poor August isn't going to like it either. You're doing yourselves a disservice here."

Julie can't imagine what could be so shocking about Reba, other than what she already knows. What she found out all those years ago. It doesn't matter, though.

"We're not leaving Lawrence Mill without it. We can't. Whatever we have to do."

"I should just burn the damned thing," Nell says. "Probably should have done that ten years ago." Julie considers the possibility of Reba's diary disappearing now, when they're so close. Going up in smoke.

"Yeah, you could," she says. "But would you do that to me? I used to confide in you. I sought advice from you. I *trusted* you."

"And look at how much that meant, since you up and left and never looked back. I don't owe you this, Jules."

"I was wrong. I shouldn't have fallen out of touch like that, I know. But, Nell, please. Knowing the truth, reading that diary. It means so much. More than anything. Please."

Nell sighs. "You'll regret this. *I'll* probably regret this. But I can see you're every bit as stubborn as you always were. I'll give you the book. For better or worse. I'll bring it by the shop tomorrow. You can pick it up there."

Julie looks at the clock on her phone. Eleven. It's not too late. "Now," she says, her voice shaky. She doesn't want to push her luck, but she also doesn't want to give Nell the chance to change her mind. She looks up at August, and he nods. "Nell, we need it now. We can come to you, or you can bring it to us."

"Jesus Christ. How did I already know you were going to say that? Give me ten minutes, and I'll be there. And for God's sake, Jules, get back in my shop and turn the alarm off. Let me give you the code."

36

I<small>T WAS THE HOTTEST SUMMER ON RECORD IN</small> L<small>AWRENCE</small> M<small>ILL</small>, and even in September, the permeating heat seeped into everything. If heat really comes in waves, like the weatherman says, then these waves were so thick as to be almost visible—pulsing, fluid snakes with hot red tongues flicking.

The air conditioner in Nell's couldn't keep up. Nell and I had been working to get all of the fresh flowers back into the cooler when Jules stopped in after her Saturday-morning play practice.

"Oh no," she muttered when she saw us rushing back and forth with vases in our arms. She backed away from the door.

"Jules!" I said.

"Perfect timing," Nell's muffled voice called from inside the cooler's open door. "Air's out. Grab a vase."

The brown window-unit air conditioner was probably older

than Nell, Jules, and me combined. It perched uselessly quiet on the windowsill.

We moved all of the fresh flowers—the ones that normally adorn various small tables around the room—into the safety of the cooler.

"Too hot in here for these. Only artificial arrangements on display until we get rid of this piece of crap," Nell says, gesturing to the monster in the window. Then she looked at Jules. "Well, well. Good to see you again. It's been what, three or four months now?"

Jules laughed. "It's only been a few weeks!"

"Feels like longer," she said. I nodded in agreement. "Guess I miss having another loudmouth around here."

Jules is only a loudmouth compared to me. I couldn't tell if I was being insulted. I had the Yellow Pages splayed open to the section labeled Air Conditioners. Nell heaved herself onto the empty stool next to me.

The best part of Nell is that she doesn't care what anyone thinks of her. It's a trait that Jules and I both admire. She never lies, except about her hair color. Her hair is short and straight, cut to match the latest style. And it's the color of mandarin oranges. It's a shade that wouldn't have passed for natural even when Nell was a girl. She would *tell* you it was natural, though, if you asked. "Always was a ginger," she'd say, laughing. And we all pretended to accept it as truth.

"So tell us about this play you're starring in. *Again*," Nell said, leaning over me as she flipped through the phone book. "Oh, that's the place. Steve Mallard runs it. Hopefully, I can talk that old bastard into giving me a deal on a new unit."

"The play is going okay," Jules said. "Lots of practice. It's *Romeo and Juliet*."

"Jules hates Shakespeare," I couldn't help but add.

"*Romeo, Romeo*," Nell said dramatically. "How can anyone hate Shakespeare? Tell me more."

Jules shrugged. "Not much more to tell, really."

"Tell her who's playing Romeo."

"Oh! Reba's old crush. Brandon Lomax."

"Uh-oh," Nell said. "Reba, you still haven't hit on that boy? He's Jen Lomax's son, right? And Jules, you're just going to go around kissing the boy Reba's had her eye on for ages?"

"I don't mind," I said with a little shrug and a smile. And I really *didn't* mind. It's true that I used to have a crush on Brandon. With his hazel eyes and glasses and wavy hair, he's attractive in a bookish, unpopular way. I never acted on it, though, and maybe that was for the best, because my desire for him seemed to have melted away in the summer heat. Ever since that day alone in the flower shop with August, *he* was the one I couldn't get off my mind.

"Deliveries?" Toby's gravelly voice made Jules and me jump. With the door propped open, we hadn't heard him come in. His jeans were ripped at the knee, and he wore a white V-neck T-shirt, his light-brown hair pulled back into a ponytail. His face was stubbly—not freshly shaven, but not yet grown into a beard.

"Jesus Christ," Jules muttered, rolling her eyes. "I forgot you're working here now."

"Yeah, and I thought *you* weren't. What are you doing here, trying to ruin my day?" He looked around, nodding at Nell and looking me up and down in a less-than-subtle manner. "Reba," he said. He made my name sound dirty as it slid out of his mouth, and I knew I was blushing.

"This might be a foreign concept to you, *Tobes*, but these are my friends. I can drop in anytime I want." Jules smirked, knowing that the nickname would grate on his nerves.

"Whatever. Never call me that again."

Nell dialed the number on the cordless phone, then looked up, the phone balanced between her ear and the cushion of her shoulder. "This is a disaster. Toby, while you're here, maybe you can help the girls move some things around."

"I charge extra for heavy lifting," Toby grumbled. "What do you need?"

I looked away from him, and something outside the window caught my eye just as Nell got an answer. She started chatting, gesturing with her hands as though Steve Mallard could see her through the phone as well as hear her. "Be right back," I whispered, then slipped out the open back door.

August was waiting outside. "What are you doing here?" I asked.

"I told you I would visit you again," he said. It had been two full weeks since he'd shown me his photographs.

"You shouldn't be here now. I'm working, and Nell and Jules are here and...you can't be here too." I backed up against the wooden frame of the building, making sure that I was out of sight. That *he* was out of sight. I couldn't help but smile.

"I wanted to...well, see you, I guess. Away from school." August stepped closer to me, too close for daylight.

"Another time," I said. I hoped he could hear the regret in my voice.

"Reba, I like you. I'd like to get to know you. I get it, how things are here. But I don't care what people think...and I'm kind of hoping you don't, either. I want to see you again, soon." There was that dimple again, and I knew he was pretending not to care too much about my response.

I don't know why I said it, other than the simple truth is that I wanted to see him too. "Okay. Meet me by the river, here, behind the shop. Tonight."

"The river," he repeated. "Okay."

"Later though, it has to be late."

"Later is good," he said, and he seemed to be breathing a little quicker. Maybe it was the heat or the fact that he was so close to me or the anticipatory look in his eyes, but I seemed to be breathing faster too.

I was a wreck when I went back inside, my face flushed, my movements erratic as I worked beside Jules. This new, wonderful secret was filling me up, and I knew I would burst if I didn't do something, say *something*. I dropped a plastic vase and jumped as it clattered around the room.

"Jules," I said finally. "I have to tell you something." I wanted to trust her, hoped I could.

"Yeah?" she said. I could see the excitement on her face. Sharing secrets does that to her.

"I met someone. A boy. He comes here…sometimes."

"What?" Jules was surprised. She may be an actress, but it's always been easy for me to read her. She held a bright bowl of artificial daisies and pulled it tight against her chest. "Why didn't you tell me?"

"It's still really new. And not what you think. It's, well, it's something no one else can know about."

"What? Why not?"

"People wouldn't like it. My father wouldn't like it. The boy I see sometimes…he's black."

Jules stopped and looked at me, her eyes wide. "A black guy has been coming by the shop? Like, when you're alone?"

I nodded, and I could feel the ghost of a smile tugging the corners of my mouth.

"What? Reba, have you told Nell?"

I shook my head, my smile disappearing.

If I'm being completely honest, I'm not sure what bothered Jules more: the idea that I might have had a romantic interest, or that said romantic interest was black. I've known Jules all my life, but I'd never thought of her as racist before, even though God knows enough people around here are. Despite her words, the label still didn't fit. Maybe the truth was a bit more complicated. For some reason, it has always seemed important to Jules that I remain as pure and unblemished as a china doll in a box on a shelf. She can be wild and reckless and free, as long as I'm not. Even when she takes me out of the box and shows me off, like those nights at Southern Saddle, she counts on the fact that everyone will see me for what I am. Untouchable. I always sort of liked it before. But now I was ready to grow up, to break free.

I won't soon forget how painfully disappointed I was in my best friend. I shook my head. "You know what? It's really nothing. I shouldn't have said anything at all."

"No, really, Reba. This isn't a Penny Decker–type situation, is it? I don't want you to get in trouble, and I don't want you to get hurt either."

"It's *nothing*," I said. "Forget I mentioned it at all." That was the first time I knew I couldn't trust Jules, not the way I've always thought I could, not the way she can trust me. She may have been right about one thing, though. This probably wasn't a path I should have been taking, and I knew it.

But I chose this path anyway.

37

Nell is wearing her housecoat and driving the delivery van with the flower shop logo on the side. When Julie approaches the driver's-side window, Nell reaches over to the passenger seat and produces a faded and water-damaged lavender book. *Reba's diary.*

"Jules, are you *sure* you want this? I can promise you that you are not expecting what's inside. It will change the way you think of Reba, the way that you think of your friendship with her. It will change all of that forever."

"Yes," Julie says with no hesitation at all. The need to hold the book in her own hands is overwhelming, and she reaches for it. Nell looks wary, but releases the journal anyway.

"Good luck to you, then, honey. I hope you find the answers you're looking for." She turns the van around in the gravel lot and drives away, her headlights fading into the night.

Julie stares at the book in disbelief, the fabric cover and some of the pages wrinkled and stiff, yellowed from water. She runs her fingertips lightly along the front, as though now that she has it, it might fall to pieces in her hands, like the honeysuckle necklace in her dream. She has to fight the urge to untie the ribbon wrapped around the book, to let it fall open in her lap and devour its contents right here in Nell's gravel lot.

"I can't believe it," August says, looking reverently at the diary.

Julie looks up at him. "We need light." She nods toward the stupid, silly park where the field used to be. Except for one burned-out streetlamp, the parking lot of Hobart Park is bathed in false daylight. It's completely deserted. They leave the car parked on the narrow paved drive and walk. Nell's shop at the top of the street is dark and quiet now, the alarm finally silenced.

August takes the lead, and Julie follows him. They'd stopped at the liquor store in Opal on their way to Lawrence Mill—*If we pull this off, I'm going to need a drink*, August had said—and Julie certainly wasn't going to argue. She twists the top off the bottle, without even removing it from its brown-bag cloak. She presses her lips deliberately against the mouth of the bottle and swallows. It's hot, and poisonous, and familiar—whiskey. He was paying attention to what she was drinking last night, and the knowledge adds to the warmth in her stomach. She passes the bottle to August, and they walk on, the two of them, alone in the starless, moonless night.

38

TOBY SPENDS TOO MUCH TIME IN THIS DAMNED BAR. WHEN the gallery's closed up for the night and his loft apartment upstairs feels like it's going to close in on him, he has to go *somewhere*. And this is the place. Doesn't even bother to change clothes, most of the time. It's a quiet, seedy, workingman's kind of joint. In his paint-spattered T-shirts and dirty jeans, he could be part of the local construction crew. Most people think he is. He could set them right, but why bother?

He's lived in this area his whole life, and yet he doesn't have many friends here. He could leave in the night, and it would be days before anyone would notice. Nell would probably be the one to discover him gone. There's no reason he should care about staying, anyway. But every time he thinks of leaving, like Jules did way back when, he feels like his boots are stuck to the asphalt of this shitty little town. The more he thinks about it, the heavier his feet feel, until he knows he's destined to stay. When he went to New York as part of the Southern Artists' Showcase, he'd thought, for a minute, that he could stay away forever, that he could leave it all behind. But before long, he felt that pull to get on back, and it's a pull he can't fight. His feet would carry him back here, whether he wanted them to or not.

He knows it's not Reba's fault, but she's trapped him here, sure enough.

Toby takes a long swig from his beer, one of several that he plans to drink tonight, now that he knows Jules is back in town. It's making him think even more than usual, making him remember how it all started with Reba.

He remembers the day he first caught sight of her with the boy. He'd been working for Nell. When that piece-of-shit air conditioner died, he'd gotten stuck moving vases of *flowers* around the shop. He was pissed about it too, fuming about women, how they tell you they need you for *one* thing, and then it turns into a hundred. He'd just wanted to get his deliveries done so he could get back home. He'd only let Molly force him into the job in the first place to keep her off his back. Molly didn't know where he got his money, though he always had some. Something shady was probably her guess, and she wasn't wrong.

Toby had just finished loading the flowers into the van, carefully, because he might not have taken that job too seriously, but he knew Nell would have kicked his ass into the next week if something got messed up on the way to a delivery. He was climbing into the van when he saw Reba around the side of the building. Damn, that girl. Off-limits, though. Too *pure*, too innocent.

Bet he could turn her wild is what he thought then. He never dreamed he'd actually get the chance.

What was she doing over there, anyway? It looked like she was talking to someone—a guy.

Maybe Reba wasn't as pure as he thought.

Whatever. He'd cranked up the van and ignored his urge to investigate. Damned deliveries had to get made. He decided he'd have to keep an eye on the situation, though, and find out what sweet Reba was up to.

He doesn't know, now, if things would have been better or worse if he'd just minded his own goddamned business.

39

IT WAS DIFFERENT THAN I THOUGHT IT WOULD BE. FOR STARTERS, the moon wasn't a helpful guide, like I'd expected in my romantic mind. Instead, I have the streetlights to thank for guiding me past David Nickel's house and out into the fields. And when I reached the fields…nothing. I wore frayed jean shorts, and the tall grass tickled my legs. The loud chatter of crickets kept me company, and I imagined them scattering beneath my feet with each step. I watched for shadows without sources. I hadn't brought anything that could be used as a weapon, not to protect me from August, but from someone else. *Anyone* else could have been out there. How was I to know what went on in the forest after dark?

I was terrified, and proud of myself at the same time. I knew Jules was out with Jake and not home, not looking out her window. But, if Jules *had* been looking, she would have seen me pushing up my bedroom window with both hands and awkwardly unhooking the screen from its pegs so I could slide one leg, and then the other, out the window. There is a row of hedges below my window, and when I climbed out that first time, their limbs scraped at my calves.

I could see Nell's shop in the distance. It was so tempting to walk to the door, to shelter and safety, to give up on this lovely idea. Maybe I'd taken on too much, too fast. But no, I wasn't giving up. I turned away from the shop and headed into the trees.

Soon, I heard the river's mellow gurgle, slow and steady like voices talking, but so low that I couldn't hear the words. The water glimmered, dark as an oil streak in the nighttime. I stood on the edge of the bank, looking around, my arms crossed nervously.

I doubted myself again. It was foolish, wasn't it, to leave the security of my house to wander into the night to meet a boy I hardly knew? It was a page straight out of Jules's book—not mine. I searched the darkness for any sign of him. What sign would there be when he arrived? If he arrived at all. *Go back*, a voice in my head whispered, pulsing in time with the veins in my temples.

I jumped when I heard what could have been footsteps. "August?" The shaky sound that came from my mouth sounded nothing like my own voice. There was no reply, only the continuous step, step, step on the twig-covered ground.

Finally, when I was preparing to run, to hide, to do *something*, I heard his voice. "Reba? Are you out here?"

I sighed, relieved.

"Reba," he said again, his voice growing closer.

"I'm here."

"I'm glad." When he reached me, he touched my arm, quickly and gently. It was more intimate than a handshake and less intimate than a hug, which I guess meant it was his way of saying hello. He lowered himself to the bank and sat, and I did the same.

"This is probably a really bad idea. I shouldn't be here," I said.

"I know. Neither should I. My mom will lose it if she catches me."

"So...what happens now?" Never having found myself in this situation before—never having been alone with a boy in my entire life (except for my daddy, of course, which was a whole different kind of awkward), I had no idea how to proceed. Should we talk? Should we touch? I wanted to touch him, to feel his dark skin under my fingertips. Should we kiss? I've heard Jules's stories before, but those salacious tales seemed to have no relation to what I was doing in that moment. Because I am not Jules, and I am not Penny Decker. I am only myself, and I was there, with him.

"I don't know." In the silence that followed, the slow trickle of the river became a wild rush to my senses, every collision of water and rock pounding in my ears. In the darkness, he was a statue, a work of art to consider. But he finally asked the question I wanted to ask him, would have asked him if, after sneaking out of my house to meet him in the moonlight, I'd had any actual courage left. "So, what's your story, Reba? Tell me about yourself."

So I told him everything I could think of, and most of it was true: that I would be seventeen soon, that I love old books, that I write poetry that no one has ever read (because it's awful, but I left that part out). That I'm not athletic, but I love the outdoors, even in the heat of summer. That I love rain, and slow music, and that I have a best friend, more like a sister really—a more adventurous sister—named Jules. Even if I can't trust her like I wish I could, I can't deny how close we are.

"Your turn," I said, when I couldn't think of anything else he could possibly find interesting.

"I'm August," he said simply. I waited for more, and he eventually continued. "Um, well, August Elliott."

"Go on," I said. I learned about his favorite things—photography and football and his little sister, Megan. He'd been a football player back home, at his old school. I wasn't surprised. I'd already seen glimpses of his muscular arms and legs. I blushed, thinking of him, and was thankful that it was dark out.

"Wait," I said. "Where is home?"

"Richmond, Virginia. I loved it there. I miss it. It's big, and full, and people are…different there. Normal. Not like here."

"You don't like it here." I was defensive, I guess. I love Lawrence Mill, loved it even as I was defying its unspoken laws.

"No, I don't."

"Then why are you here?"

There was a long pause before he replied. "I didn't have a choice. My dad's job. He was transferred here."

"Transferred?" That word. I'm a smart girl—at least, I think I am—but I hadn't seen this at all. Were there clues I'd missed along the way? It seemed so obvious all of a sudden.

This was a thousand times worse than Penny Decker and James Edgemont. My throat was dry, even in the moist heat, and I realized I'd been given a piece of information that I really, really didn't want. I'd heard that word, *transferred*, too many nights from my daddy's mouth over dinner.

"He was a manager, or something, at the headquarters of this textiles manufacturer. They sent him here to oversee—"

"The mill," I interrupted, feeling the familiar mottling of my damned cheeks. With the timing, I should have guessed it from the very beginning, from that first day in the fields. The sound of the river pounded against my ears, angrier than before. "Your dad works at the mill." I thought about the day I first saw the flash of August's camera. The same day my daddy was denied the promotion.

"Yeah."

I was afraid. Not abstractly, but literally, absolutely *afraid*.

"Why?" August asked. "Is that bad?"

He settled his hand against my knee, but I jumped involuntarily, my ankle scraping against a rock. I ignored the urge to scramble to my feet. "Nothing," I whispered, because I couldn't bring myself to tell him. "It's nothing." I had no idea what to do next.

My heart—my head too—filled with dread at what would happen to me if I was caught, because my sin had become so serious. Sneaking out of the house. To meet a boy. The son of the man my daddy despises.

I could tell August felt it when I changed, how I turned quiet and uncertain. Our arms touched, but I hardly spoke again, isolated as I was with so much more to consider. When I left him, I ran faster than I thought I could, wasting no thought on the scratchy tall weeds whipping against my bare legs, my hair lashing against my face.

He'd put his hand in mine. His eyes had been so hopeful (did I really see that, in the darkness, or was it my imagination?) when he asked to see me again. I'd looked down at my hands, felt his skin against mine, soft and cool. I saw that connection, and I ran. As if my life depended on it. As if *his* did.

40

"WAIT, GO BACK," AUGUST SAYS. JULIE STOPS READING. SHE'S sitting on a yellow curb, and August is pacing back and forth in front of her.

"It's too much, isn't it?" she says. "It's...it's..." She trails off.

"So she tried to tell you about me, early on, in the flower shop, and you reacted that way?" he asks.

She looks down, embarrassed. "I did."

"Which was it for you? Was it a race thing, plain and simple? Are you like that, Jules? Or was it what Reba said...something deeper?"

Julie knew this would happen if they read the book, knew she would have to confirm her own screwed-up notions. "It's horrible either way, isn't it? But it was the latter. I needed her to stay innocent. That made it okay, somehow, for me to be...who I was. Like she was *good* enough to make up for the fact that I wasn't."

"That's messed up," he said.

"Yeah, I know." She stands up from the curb and wanders to the playground. August follows.

"Why *were* you that way, Jules? You didn't have to be like that."

"I don't know." It's too much to explain. She'd only really started to understand, during a few months of therapy after Beck was born, that her behavior back then was all tied up with losing her parents early, and not feeling loved by Aunt Molly, and being convinced that she was supposed to be somewhere else, and feeling like nothing she did in Lawrence Mill really mattered.

She'd had some sort of twisted maternal instinct where Reba was concerned. It was the kind of love you'd get from a mother who relies on you to fulfill her own dreams, who puts you on a pedestal, who has expectations you can never achieve. The *worst* kind of mother. She doesn't know why Reba had spent any time around her at all.

"Those nights with her," August says. "I've never been so afraid, and so excited, and so…happy." He settles beside Julie into one of the swings on the playground, beneath a large fluorescent streetlamp that illuminates everything like a grotesque moon. They pass the bottle back and forth. "I had no idea she was going to be so important to me. But she was so…" He shakes his head. "She had me," he says. "I don't even think she knew what she did to me."

"It was mutual, I think." Maybe she's trying to comfort him, or maybe it's true. It *seems* true, based on what they've read so far.

"Maybe sometimes you just know."

"I guess."

"You've never felt that?" he asks.

"I don't know," she says, using her feet to push her swing backward. "Maybe it was like that with Evan and me. It's hard to remember now."

"Evan? Beck's dad?"

"Yes. My ex-husband." She flinches when she says it—the words still taste so sour.

"And you've been divorced…"

"Five years," she says, looking away. "He…left, before she was born."

She clenches her fists around the plastic-covered chains of the swing set, afraid that she has given away more than she wanted to. That now she will have to tell him the whole story. And she doesn't want to.

"It was my fault, though," she whispers. "Everything was my fault."

Two full, aching weeks after that first kiss, Evan and Julie were paired together to perform a scene for their acting class. The scene they'd been assigned was from a play workbook. It was an argument between lovers, and they laughed as they practiced their roles at the beginning of class.

Evan had the first line. When he started, the whole class watching, she was genuinely startled at the harsh cruelty of his voice. Because he was *that* good. She forced her tone to sound mean and ragged, and she fell easily into her role. But she felt it, the growing competition between them. Until then, they'd complimented each other on their respective monologues, discussed the merits of certain movements, certain vocal inflections. They'd never been compared, side by side.

With the intensity of the scene, their voices rose until they were shouting, and though it could have been a real fight, it was only the two of them putting everything into it. The desks were a foot or so away from where they stood, or marched, or pointed, but it took only a few short moments of the mock heated debate for everyone else to disappear. For the room to disappear. Evan's blue eyes were hot, the color of lit coals before the flames appear. Julie had the last line.

"I hate you!" she screamed, and her hand flew out to hit him, a fake slap that ended the scene. Evan caught her by the wrist, luckily, because the moment had become so intimate, so real, that she may have truly hit him. It happened so quickly—Evan grabbing her wrist, pulling her into him, their mouths crashing together.

"Yeah!" yelled a boy a few rows back. The rest of the class started to cheer. No one else had read the script (except the teacher, who looked quite alarmed), so no one knew that the kiss wasn't part of the act. Pure improv, Evan said later, a knowing smile on his face.

Julie gathered her books and was out of the room before the class finished clapping. She could feel Evan behind her. And then they were laughing and kissing in the hallway, her back against the wall and Evan's hand on her cheek. "You are amazing," he said, and she laughed.

He lived in a studio apartment, a tiny room with brick walls. They dropped their school things as they barrelled through the door, arms wrapped around each other. His bed was a mattress with no frame and white sheets, all knotted together, unmade. He wore a long-sleeved white T-shirt beneath a short-sleeved blue one. They twisted together as she pulled them over his head. His jeans were brown-belted, the metal clasp pressed against her stomach as they held each other in the middle of the room.

His sheets were soft and his skin hot like an iron that could press away her flaws and leave her smooth and bright white and perfect.

☙

"So, you *have* felt it," August says, as they walk, slowly, clumsily, on the oval-shaped asphalt that sits unnaturally on the plot of land behind Nell's. This place used to be covered with untamed grasses as high as their knees. Weeds are already breaking through, taking back the land.

"I don't know," Julie says. "I don't know what it was. It all feels like madness now."

"Love?"

"I thought so. Then."

"So, what happened?"

"Reba happened. Life happened."

"But Reba was before," he says, clutching the half-empty liquor bottle in its brown paper.

"It never goes away. Things like that, they never do."

"I guess I get that."

She changes the subject. "You must have hated living here."

"Come on," August says. "How could I like it? When we started looking for houses, it was *suggested*, pretty directly, that there was a certain side of town for us. You read about that kind of shit, and I mean, I'd been discriminated against before...but it was all subtle stuff, you know? And then we move here, and what's the first thing they tell us? Know the boundaries. Didn't anyone think that was wrong?"

"Some people did," Julie said, sighing. "But for most of us, it's just how things were. People like Mr. McLeod and Aunt Molly and Mr. Nickel kept pushing the kind of behavior that they grew up with... and we bought into it, some of us, without questioning. Maybe it's better here now, who knows?" After all, Maggie Harris hadn't batted an eye at seeing August in the hotel lobby, even if he *was* the only black man in Southern Saddle.

Julie hopes, at least, that things are different.

41

I'D BEEN COUNTING DOWN THE DAYS UNTIL MY BIRTHDAY. Seventeen seemed magical and elusive; ever since Jules turned seventeen at the beginning of summer, I could hardly wait to do the same. Not to mention that everyone else in my grade had *already* turned seventeen. Some of my classmates were on the verge of eighteen. It was a happy miracle that I'd made it into this class at all, that I wasn't a junior right now, instead of a senior.

This morning (or yesterday morning, since I'm writing this so late), I was pleasantly surprised to see Jules waiting for me outside with a chocolate cupcake smeared with frosting and covered in sprinkles, with candles in the shape of the number 17 smashed into the top. It's a tradition, a thing that we do every year. Since we were kids, we've been baking birthday cupcakes for each other. Before Ted left and Molly turned so bitter, she'd even get in the kitchen and help Jules make cupcakes for me when it was my birthday. These days, though, Jules makes them alone.

The treat was delicious, and the gesture, though familiar, was even sweeter. Jules is still my best friend and I can't hold a grudge against her, even if I know enough now to keep my secrets close.

Also, I hardly see Jules anymore, so even if I *had* decided to hold a grudge, there is a possibility that she wouldn't have noticed. Not even Southern Saddle is enough to tempt her away from play practice these days, and I've been busy myself, working afternoons at Nell's.

Jules and I walked to school, through the fields, and I gingerly nibbled the cupcake, trying my best not to cover my entire face in frosting. Jules (always the performer) sang "Happy Birthday" to me in front of everyone in English class, and for once, I turned a shade of red that had more to do with happiness than embarrassment.

All of this attention from Jules made me feel guilty that I couldn't tell her what I had planned, but I wasn't changing my mind. Jules wouldn't know, wouldn't even guess, even though she sits in the desk right beside me and it was all right in front of her face, if only she was looking closer.

August didn't speak to me, has never dared to speak to me in class once he realized that it just isn't done. I've never thought of it before, but apparently, things aren't like this everywhere.

I had tried not to think of him. Really, I had. I even tried to rekindle some small feeling for Brandon Lomax, who is also in our English class. But those feelings seem very far away, a little-girl crush. And this, this feeling for August—this feels like much more.

I sat up straight, one hand in the pocket of my pink cardigan, where a folded piece of paper was lodged. I'd written it at midnight, when I decided to follow my heart this once and see where it leads.

It was so sneaky, so sly, that I couldn't believe I was really going to do it. But I *did*. The bell rang; class was over. I invited Jules over for my birthday dinner, and we walked to the door for our next classes. Just as Jules started to walk away, just as she turned her head, I accidentally (on purpose) walked right into the boy from class.

"I'm sorry," I mumbled, one hand on his arm.

"It's okay," August said, smiling. "You all right?"

"I'm…" I opened his palm with my fingers, dropped the note into his hand. And then walked quickly, quietly away, feeling equal parts thrilled and terrified.

There was a simple birthday celebration, with a dinner and a puffy white cake with frosting light as air, courtesy of my mama. My daddy was still sulky. If possible, he seems to be growing more and more upset as the days pass. Even on my birthday, he couldn't help but raise his voice, yelling about his boss questioning him in front of coworkers. He'd started drinking beer with dinner instead of Mama's sweet tea, and he got louder with every beer. Jules left after the cake, and after presenting me with a gift—a silver necklace with a dangling half-heart charm with the word *best* written across it in neat cursive. Jules kept the other half, the side that said *friends*. I'd admired it at Claire's over the summer, one of those times when we went to the mall before Southern Saddle.

Maybe it's cheesy, but I truly love it, and it made me think that maybe eventually, at some point, I'll be able to confide in her again. I put the necklace on right then, and I haven't taken it off since. My parents gave me a new dress, something girlish that my mama must have chosen, white eyelet, more fitting for a girl of twelve than seventeen. I left it lying on the bed—it kind of matched the bedspread—when I crawled out the window.

My stupid gypsy skirt made it difficult to slip out the window, and I cursed as I scrambled out, promising myself that I would wear something more suited to this next time. *If* there was a next time. I realize I'm not an easy girl to get to know. Maybe he wouldn't want to keep seeing me. I *had* run off the last time we were together, after all.

It's funny how sometimes the darkness settles around you, and you forget to be afraid of it. I welcomed it this time, a cloak to keep me concealed from the eyes of those who would…what? What would they do when they caught me? And who are *they*? My parents? My friends? Someone else entirely? I didn't know, and on my birthday, I didn't want to care.

He was waiting for me when I got there, and he was holding something in his hand.

"You," I said. It has become my quirky little greeting for him.

"Happy birthday," August said, presenting me with a book. I held it close to my face so I could see it better. It was a journal, small and lavender with a deep-purple ribbon holding it closed. The inside was empty, pristine. "For your poems," he said, but I have enough notebooks for poetry, and I already had this desire to tell the story, to put on paper all of the things I wish I could tell Jules, but can't.

"How did you know it's my birthday?"

He smiled. "Your friend, singing today."

"Thank you."

I touched him, his hand, felt the smooth texture of it, and listened to the sounds of the river. And then I was closer, my mouth *too close* to his and lingering for an instant before I kissed him.

I started writing the moment I got home, wanting to capture every moment—from the first flash of August's camera up to now—of this crazy *whatever-it-is*, and now the sun is coming up and soon it will be time to get ready for school. But the words are here, and that's the important thing.

What will become of all of this?

42

JULIE AND AUGUST STAND NEAR THE RIVERBANK, THE TREES gone now, all cut down—for aesthetic pleasure, Julie guesses. For someone's aesthetic pleasure, at least.

"It was all my fault," August says, his voice breaking. He grabs Julie's hand, grips it. His eyes are bloodshot; they've been at the park for what feels like hours. The nearly empty liquor bottle dangles from her other hand. "Listen to me, Jules. This was all my fault. If she'd never met me, she'd still be alive, damn it. It was the only time in my life that meant anything." His voice rises. "But I would take it back, every piece of it, every bit, every kiss, *everything*, if it would bring her back." He grabs the brown-bagged bottle from her hand and throws it, hard, into the river. It jingles, melodically, satisfactorily, as it smashes against rocks that Julie can't see. "Why can't it bring her back?" August shouts.

Things have begun to blur, but still, Julie sees it. Behind August, to his left, the new footbridge.

"It wasn't your fault," she says. "It was *my* fault. Because it was me. I did it." Her voice cuts through the cool air like scissors through paper.

"Did what?" August says, his voice filled with confusion, and she can tell that he doesn't understand—because if he understood, he would hate her. And she deserves it.

"Reba didn't commit suicide. I *killed* her."

43

IT GOES SOMETHING LIKE THIS: WE DON'T TALK MUCH ABOUT school, because we don't have any of the same friends. Class assignments drift into our conversations occasionally, but mostly we swap things. He brings me books, his favorites, worn covers a testament to the pressure of his fingers, particular phrases underlined. He likes classics— *Catcher in the Rye, The Sound and the Fury.* He's a reader, like me, which makes me like him even more. Sometimes he brings me a book I've read before, but I don't tell him so. The stories take on different meanings in the context of *him*, of his scrawled notes in the margins. I bring him poems I've written, which I never thought I'd share with anyone, and he manages to say nice things. He brings me photographs, images he has captured of Lawrence Mill and of his former home in Virginia.

I'm completely smitten. I am filled to bursting with happiness.

One night I told him about the rickety bridge that connects the riverbanks, and how Jules and I broke it when we were children.

August and I were sitting on the gently sloping bank of the river, facing what was left of the bridge. I'd like to have sat on it, swinging my legs back and forth in the air, but it is unsafe in the dark, even if you know where the broken board is. I told him about how Jules had cut her leg, badly, years ago when that plank gave way beneath her, the long gash starting at the base of her shin and crawling up to her knee.

Molly and my mama warned us a hundred times after that against playing on the bridge. No one ever repaired it. My daddy had promised to, back then, on a weekend maybe, whenever there was time. But there never *was* time, I guess, and the bridge stayed damaged, arching, lazy and pretty and unstable with the seventh plank loose and dangling. The rail on one side had been broken long before, by someone else who knew the secret of the bridge even before Jules and I did. August said he'd like to photograph it in the daylight, with the sunshine sneaking through the trees.

"Why pictures?" I asked him. "What makes photography so special to you?" His legs were splayed and I leaned against him, my back pressing into the reassuring weight of his chest.

"Because things disappear."

"That's optimistic," I said, teasing him.

"It's realistic. With a camera, you can catch things. Stop them in that perfect place, perfect time. Photographs...they keep you from forgetting." He grinned. I kissed his cheek.

"Why poetry?" he asked me.

"Because there is a word for everything." I believe it too. People say things like *There just aren't words to describe it* and *Actions speak louder than words*, but I don't think it is true. There are words for everything, and nothing could possibly speak louder.

44

"You didn't kill her, Jules." August's voice is raw and hoarse. "Reba killed herself. She jumped off the bridge because she thought I'd abandoned her. She waited for me, and I wasn't here. That asshole, her father, was burning down my family's house." August laughs bitterly. "He didn't even know about Reba and me. It was all about him. Because of him, I never made it here that night. I never made it to her." He closes his eyes, as if the words hurt.

"You're wrong." Julie thinks of the newspaper article about Reba's death, with Reba's school picture right there on the front page. "She didn't jump. I *was* there that night. I *pushed* Reba off that bridge. I killed her, really and truly. It was me." Tears are a sign of weakness, but here they are, trickling stupidly and uncontrollably down her face. "And, God, I am *so, so* sorry."

August is watching her, the expression on his face one of pain and skepticism. "You didn't kill her, Jules."

"I did."

Finally, she can see it start to sink in, this awful truth. But still, the anger doesn't come, only surprise. "But why?" he asks.

"I don't...I don't know." Her memory of that night is hazy, twisted. Because she can see them, the two figures arguing on the bridge. And one of those figures is her, even though it feels like she is watching from far away.

"You said you killed her. If that's true, then tell me why. You loved her. Why would you have done it?"

"I don't know. I don't know!" Her sudden shout startles them both. She can see her own shadow spilling out beneath the street-light, a larger, darker version of herself. She closes her eyes, tries to remember the night Reba died. "I'd been drinking. A...a lot. It was the night of the school play. I saw her sneaking out of her window, and I knew she was coming...here, to the bridge, to meet you. I'd always been envious of Reba, of how perfect she was, and then she wasn't perfect anymore, but she was in love. She had you. Anyway, I got it into my head that I should follow her, and so I did."

"What happened then?" His voice is quiet, so low that she can hardly hear him above the slow slide of the river beneath them.

"I don't remember it all. I must have startled her. We argued—on the bridge, I think—and I-I pushed her."

"What did you argue about?"

"I don't know. You, I guess."

"And then what? Did you try to help her?"

"I..." She is a coward, an evil, useless coward. "I ran."

"You *ran?*"

She nods, trying to pull herself together, trying to prepare herself for his wrath.

"Do you *remember* pushing her?"

"Not exactly. But I did it. I'm almost sure of it."

"How do you know?"

"I was there. I know I was there, and he said if it wasn't for me, she'd still be alive."

"Who's he?" When she doesn't answer, he says it again. "Who's *he*, Jules?"

She doesn't remember pushing Reba, not the act of it. But he told her it was all her fault, and she *does* remember being there, remembers that volatile scene on the bridge, remembers seeing Reba tumbling down into the water. She feels guilty enough for it to be the truth. It *is* the truth. But August is looking at her as if it isn't true at all, as if it just doesn't sound right.

"Toby." Her memory of *that* day is very clear, of the hospital bed she was lying in when he told her what she'd done, when he showed her the newspaper article with Reba's smiling face. Of the vicious growl of his voice, his red-rimmed eyes.

August grabs her by the shoulders and finally she sees the anger she's been waiting for. "Someone told you that you *killed* a person, your best friend in the world, and you just *believed* them?"

It's momentarily tantalizing, this idea that maybe she didn't do it after all. But it can't be real. She already believed she killed Reba, even before Toby confirmed it. "Why would he have told me that if it weren't true?"

"Great question," August says. "Why would he?"

Julie sits down on the riverbank and puts her palms to her forehead. She wishes she hadn't shared the whiskey with August, wishes she could think clearly without the fog of alcohol. Here, at the bridge…it feels like that night. Why would Toby have lied? Toby had nothing to do with Reba, with what was going on at that time.

Except…that wasn't entirely true, was it?

It occurs to her that the only place she might find answers is in the diary. But if Toby is in there, if her own flesh and blood is involved in this somehow, then she needs to know, needs to understand, before she shares it with August. She has to read the diary, all of it, no matter how painful it is, no matter how much it hurts her.

"You need to talk to Toby."

"Yes." Except, she isn't sure she really wants to. Not until she finishes the diary, at least.

"Let's go. You said he's still here in town, right? You know where to find him?" August's hands are on his hips; he's full of drunken bravado. "Let's go now, find out what he knows, and *why* he knows it."

"It must be two a.m.," she says. She shakes her head. "I'm too tired to think right now. We can track him down tomorrow. Let's go back to the hotel, okay?" She remembers leaving in the car a snack-size bag of pretzels from the airport. If she gets something in her stomach, she should be able to make the drive. It's not the smartest decision, and she'll be disappointed at herself in the morning, but right now, all she wants is to get as far away from Hobart Park as possible.

August opens his mouth like he wants to argue, but then he shrugs. "Okay. Whatever you want."

45

ISN'T IT WONDERFUL, BEING IN LOVE, OR AT LEAST FEELING something that might, maybe, possibly be love?

It doesn't matter that, now that the meetings with August have become more and more frequent, I wake dazed, sleepy-eyed, and squinting, with my mama knocking loudly at my bedroom door. It used to take only a light tap to wake me. At school I am tired but smiling, secretive, and carrying around this lovely lavender notebook that Jules never thinks to ask about. It's a piece of August, the only piece I can carry with me publicly.

If it wasn't for the play, if Jules wasn't engrossed in the life of fictional Juliet, then maybe I would worry. Maybe I would be more careful. But she's hopelessly distracted. Does it make me a bad friend to say I'm glad?

I spend each day looking forward to the nights I know I will spend with August. We have a marker, there by the river, a meeting spot—the little broken bridge I pointed out to him in the beginning. We sit on the banks and talk, and kiss, and do other things on the rocky, grassy slope. Just the thought of which makes my entire body flush.

It's been this way for a while, now. I sneak home in the early-morning hours, sometimes barely making it through the front yard and back into my window before my daddy leaves for work at five thirty. My jeans (or skirts, or shorts, depending on the weather) have gravelly rocks stuck to the back that I shake off onto the carpet of my bedroom, then gather into my hands and toss out the window. There are grass stains on my clothes from clinging carelessly to him as we roll along the ground in darkness. When I wear shorts, I come home with scrapes and scratches on my legs, mostly from the rocks on the bank. I hide them with long skirts and jeans, but I wear the thin scars like jewelry that he can never give me. I am proud, though no one can see.

46

JULIE AND AUGUST LEAVE EACH OTHER OUTSIDE THE HOTEL
elevator, with a plan to meet back up in the morning, to talk to Toby
and to finish reading the journal. But when Julie has the door to her
room closed and locked, she turns on every light, starts a pot of coffee,
and sits down at the tiny table with Reba's lavender diary.

Then, armed with her own memories from ten years ago, she
begins to read.

47

IT HAPPENED, TONIGHT. A CURTAIN HAS BEEN LIFTED, AND NOW I know a little bit more about the kinds of things Jules is always hinting about.

Except maybe it wasn't like the things Jules does at all, because nothing has ever felt so real before, so sincere. I know I should have been afraid, but I was a wildflower, unfolding in the darkness beneath the sunshine warmth of his hands.

48

A HOT SHOWER DOESN'T HELP AUGUST UNWIND, MAYBE BECAUSE the water coming from the showerhead is lukewarm, headed rapidly toward cold.

He wishes he had a cigarette. He's not a smoker, but every now and then, when he feels like this, he buys himself a pack. He imagines himself now, sitting near the opened window, cigarette smoke drifting out while he regains his equilibrium.

As the cool water falls languid against his back, he thinks of Reba's hands on him, thinks of the first time they made love. He wasn't prepared, couldn't have hoped for such a thing. He hadn't brought a condom, and she didn't ask him for one. Things had gotten out of hand. One minute they were fooling around like always, and the next minute, they were doing something more. It surprised them both. And it was fast, and he was embarrassed. He's even more embarrassed when he thinks about it now.

"I'm sorry," he said afterward, shaking his head.

"For what?" Reba was so innocent that she didn't know yet how it was supposed to be.

He'd felt her tense up, and he'd whispered, "Are you sure?" She'd nodded, but her teeth were clenched and maybe he should have stopped. But she was clinging to him, pulling him closer and closer. The wild honeysuckle bushes framed her head like a halo.

He hadn't thought to bring a blanket. He'd been careless, and twigs and pebbles and dirt clung to the back of her knees and calves. A trail of liquid, thick and pearly, marred her thigh. He vowed, then, that he'd never do it this way again, not with her. She deserved better.

His undershirt was missing, and he fumbled for it, then used it to carefully clean the mess from her thigh, folded it, and wiped gently between her legs. He'd known it would be her first time, should never have let things get so far. He could have made it perfect for her.

She was quiet while she slid her underwear and skirt back up over her hips, tank top over her head. He dusted debris from the back of her shirt, then dressed himself, leaving the undershirt crumpled beside them. He sat behind her and pulled her up so that she leaned back against him. She was trembling, light as the flapping of a moth's wing against his palms. He buried his head in the place where her neck met her shoulder, her hair falling into his face.

"Reba," he whispered in her hair.

When he said her name again, she nestled against him and whispered, "Shh…"

August turns off the shower faucet and rubs the rough hotel towel furiously against his body, like he could shake away the memory. He doesn't want to be alone with it, with these memories of her. He wonders if Jules is awake, what she would do if he knocked at her door. He toys with the idea of it for a moment, and then gives up on it and starts to dig through his suitcase.

There's got to be a cigarette in here somewhere.

49

OH GOD. I'VE BEEN CAUGHT.

I was meeting August at the river tonight when the rain began to fall, splashy wet missiles exploding against my face, my white tank top, my thin jacket.

"Reba, let's go home," August said, hands on my arms. "It's late. It's horrible out here. We can come back tomorrow night."

"No." For me, it had to be tonight. It was the first time I'd seen him, outside of school, since we did…what we did. In the days since, I had almost convinced myself that it hadn't really happened, that it was nothing more than a lovely dream. I needed it to be real, needed to touch him again.

"Follow me," I said.

I led the way to Nell's shop and reached for the set of keys still nestled in my jacket pocket from work that afternoon. August and I were soaked, water seeping into our clothes and skin, by the time we crossed the field and reached the shelter of the covered wooden porch. The back door creaked as I turned my key in the lock and pushed it open.

"We'll be dry in here," I said.

August looked around, uncertain. "Reba, should we be here?"

I could feel my skin buzzing. I felt timid, but I wanted him all the same. "No. No, we really shouldn't." I shut the door behind us anyway, twisted the lock, and pressed myself into August's arms.

50

"HERE YOU GO, DARLIN'," THE BARTENDER SAYS, AS SHE SLIDES another bottle Toby's way. The bar is mostly empty tonight, and he's been occupying this stool for hours. How many beers can one guy drink, anyway, before sleep overtakes him? For him, it's a lot. He could up the ante to something stronger, and maybe he will, if these damned thoughts don't go away.

"Hey, Toby," the bartender says. Shit, she knows his name, and he can't think of hers to save his life. He's always been bad with names. "Want to talk about it?"

He doesn't reply, but his glare says enough, he's sure. Better that he doesn't know her name. He doesn't want to talk about it. He *never* wants to talk about it, but every now and again, it seems like she can't help but ask.

The beer signs glowing red in the window are giving him one hell of a headache. He rubs his temples with his fingers and thinks of the night he learned Reba's big secret.

He'd left his cell phone at the damned flower shop that night, and he couldn't do business without it. He had to be available at all hours. That was why he'd bought the thing in the first place, wasn't it? No one else had a cell phone then; Molly still had that goddamned car phone thing that looked like a suitcase lying around somewhere. Jules had been so jealous when she saw his new phone. He liked the idea of having something that she wanted. She'd been a pain in the ass ever since she moved into the house.

So he got the cell phone, and what did he do with it? Left it at the shop when he went to pick up his deliveries. It was late when he remembered, middle of the night almost, but all of a sudden it hit him why his phone wasn't ringing—because he didn't have it. And that girl was supposed to call, the sexy one with the coke habit. He'd been sliding freebies her way here and there…when she made it worth his while.

It was raining buckets, and the car wouldn't start when he tried to crank it. Time to upgrade was what he'd been thinking, not that it helped him then. Walk to the shop in the rain, or get his phone the next day? He thought of the sexy blond—Cara, she said her name was, but he never knew for sure. People gave him fake names all the time, made them feel safer or something. He slammed the car door and started in the direction of the shop. He'd never been one for walking that path, but he'd seen Jules and Reba do it plenty of times. He was drenched by the time he got to the old guy's house—Nickel, his name was. His boots and the bottoms of his jeans were covered in mud and wet grass and who knew what other shit, and the whole thing was starting to put him in a really bad fucking mood.

His mood sure didn't let up when he reached Nell's, soaked to the bone and reaching into the pocket of his wet jeans for his door key, and he saw shadows moving inside. "You've got to be kidding me," he mumbled. What the hell was he supposed to do, confront an intruder in Nell's shop? Be some kind of hero? Why would anyone want to rob Nell's, anyway? Not exactly like she was bringing in the big bucks. He probably brought in more in one good night of dealing that she did in a whole week of running the store. Stupid high school kids, maybe. He leaned in closer to the window to get a better look. And about pissed his pants when he saw them.

He could see almost everything in the red glow of the Exit sign. Pretty little Reba—he'd know that hair anywhere. *Virginal* Reba, or so he'd thought. He'd been wrong, though, because there she was, up against the wall with her arms around some guy. That dark skin in the red light, all over her. Those fingers pushed her tank top over her head, and he'd been right all along—there was a hot little body under those clothes. *If Jules could see this*, he thought, chuckling to himself. Jules had this messed-up idea then, God knows how she came by it, that she could screw around all she wanted, sleep with all the boys in town, as long as she stuck to pure, sweet Reba like glue. Like all that purity would rub off. *Looks like all that purity is out the window, baby.*

Well, well, well. It was a good show. Reba wasn't the prude he'd thought she'd be, and he'd thought about her that way hundreds of times. He could see it on her face when the guy finally got inside her, pleasure and relief and anguish all mixed together—and damn, he wanted her looking at him that way. He could hear her moaning, softly, through the window. He'd have liked to make her moan like that. Louder. He'd have liked to make her lose control.

But what the hell was she doing with that guy? It was some serious shit around these parts, especially then. Black guys didn't mix with white girls. Especially not with white girls like Reba. It was no secret that her daddy was as racist as they came, part of the generation that still thought that way. Toby didn't give two shits about color (still doesn't). He may be a lot of things, but he's not a racist. Still, it was pretty messed up on Reba's part—dangerous too. Her daddy could have actually killed the kid. It was a serious secret, not like the girls sneaking out to play at Southern Saddle, not like the things Jules got up to when Molly was away.

The girl had gotten herself in deep. If anyone found out, there would be hell to pay...and the only thing standing between that big secret and the rest of the world...was *him*.

51

PUTTING THE WORDS ON PAPER MAKES IT MORE THAN JUST A BAD dream. But I have to get it out.

The rain had stopped, but the ground was wet and my feet were making squishing noises as they sank into the muddy grass, and it made the walk home *sound* so much louder. I felt equal parts blissful that I'd seen August again and anxious that it was over now, and I was going home alone. My clothes were uncomfortable, stretched loose from taking them off and then putting them back on in their dampened state. I hope I cleaned our footprints well enough from the floor of the shop.

I had barely lifted myself in through the windowsill when I heard a casual cough. I jumped, and a thousand thoughts rushed through my head. My daddy. Oh God, I was dead. And August too. I'd have to lie. *Think of a lie, think of a lie.* Poor planning, really, not to have thought of the story I'd tell, if I *was* ever caught.

I looked up, would rather have died than face him like this, but it wasn't like I had a choice. Except it wasn't my daddy. It was *Toby*. Toby, in my room, sitting on the wooden vanity chair in the corner. Lounging, more like, because even though his hair was wet and wavy, he looked as attractive as ever, and completely at ease.

"Hey there, *Rebecca*," he said, breathing my name, my grown-up name, and I was nearly frozen with terror. He knew.

"What are you doing here?" I asked. I wrapped my arms around my body, fully aware, now, of my wet, white tank top. Toby had never, in all of the years of my friendship with Jules, been in my bedroom.

"Hope you don't mind that I'm here. The window was open. I was surprised to find that you weren't here, though." He laughed, a low chuckle. I looked down. "Actually, no, I wasn't surprised at all. I knew you weren't here, because guess what happened to me tonight?" When I didn't respond, he continued. "I caught one hell of a show over at Nell's."

I wish I could have kept the color from my cheeks, but I felt it, slow heat rising up from my chest. I was probably pink all over, scared and embarrassed and other emotions I couldn't put a name to, not with Toby's eyes looking me up and down suggestively.

"What do you want?" I whispered.

"Little Rebecca. I used to think you were so innocent. Doesn't everyone think that? I wonder what they would do if they found out it wasn't true. I wonder what your daddy would think if he knew you'd been out all night fucking a... What's that word he likes to use?" He trailed off.

I don't know if it was the crass, rough-edged way he described what August and I do together or the fear of it all coming out into the open, but I felt my eyes welling up. Tears wouldn't help me, though. There is so much more at stake than even Toby realizes. It wouldn't take much for my daddy to make the connection that the boy I've been seeing is the son of his boss. And then August would be in real danger. What was it they did to James Edgemont? Started a fire in his family's front yard? Daddy wouldn't settle for that.

"I didn't know you could be so cruel," I said, which wasn't true. I've always suspected that Toby could be this cruel, and then some. "Why would you do this?"

"*Life's* cruel, baby." He stood, walked to me, primal in his approach, and I felt suddenly like prey. He touched me, shoulder to jawbone, softly with his rough fingertip. "You know…I've always been good at keeping secrets." His breath was hot against my neck, and I knew I should step away, but an uninvited tingle spread along my skin. I should probably have screamed at him, but it would have wakened my parents, and then what? They'd burst in and find Toby in my bedroom, and things would be bad anyway. God, I was so tired, hadn't slept in so many hours, and my bed looked so inviting and everything was going to hell in a handbasket, and I didn't know what to do, only that I had to protect the only thing I've ever thought of as precious. August.

"Just tell me what you want, Toby," I said wearily. He slid his finger underneath the strap of my tank top. "Are you trying to…I don't know, blackmail me, or something?"

He froze, his finger warm against my collarbone, and then he removed his hand completely, and I was shocked and disturbed by the way my body tried to betray me, tried to move closer to him so he would touch me again. Was I so addicted to affection now that I'd take it from anyone?

"No," he said, his voice quiet. "No, not that. Guess I'm not as cruel as you thought. Break it off with the kid, though, Reba. You're in way over your head."

Everything felt surreal—Toby close enough for me to breathe him in, the whiskey on his breath, my clothes sagging against my skin, the suffocating whiteness of my bedroom. I thought of the word *savage*, of the way people behave when they have something to protect, of the way instinct moves them.

"I know," I whispered. "You're right. I'll break it off, if you promise not to tell." Trusting Toby was a risk, especially when I knew I couldn't bear to end things with August. It was a dangerous game to play, but the words rang true enough. Toby seemed to believe me, anyway.

52

WHEN HE FIRST SAW REBA AND THE BOY TOGETHER ALL those years ago, Toby thought he'd hit the fucking lottery. What a punk kid he was. He thought he was going to finally get a chance at her—he had the ammo, after all. Truth is, blackmail was the only thing on his mind when he climbed through Reba's window. But when he looked into her big, scared eyes, heard that frightened voice... Well, he couldn't go through with it. Couldn't be that guy.

He could see it, though, that ache to be touched, not just by her little boy toy, but by someone who knew how. The way she shivered when he ran his finger along the delicate line of her neck.

If he could be patient, he thought, maybe he'd have his chance after all.

53

I HAVEN'T TOLD AUGUST THAT TOBY KNOWS. I DON'T WANT HIM to think we're in danger. I don't know what he would do. Maybe he would go after Toby, which would be stupid. August may be bigger, but Toby's not the type to put up with threats. More than that, I'm afraid that August might end things, that he'll want to walk away when he understands, fully, how volatile Toby is, and what my daddy could do if he found out about us. I don't want to lose August.

I didn't think about how easy it would be for Toby to check up on me, to see if I was telling the truth. His window overlooks mine, and now he knows to look, to see if it's open.

"You lied to me," he said, when I scrambled through my window and saw him sitting in the chair a second time.

"Yes," I said. I may have been afraid of Toby, but it seemed stupid to deny the obvious.

"Why?"

Why would I lie to him, he meant, when he has dirt on me that he could spill at any time. "You should really stop sneaking in like this," I said.

"Yeah? You should stop sneaking out."

"You know, you have secrets too." I know about his drug dealing. Jules told me a long time ago.

"Yeah. But nobody cares about my secrets, Reba. I bet your mama, and your daddy, and Nell, and Jules... They'd all have something to say about yours."

I turned my back on him and tried to pretend he wasn't there. As if that were possible. I put the Fiona Apple CD on with the volume turned down low so it wouldn't wake my parents, and I sat on the floor, back against the bed. I wanted to take off my dirty clothes, stained from the riverbank, but I knew I couldn't with him watching. I don't know what's wrong with me, but the feel of his eyes on me made me feel...important, or something. I was aching to pull out this diary, to write about my night with August. Odd that now that Toby is finally gone and I can write freely, he's the one I'm writing about.

His head tilted back against the little vanity chair, his eyes drifting closed to the slow rhythm of Fiona's sultry voice. I studied him. I've never told Jules that I'm sometimes mesmerized by Toby. He's *sexy* in a grown-up way, in the way of underwear models or men in cologne ads. In the way that makes you uncomfortable, because you know he's seen and done the kinds of carnal things you can barely imagine. Even writing it down feels wrong; it would be too weird for Jules to know how I think of him. But I *do* think of him, and the idea that he was here, in my bedroom again, was making me feel a strange way.

"Toby," I whispered. He couldn't fall asleep here. I got up and leaned over him so that I was whispering into his ear. The smell of him, whiskey and cologne, was overwhelming. "Toby, wake up."

"I'm awake," he said. He was close enough to kiss. Helplessly, I leaned in, and then, when I realized what I was doing, what I *wanted* to do, I jumped backward, hoping he hadn't noticed. But the smirk on his face told me he had.

"Go home," I said.

I watched him stand, stretch, look me over one last time before he swung a leg over the windowsill. "Wait," I said. "Are you going to tell?"

Toby paused, halfway out my window. It isn't fair that he is so much more graceful exiting my window than I am, when I've had much more practice. "What makes him so special, anyway?" he asked. "You think you love him or something?"

I shrugged. "Yeah, maybe."

Toby shook his head. "You don't. Tell you what, *Rebecca*." He raised an eyebrow. "Next time you feel like going to see him…come see me instead."

"Why would I do that? So you don't tell?"

"No," he said. He was doing that thing he does, looking at me like he knew more than he should. "Maybe you're curious. Something tells me you want to."

"I don't."

"We'll see." And then he was gone, and I quietly slid the window back down and pushed the latch into place.

I'm not going to do that, though. I'm not going to go to him, and I'm awful for even thinking of what it would be like. For even imagining it.

54

Julie can't believe what she's reading. She screams, trying in vain to purge this frustration, this anger. Her voice is loud and satisfying in the confines of her hotel room, but it isn't enough.

Toby. All of this time, and she never knew, never even guessed. She knew about Reba and August—hadn't she seen them together with her own eyes? She was blind, though. Stupid. Toby had been a player in this screwed-up production from early on, and he'd never told her. He *lied* to her about it.

She's starting to realize that she doesn't know this story nearly as well as she'd always thought.

55

I WASN'T FORCED, WASN'T PUSHED. IT WAS ALL MY DOING.

Toby opened the door before I could knock, my right hand frozen in the almost act of it. He seemed surprised, but not for long. Then he was smug, looking me up and down in his way. His eyes told me that he'd like to devour me, and I thought of eating, of consuming. I thought of wet, ripe fruit, sweet peaches hot from the sun, dark plums. Things with skin. He was wearing a T-shirt, maybe blue, maybe green, hard to tell in the moonlit darkness. It was late, and the lights were off inside Molly's house. I followed him into the shadowy living room. I couldn't see, but my feet knew the way. Almost as though I was there to visit Jules like always, not there for him, for…for… I didn't know why I was there.

I was fast behind Toby. Jules was at another drama club member's house rehearsing, but who knew when she would be back? I couldn't bear to face her, to have Jules find me in her house like this, with Toby. What lie would we tell?

His room was hazy, black light glowing in one corner and thin tendrils of smoke rising from an ashtray on his nightstand, his eerie paintings covering the walls. Why do they call it a black light when it glows blue in a dark room? I hadn't been in his room in years, since I was a kid and Jules and I would sneak in when he wasn't home, would snoop through his things with childish curiosity. He represented, to us, the entire world of boys, of mysterious *boyness. Stay out of my stuff, shitheads,* he said to us the one time he caught us there. He was eleven.

"I'm here," I said, after he shut the door behind us. My arms were folded across my chest, fingertips rubbing the soft texture of my sweater as if it could provide some comfort. I wore a sweater and jeans, though God knows it is still warm enough for tanks and tees. Indian summer, they call it, even this late in the year.

"Yeah, I noticed that." His voice was low, quiet. Was he nervous? "*Why* are you here, though?"

"You…you told me to come. I thought you wanted me to… I just wanted to *see.*" After a quick glance at his bed—unmade and messy with gray covers—I intentionally faced away. I looked instead at the strange art he had painted onto the walls. In front of me was a hummingbird, muted shades, long beak slipping into some delicate flower painted in light colors with crimson along the edges. Toby flipped on the radio, and suddenly there was music in the dim room. I stared at the walls, waiting.

"Why do you do this?" I asked, gesturing to the walls.

"Paint?"

"No, not that. Why do you paint *here*, on the walls, and then cover it all up?" Jules and I have seen him do it dozens of times over the years.

"Why not?" he said with a shrug.

"Do you even take a snapshot when it's finished?"

He shook his head.

"Why?"

"Shit, Reba, I don't know. It doesn't have to last, you know? If it did, I'd probably lose interest. Its only value lies in its impermanence."

"Deep," I said. "It's fascinating, you know."

"Whatever." He touched me from behind, hot hands on my shoulders, and I jumped. "Calm down, little Reba," he murmured, his voice losing some of its usual edge, his lips against my earlobe. "Here." He handed me some sort of cigarette, orange tip glowing in the dim light. I thought of swallowing it, of hot, bright fire melting like tangerine on my tongue.

"I don't smoke."

"You do now. It's a joint. Help you relax. Loosen up." He drew out the word *loosen*, and it sounded sexy and scary at the same time, slipping from his Southern mouth. "Go ahead."

"I don't want to," I said. "I don't want that."

"You don't have any idea what you want," he said. "Take it." I took it from his fingers. He'd been right before. I *was* curious about all of it.

"Put your lips on it," he said, and I did, sipping the smoke into my lungs. I thought of summertime and sweet tea and straws with candy-cane stripes. "Hold it in," he told me. I held it, longer than a normal breath but not so long that I felt my lungs would burst. "Now, let it out." A cloud of pearly smoke unfurled from my open mouth. All of that, inside me. "Good girl."

"Yes," I said. He was right—I *did* want it. It didn't take long. I felt like a tight ball of yarn unwinding. "More."

"No. Not yet. Not tonight." He put the joint down on his dress-er—no ashtray—and I thought of fire, of things burning. Of embers. He was behind me again, hands touching me, moving from my shoulders to my elbows and back up again. I could feel the heat of his hands through my sweater. I was so warm all over, and I wished I'd worn something lighter. I closed my eyes as his hands traveled over my breasts. Toby's touch wasn't like August's at all, not hesitant and respectful but certain, hungry. His hands slid lower, serpentine, one arm snaking around my waist and the other hand gliding along my denim-covered thighs.

His grip on my waist tightened and he pulled me against him. His hand was at the crotch of my jeans, and he was rubbing me there. I could feel his fingers and the stiffness of denim and the cotton of my panties all at once. "Reba," he hissed into my neck as he held me tight against him, his mouth on my shoulder, on my ear, on the back of my neck with my hair flipped easily out of his way.

"Do you want me to stop?" he asked, his voice rough. I opened my eyes, but didn't respond. He rubbed his fingers into the seam of my jeans and I could feel his touch on me and inside of me and everywhere. I tried to hold it in, but the quiet moan escaped my traitorous lips. I knew I shouldn't be there.

"Rebecca, do you want me to stop?" And then he did stop, stilled his hand and his mouth and waited, and the quiet tingling inside me slowed and my breath was heavy to my ears. "Tell me," he said. "Tell me to stop."

"No," I whispered, so quietly that he leaned his head forward to hear me clearly. "Don't."

"Black Hole Sun" played on the radio but I didn't think of sunlight, didn't think of anything in that wild darkness. I lived in the feel of his fingers on me and the sight of the intimate puncture of the hummingbird's beak into that soft flower, so vivid in my arousal that its wings seem to beat, to hum against every inch of my skin.

I could feel his breath on me, hear it ragged against my ear. "When you leave here," he growled, "will you go to him?"

My voice was shaky, distracted. "No."

"Just me," he said. "Say it." He gripped me harder. "Tonight it's just me."

"Just you." It was a sigh, a moan, a whimper.

"Again."

"Just you," I said. "Just you," repeated over and over as I came faithlessly against the hot concave of his hand. And then I was quiet.

I started to tremble as it wore away, that savage pleasure I never meant to experience. Or did I? I'd come to him of my own accord. A bewildered, guilty gasp escaped my lips.

"Shh…" he whispered, full lips kissing me where my neck and collarbone met. He released me, and I felt as though I might collapse. "Go home, Reba."

I ran out of his room and through the front door into the night. I scrambled clumsily through my window and curled up on my bed in the deceptive safety of my bedroom, covered in warm lamplight and shame.

And now, here I am, confessing it all.

56

I WASN'T READY TO SEE AUGUST AGAIN. I NEEDED MORE TIME TO rid myself of Toby's touch, in case August looked at me and saw traces of Toby left behind. But I couldn't exactly tell him that, so I'd agreed to go along.

August took me to see the new house his family was building. It is in the newest neighborhood in town, upscale, something my mama and daddy could never dream of affording. It has only been a few days since Toby, and I was confused, right and wrong blurring inside my head and my heart and my body. I was covered in gray, every inch of me. I didn't want to end things with August. Toby was right. I *had* been curious. And now I knew, and it wouldn't happen again.

It was a risk to go with August, in public, to his future home. It meant a drive through town in the front seat of his car. But I went willingly; I owed him even if he didn't know it, and it was raining out, with hints of an approaching storm. I remember, all too well, what had happened last time it rained. I felt hot thinking about Toby, and I was repulsed by myself, by my body's reaction, how he'd reduced me to a quivering mess, fully clothed, with only his touch. There was something about him, though, about the *way* he touched me. Like I was not made of glass, like I wouldn't crumble beneath his hands. Like I was a woman, and not the timid girl everyone believes me to be.

I could feel August glancing over at me, and I knew he could tell that something wasn't quite right. But I couldn't tell him what I'd done. I don't want him to think of other men's hands on me, don't want him to know how much I liked it.

So, I said nothing. I knew what August must have been thinking—that I had doubts, that I doubted my decision to be there with him. I tried to relax as we got closer to the house, and when we arrived, I could see why he'd suggested the place. It was only a skeleton still, plywood and exposed beams, surrounded by dirt that had turned to mud in the light rain. But no streetlights, not here. Not yet. No light at all, and no reason for anyone to take a second glance. His car, pulled into what would eventually be the driveway, seemed hardly visible should anyone pass by, which in itself was unlikely, given the hour.

He carried a soft blanket—he'd bought one soon after the night we first made love on the riverbank. He spread it out in what would one day be the dining room, after first checking to make sure that no wayward nails marred the makeshift floor.

"Here," he said. "Want to sit?"

I did. The blanket was smooth against my palms. He settled beside me and we looked out into the rain from the rectangular-shaped hole in the wall where the french doors would be. He put his arms around me, and I tensed up.

"Is something wrong?" He pulled his arms away.

"It's…" I don't know what, exactly, is wrong with me. I don't understand myself. "I'm just worried about my…shoes," I stammered. What a stupid, made-up lie. "They've got all this mud on them, and I don't want to make tracks…when you take me home. The driveway, my room. Mama might see."

"Did that happen last time, after Nell's? Did you leave any tracks?"

"No." It had been far worse than footprints.

"Then don't worry. We'll clean them up before we leave, I promise. I've got napkins in the car. Don't worry, okay?"

The tenderness in his voice made me want to hide my face. "Okay." I sighed and leaned against him. And then our mouths were pressed together, and his hands were tangled in the curls of my hair. I was suddenly so filled with affection toward August that I wished *I* could be inside of *him*, wished he could swallow up all of me and that he would know my betrayal and also know that I didn't do it on purpose. I just had to know.

I wrapped my arms around him in a fierce embrace, and we lay there, side by side on the blanket, my head against his chest so I could feel the *thump-thump* of his heartbeat.

"Are you sure?" he asked later, like he always does. As if I might change my mind. I nodded, though, touched my lips to his and clung to him. There were no leaves to crunch beneath us; there was no wall against my back like at Nell's, only our arms wrapped around each other and the rain now falling in sheets. I was comforted by the sound of water, as steady as if it were the river rushing below us.

57

I SAT ON THE EDGE OF TOBY'S BED, IMPATIENT FOR THE MOMENT when he would touch me again and all of the thinking, the doubting, the wondering *What in the world am I doing here again* would stop.

I went back there. I know it's wrong, and I went back there, anyway.

He handed me the joint and I took it this time, no objection. I breathed it in, exhaled, and did it once more before he could stop me. He didn't have a shirt on, and I wished he did because my eyes were drawn to his chest and I didn't want them there, tried my best to look anywhere else. Why does he have to look so good? He is smooth and muscular, and I wanted to slide my palms against the firm tanned skin of his abdomen—and I hated myself for it.

"What do you want from me, Reba?" he asked, running a fingertip lightly up my arm.

"What? I... Nothing. I don't want anything." I looked down at the rough beige fibers of the carpet on his bedroom floor, at his brown flip-flops in a neat pair against the wall in one corner. The hummingbird on the wall, claiming ownership of the flower, lightness of petals marred by the crimson seeping in at the top, deep red like blood. I thought of bloodletting, of virgins, of sacrifice. The radio played "Wicked Garden," and I felt myself blushing. I was wearing a tank top this time, blue, and jean shorts, but I still felt so hot, like my skin was teeming with tiny fires burning in different places: the base of my throat, my exposed shoulders, the tops of my thighs.

"You do. Show me. Touch me." He took a long pull from the joint and put it in the ashtray on his nightstand. I looked up at him, hesitant, and he grabbed my hand in his own and pressed my palm firmly to his chest. He sighed, his dark-green eyes closing and something like a hiss slipping from his mouth. I thought of snakes again—he made me think of serpents. Maybe it was all the temptation, things I didn't know I wanted.

I thought of the word *resist*; my mind tripped over it. To abstain from, to oppose. But the opposite word, which has always felt so delicate and exotic on my tongue, fits him better, his head tilted back against the headboard as I cautiously explored the tight muscles of his stomach, the top of my thumb grazing the copper coin clasp of his blue jeans. *Irresistible*.

"You're nothing like him," I said bitterly.

He grabbed the front of my tank, balled it together in his fist, and used it to pull me against him hard and fast, his lips colliding with mine in a rough, frantic kiss. The stubble along his jaw scratched at my lips, and I felt raw. I wanted to hurt him, and at the same time, I wanted my hands all over him. We would surely drown, together, in this heady mix of disdain and desire.

"Jesus Christ," he gasped when he pulled away from me, looking disarmed for once in his life. "Go, Reba," he said. "Go home."

My skin was buzzing with lust and power. The way he was looking at me made me feel like what he'd told me before was a lie, that he didn't own me but that I owned *him*.

"No," I said. It felt like someone else, another girl lost in this perverse wonderland, who crossed her arms like an *X* across her front and reached for the hem of her tank, pulled it slowly over her head, tossed it to the floor. "You want me, don't you?" I whispered. It sounded like a taunt, like a challenge, like it came from a mouth that didn't belong to me. "Then tell me what to do. Teach me. *Show me.*"

And he did.

58

EVEN BACK THEN, JULIE KNEW REBA WAS HIDING SOMETHING. She could feel it, like Reba had grown a shell (something with scales, with spines) over her skin to keep Julie from seeing the truth. In the years since, Julie always believed it was the secret affair with August. But that was only one tiny part of it.

There was a day, back then, when play practice had ended early and she'd caught up to Reba as she was closing up Nell's. They'd walked all the way to the Thomas Pharmacy and Car Care for ice cream and then back through the field, but they were each sullen, lost in their own private thoughts.

"Tell me about practice," Reba said, or something like that, when they were by the river. But Julie could see she was distracted.

"Oh, well, you know…just practice. Actually, I'm getting pretty good at being Juliet, even if she *is* completely pathetic."

"Do it," Reba said.

"Do what?"

"Show me. Be her. Be Juliet."

"No. That's for the play only. Besides, you'll see it soon enough." The truth was, she'd gotten a little *too* good at being Juliet, and she was embarrassed by the sweet tone of her voice, by the way she could infuse her words with emotion, as though she could make love with words alone. It had become very intimate in a way she wasn't comfortable with. She had started to wonder what, exactly, made her so good at *faking it*.

"Jules," Reba said. "There are some things I need to tell you." Her eyes kept darting to the riverbank, so much so that Julie found herself spinning around periodically to make sure there was nothing back there worth seeing.

"Okay." She crossed the bridge, jumping over the loose plank, and then she was on the bank next to Reba. She remembers wondering why Reba's eyes looked so tired, why her lips were strangely plump and chapped, as red as if she'd been eating berries.

"I'm not who you think I am."

"Huh?"

"I'm not who you think I am. Not anymore."

Julie studied Reba's worried face. "What do you mean?"

"Have you ever been in love, Jules?"

The words hit her like a slap. Because she didn't love anyone at all, except Reba, and that was a whole different thing. None of the men Julie had ever been with had been able to make her care, and only a few had tried. When they touched her, she felt alive, but the sensation was brief and then she was empty again. It was part of the reason she was so upset about the play, about being so good at pretending. She knew for a fact that she'd never been in love, and she knew with equal certainty that no one had ever loved her.

"No," she said. "No, I haven't." Not in real life. She felt regretful suddenly, in a way she never had before, about the things she'd done with her body without the mythic thrill of love behind it all. She knew that Reba was trying to share something with her, but she didn't feel like talking anymore. Not about this.

"I think I'm going to go home now, okay? Let's talk later."

She left Reba behind, a surprised expression on her face. Twigs from tree limbs slapped at Julie as she worked her way through the woods, her shoulders sagging beneath the weight of some strange sadness.

Julie has thought about this conversation a hundred times over the years, has wondered what Reba might have said to her then, what she may have confessed, had Julie not been so self-absorbed. She always assumed it would have been about August. But Reba was hiding so much more.

59

I CAME SO CLOSE TO A CONFESSION TODAY ON THE RIVERBANK. But Jules…she didn't want to hear it. Almost as if she knew that whatever I had to say would shatter her illusions about me. I had barely even begun when she ran away, and I was disappointed and relieved at the same time.

The truth is, I don't *want* to confess. I feel evil and reckless and distraught about the things I've done with Toby, with August too trusting to know any different. But the feeling of having them both close to me, of having these shameful, delicious secrets…is exhilarating.

And wrong. I know it's wrong.

How do I let them both inside me so easily? All of my life, I've been caged like a little bird, but I didn't see it, didn't know I was waiting for someone to come along and set me flying on feathery wings. There's August, who slipped into my heart and made it open for him. And there is Toby, who touched me once and made me uninhibited and wild. Free. What's wrong with me, that I want Toby's hands on my body, when August would touch me only with tenderness? August, who looks at me and sees only goodness.

When I am with August, it doesn't feel like it's wrong. But when Toby's lips are on my skin and the strands of his silky hair are caught between my fingers, I feel alive. With him, I don't have to be someone's ideal. When we are together, we are *more* than good, or bad, or pure, or sinful. We are above all of that. We are filled with lust and power, and when we touch, the feeling only multiplies over and over, and it only gets more intense. It only gets better.

Surely I'm not some sex-crazed teenager. Surely no one has ever felt this before. So here's the troubling part: being with Toby doesn't feel wrong, either.

I don't know if I love them or if I hate them both.

60

Toby leaves cash on the bar and starts the walk home. Maybe now that he's good and wasted, he can sleep, let all of the memories go for a while.

Like there won't be dreams. Nightmares, more like.

Most of the little shops in downtown Opal are closed for the night, though the pizza joint and the redneck pool hall still seem to be going strong. The city is trying to revive the downtown square, make it artsy, add more boutiques. Sometimes, it seems to be working. Tourists show up on the weekends, in the spring and fall when it's not too hot out, looking for the small-town experience. His art gallery was featured in *Southern Living* a few months back. A woman who makes artisanal soaps just moved into the building next door. But after dark, it's the same old rough crowd hitting up the same old rough places.

It is what it is.

Back then, he didn't care about all of that shit. When there was Reba. When she was his, more or less. Less. That girl made him feel strange things, think strange things. She got to where she'd come to him damn near every other night. Who knew how she made time for the other guy. She still did, though. When she was in Toby's arms, he couldn't stop himself from asking, *Does he touch you like this? Does it feel the same?* Always the answer was no, except when he asked if she loved the boy, and then yes. Always yes.

But Toby had his own ways of making her say yes. He'd always known she'd be good; he just had no idea *how* good. He might have thought about blackmailing her once, but he didn't even have to, and he was glad. Better for her to come to him of her own accord.

No fucking reason he should have wanted it to be more. All the dirty, sexy things they did together, and he got the feeling she didn't even like him. *Wanted* him, though, and that was enough. He knew he did something to her that no one else did, not the boy, not anyone. When Toby touched her, she came…undone. And then she dressed and she had that look in her eye, like she despised him, but she despised herself more. It shouldn't have mattered that she was always leaving; he shouldn't have wanted her to stay, shouldn't have wanted to calm her, to somehow make it all better.

He'd started painting her by then, on his bedroom wall. It was big, the biggest thing he'd ever painted at that point. He figured she'd shit a brick if she realized it was her, so he was saving the face for last. He'd covered up a blue-painted waterfall to start the new project, so that with the rough sketch, she looked like she was lying in a pool of water.

It still fucks with his mind, thinking of how he started painting her that way. Like he mapped out her death, like he killed her without even knowing it.

61

AUGUST INVITED ME TO HIS HOME LAST NIGHT, HIS TEMPORARY home at least, until the new house is finished. Lamplight cast a welcoming glow, but I tiptoed like an intruder.

"It's lovely," I whispered. On the outside, it was no more than an aging mill house, its color indefinable at night, even with the beam of the porch light. But the inside was filled with beautiful treasures, dark wood and tall floor lamps with thick stained-glass shades like church windows. His parents have good taste.

"You don't need to whisper," August said. "There's no one here except us." But his voice was low too. Our world together had so far been made up of only quiet words and soft embraces, and we didn't know how to speak normally to each other. "It's just the rental," he said, closing and locking the door carefully behind him. I heard the *click, click* of the lock and remembered, again, how risky it was for me to be there. I wandered through the house, feet silent on thick-padded oriental rugs. "The new house should be finished soon. My dad hopes it will, at least."

"Where are they? Your family?" I was sure he had told me already, when I was lost in my own complicated thoughts.

"Back in Virginia for a wedding. I talked Mom into letting me stay behind. She assumed that I had made some new friends I wanted to hang out with. Like I was 'fitting in' or something."

He moved closer to me. It was the first time we'd been alone together indoors since the night at Nell's shop, which is tainted for me now that I know Toby was watching. I felt awkward in August's home, uncertain of what to do, how to behave.

He led me to his bedroom, and I sat on the very edge of his deep-blue bedspread. A row of trophies lined his dresser. Many had little brass football players perched on their stone ledges. His camera sat beside the trophies, atop a stack of books on photography. I shouldn't have thought of the differences between this room and Toby's, but I did. August's room *seemed* safe and warm, but I didn't feel that way myself. I felt out of place, like I wasn't supposed to be here. Like it was wrong, somehow. When I'm in Toby's room, I always feel like I have fallen into some other, darker world, those strange paintings covering the walls, the unsettling black-light glow, the light odor of marijuana. Wilder. I am a different person there.

August sat beside me, and I stared at the knees of his dark-blue jeans. When he kissed me, I opened my eyes and found him looking back. He watched me with reverence, eyes on mine as he tilted me slowly back against the bed, and I wanted to enjoy it but I couldn't, not with an image of Toby so clear in my mind that he may as well have been there with us. August wouldn't take his eyes off me, and I wished he would have; I didn't like the idea of those deep-brown eyes watching me and seeing this lie, seeing something pure and beautiful that doesn't even exist. For the first time, I felt angry with August, angry that he couldn't see the truth, that he would be so foolish as to put his young heart in my unfaithful hands.

I couldn't stop thinking of Toby.

Afterward, the pull to confess was so strong that I told August about my daddy instead, about the lost promotion, about his outrage. About how foolhardy it is for August to spend time with me. He didn't seem as surprised as I thought he would be—maybe he'd somehow put it together himself. But part of me hoped he would listen anyway, that he would leave me alone, leave me behind.

It would probably be for the best.

62

Toby turns the key in the door of the art gallery and stumbles inside. Walking is confusing at this point, though, and before he knows it, he's tripped himself up. He lands on his hands and knees on the hardwood floor. Times like this, he wishes he was still into drugs. Pills would have been faster, might have saved him from the goddamned headache he knows he'll wake up with tomorrow.

In the darkened room, Reba's eyes stare out at him from a dozen paintings. He hates it, her looking at him like that, but he loves it too. He must, to keep painting her again and again. Reba in the river, Reba in the woods, in her bedroom, on the bridge. Tonight, his eyes are drawn to a painting of her standing in his old bedroom, by the edge of the bed. There's no drug powerful enough to block out the memory of that night, over a decade ago now.

Thanksgiving night—a risky time for her to have been sneaking out, but there she was. It was dark in his room, and for the longest moment, he couldn't figure out what woke him up. Then his eyes adjusted and he saw her there. His window was open, and a November breeze seeped in. His sleepy brain thought she must have somehow climbed in through the second-story window, but no.

"The front door was unlocked," she said in a low, breathless voice. She snapped on the radio on his nightstand. She was wearing little gym shorts and a tank top, no bra, with a big cardigan sweater over her arms. What was she doing there? Had she lost her goddamned mind?

"Lucky you didn't run into Jules," he mumbled. "The only other person who would sneak around at this hour on Thanksgiving lives in this fucking house, you know."

"Shh." She held a finger to her lips. She didn't usually show up like that, especially not that late. The whole scene had this weird, dream-like quality, almost like he'd taken something before bed. He hadn't, though.

"Reba, what are you doing here?"

Before he was even fully awake, she was straddling him, her mouth clumsy and frantic on his. She kissed him hard, teeth scraping against his lips, and he was confused—was she angry, or horny? She kissed him, bit him, his lips, his neck, his ears. His hands caught her hip bones and pulled her to him, the thin sheet separating her body from his. "Jesus Christ, Reba," he moaned.

"It's your fault," she whispered into his ear as she attacked him with her mouth, her fingernails scraping at his arms. He tried to understand what she was saying, but she wouldn't let up, and he was scared shitless and more excited than he'd ever been in his whole goddamned life.

"What?" he gasped as she pulled the sheet out of the way and reached for him. "What's my fucking fault?"

Her eyes were watery when she looked at him, and he didn't know if she was going to fuck him or cry on him. "It's your fault I'm like this," she whispered. "You made me this way, didn't you? You turned me into this."

He was wide awake and on top of her before she knew it, sheet tossed to the floor and her wrists pinned above her head with his left hand.

"Uh-uh," he said, his free hand roaming her body. "I didn't make you come here. I didn't do a thing, other than give you what I knew you wanted."

"Don't," she said as he pushed down her shorts. "Don't," she repeated, as she arched herself up to him.

He didn't know what her game was, but he didn't like it. "Reba," he said, his voice harsh and confused. "Do you want this or not?"

He couldn't tell if she was crying, didn't know what he was supposed to do. Hold her? Tell her it was going to be okay?

He really didn't need this shit.

"Say yes, Rebecca," he groaned into her ear. "Say yes, or this stops." He'd been holding her down, but he eased up, pulled away. Let go of her wrists and, for some reason, trailed her collarbone with chaste kisses before looking at her again.

Her wide-open eyes were killing him, that look of lust and terror and God knows what else. Her wet, raw lips parted, and the curtains rustled and moonlight shone on her gorgeous face while "Glycerine" played on the radio.

"Yes. Yes." Her legs wrapped around him and pulled him in close, and it was the sweetest fucking place he'd ever been.

Sad thing is, he's thirty years old now, and he's still never had anything better. There *is* nothing better than her. He collapses onto the floor of his gallery. He can feel her eyes on him, and he knows it isn't real, but it's soothing all the same.

63

JULIE JUMPS AWAY FROM THE DIARY, HER FINGERTIPS TINGLING
as though the pages have singed them. She looks around, surprised
to find herself still in this hotel room and not in the Lawrence Mill
of ten years ago.

She leaves her room in a hurry, barefoot, without really knowing
where she's going, only that she has to put some distance between
herself and that damned book. The hotel carpet is flat and firm
beneath her feet, and when she presses the button for the elevator, she
finally knows where she's headed. She takes the elevator to the third
floor, the highest floor of the hotel, and then turns down a hallway
that she knows leads to the back staircase. There's a metal ladder
there, and if she climbs it, she'll find herself on the roof. She's been
up there only a few times, with men she met at Southern Saddle back
when she was a teenager. But it seems like a place where she might
find some clarity.

She climbs up, her bathrobe sweeping against the metal rungs. The
trapdoor is heavy, but she manages to push it open. It's deserted up

here, as she knew it would be, the concrete of the roof level coated with rain-washed yellow pollen and a line of bulky air-conditioning units humming along the perimeter of the roof. She finds a corner and sits. The white hotel bathroom will be covered in yellow after this.

She'd stopped reading just before the Thanksgiving entry. She wasn't ready. That Thanksgiving night is vivid in her mind. The night she caught Reba, though she had no idea what she'd actually caught her doing.

Back then, Julie and Toby shared a hallway bathroom. At night, when Toby was home and Molly was away at work, Julie crept like an intruder down the hall when she needed to pee, using her hands and the sliver of light that escaped from under Toby's closed door to guide her through the dark hallway. It wasn't Toby himself that she was trying to avoid (not that she ever welcomed his company). But Toby, at least, was an enemy she knew. What made her hurry was her attempt to avoid, whenever possible, accidental interaction with one of his "clients," either accompanying him up the stairs to his room or slipping out of his bedroom, product in hand.

He invited them into the house with no thought of danger, no worry of hidden policemen or drug-induced threats. Julie couldn't believe that Molly didn't know, that she hadn't heard rumors. But maybe she had. Maybe she only pretended not to know about Toby's dealing and Julie's late-night adventures. Easier not to deal with it. Or maybe no one talked at all, maybe Julie was just paranoid. Maybe no one cared enough to talk.

It would happen, occasionally, though, that Julie would be opening her bedroom door or the bathroom door at the exact moment someone was coming or going. And she couldn't resist watching, couldn't resist seeing who would come to a college kid's house in a small-town neighborhood in the middle of the night, pockets filled with wadded-up twenty-dollar bills, to get a fix. Mostly they were the usual suspects—Toby's friends, long-haired boys in bands. But sometimes she was surprised. The middle-aged manager of the gas station on the corner of Magnolia, the cashier at Piggly Wiggly. Her tenth-grade science teacher.

But the biggest surprise of all came that Thanksgiving night, when she stood in her bedroom with the door cracked and watched the lovely blond-haired girl hurry from Toby's room, arms across her chest and eyes to the floor.

Julie's world crumbled as easily as a handful of dead flowers. As soon as she heard the front door click softly closed, she banged her fists against Toby's bedroom door, the noise of it echoing down the hallway. When he didn't respond, she flung it open on her own.

"What the hell did you do to her?" she asked, struggling to keep her voice at a reasonable level despite her panic. Toby loved to get under her skin. The room was smoky and completely dark, except for the moonlight slipping in through the window.

Toby flicked on the bedside lamp. There were things everywhere—a square mirror lying flat on the nightstand, wayward bits of powder clinging to it, sheets and pillows strewn about the floor. She could see newly painted vines, so detailed, crawling up one wall, and the start of a woman—lithe legs, pink-painted toes, slender thighs—on another. Toby was lying on the bed, body twisted from leaning to turn on the lamp and naked except for boxer briefs, black. "Jesus fucking Christ," he mumbled. "Doesn't anybody knock anymore?"

"What did you do to her?" Julie shouted, quickly losing the fight to control her emotions. She picked up a pillow and hurled it at Toby, and it hit him in the face. She couldn't imagine Reba, her Reba, in that room, with Toby. Toby, who dealt drugs and got high and painted full walls with tiny paintbrushes.

"What are you talking about?" Toby sat up in the bed. His chest was streaked red with scratches, like he'd been fighting someone. Like someone had been fighting him.

"I saw her leaving your room. I saw her. Why was she here, and what the hell did you do to her?"

"What? Nothing. She wasn't here," he muttered.

"Don't lie to me." Julie snapped on the overhead light, and the room was bright with artificial daylight. Toby covered his eyes with his arms.

"Fuck you, Jules," he said. "Go to bed."

"Tell me. Tell me what happened in this room, or I will tell every single person I know about your little drug business." Her face burned red; she could feel it. She hurled another pillow at him. "Why are you so scratched up? Did you hurt her? *What did you do?*"

"Goddamn it, stop!" he yelled, throwing a pillow back at her. "I thought you wanted to know about her, not me. And I didn't *do* anything to her. Nothing she didn't want, anyway." He leaned back against his headboard and closed his eyes.

"What does that mean?"

"What do you think? You're the one going on and on about my 'drug business.' The girl's got a habit, okay? She's a client."

"She's *what?*"

"A client." He looked her up and down. "Happy?"

"I don't believe you."

"Believe it, baby. Nothing heavy, a little pot here and there. So, relax already. Maybe you could use some yourself."

"Why? Why would she do that?"

"I don't know, Jules. I'm her dealer, not her therapist. She wants it, I've got it."

"It's three thirty in the morning. Why now?"

Toby rolled his eyes. "Isn't it obvious?" She didn't answer, because nothing was obvious anymore. Five minutes before, she would have sworn that her best friend would never touch drugs. *Obviously.* "Because she doesn't want you to know."

"Reba doesn't do drugs."

"She does now."

"Why is your chest all scratched up?"

"When did you get so damned nosy?" he asked, leaning forward. "Unrelated, Jules. If you really want to know, I had a date tonight. Earlier. With a girl who likes it…rough." He laughed. "And who am I to deny her?"

"You're disgusting." Her voice was low and scary, even to her own ears, when she said, "If you sell Reba anything that hurts her in any way, I will find out about it, and I will hurt *you.*"

"You're so full of shit. I don't believe a word that comes out of your slutty little mouth."

She narrowed her eyes at him. "Believe it, baby." She slammed his bedroom door behind her and stomped back to her room.

"Turn off the fucking light, Jules!" he yelled, but she pretended she didn't hear.

64

JULES LOOKED ME IN THE EYE WHEN WE MET AT THE FOOT OF Molly's driveway for school. I felt scrutinized, like a math problem where the answer is wrong, and I wondered what she knew. I didn't have to wait long, because Jules has never been the subtle type.

"I saw you," she said.

"What?"

"Leaving Toby's room on Thanksgiving night. I saw you."

I could feel my eyes widen. "Jules, it's not what you think…" I'd been so desperate for Toby, so stupid, that I'd forgotten to be careful. I'd *needed* him. I didn't even check, when I was leaving, to make sure Jules wasn't around. It was my own fault.

"You don't have to make excuses. He told me about the drugs."

"Whatever he said… Wait, what did he say?"

"That you do drugs. Pot. That he's your dealer. Is that true? Unless you were doing something else in his room that night."

Toby has made me careless; both of these boys have. Confused me, messed with my pretty, simple world. And now Jules has caught on.

But Toby… He lied about it? Why? "I don't know…" I said weakly, my voice trailing off as I tried to think of what to say next.

"I don't understand you anymore. We tell each other everything… At least, I thought we did. What's with the hiding?"

My only experiences with drugs are the nights when Toby passes me a half-smoked joint, sometimes before we do…what we do, sometimes after. What to say next… That I wasn't really doing drugs after all, that I was seducing Toby that night? That we were making love in his bedroom? I *want* to think of it as making love, because it sounds less depraved when I turn the phrase over in my head. But I know that what we do together is something completely different, something bigger and more complex than that. Making love is what happens when August and I are together, and it feels like betrayal to use those same words, even in my mind, to describe the things Toby and I do to each other.

"Um…I don't know. I guess I'm just trying it out, Jules. I've been kind of stressed lately. My dad and the job thing, and school, and…I don't know, stuff. Don't make a *thing* of it." I don't usually talk to Jules this way, and I could see that she was taken aback.

"I'm not making a *thing*, Reba, I just didn't…know that you were doing that." She looked hurt and…something else. Jealous?

"Oh," I said. "You've never done it before?" I assumed that Jules has tried all kinds of different things, what with all of the experiences she's had with the older guys and the alcohol.

"No," she says. "You'd know if I had." It was a lie, though. I know that Jules keeps plenty of things from me, always has. Protecting me, I bet she would say if I were to call her out on it.

"Probably not," I said bitterly. "We don't really see each other anymore. You're busy, remember?" It was the easiest way I could think of to let Jules know that things are different now. I can't confide in her anymore, not without all of this judgment.

I bet that if she could, she would keep me sweet like the untouched bloom of a flower forever.

"It's not like that," Jules said. "You know it isn't."

"I know." I sighed. "I'll see you in class, okay?" And I sped up, walking as fast as I could. Jules didn't even try to catch up.

There are so many secrets now that it's hard to keep them all straight.

65

JULIE JUMPS WHEN THE DOOR TO THE ROOF GROANS OPEN. Dazed from reliving her own violent memories, it takes a moment for her to recognize that the person climbing up onto the roof is August.

"Hey," she says. This time he's the one who's startled. He looks around, finally sees her in her little corner. She leans back against the cool concrete roof. She's wearing pajamas beneath her bathrobe, and she tugs the robe tighter around her body, modest suddenly in his presence.

"What are you doing up here?" he asks. He's wearing the same clothes from earlier, except that his shirt is untucked, top buttons undone.

"Just needed some fresh air…a place to think," she says.

"I can go, if you want to be alone." He hovers near the door.

"No. Stay." She should tell him about Toby and Reba, but she's still in shock herself. She doesn't know how to say it; she hasn't processed it yet. August leans against the concrete wall, rests his elbows there, overlooking the city.

"There's no way you killed her, Jules," he said, "if that's what you're thinking about."

For the first time, she wonders if that could be true. She's been wrong about so many other things, hasn't she? But even this recent revelation about Toby and Reba isn't enough to absolve her. It doesn't change the fact that Julie *remembers* being in the forest, *remembers* arguing with Reba.

"How'd you know this was up here?" she asks.

"Didn't. Just guessed. The office building where I rent workspace has a rooftop like this. No one ever goes up there but me."

It strikes her, then, how little she knows of him. It's probably better that way, but she finds herself wanting to know more. The only genuine details she has about him come from Reba's diary, from when he was a teenager. She thinks about how much she, herself, has changed since those teenaged years. She doesn't want him thinking that's who she is anymore.

"Tell me about your work," she says.

"It's…you know…work."

"Do you like it?"

He nods, shrugs. "Yeah, I like it. I mean, it's what I always thought I would do, taking pictures, so it's good." She doesn't have to ask what's missing from his life. The loneliness emanates from him; it enrobes him, makes him seem like some kind of martyr.

"Do you date, August?" He doesn't look at her, doesn't answer.

"I mean, I know you said that you haven't had anyone special… not since…but do you date, ever?"

He shrugs again. "I guess. I'm not celibate, if that's what you mean. But they know I'm not looking for a relationship. I…you know, I can't."

It isn't fair. Julie had always thought August changed everything for Reba, but she can see now that Reba also changed everything for him. In an alternate world where they had never met, August could be out there somewhere, happy, at peace. He could be tangled in a lazy embrace on a sofa, watching TV with his wife while his children slept upstairs. He could be a completely different person from the one standing before her now, the loneliness and guilt and anxiety wound through every cord of his muscles, from his tight shoulders to the clench of his hands atop the low wall overlooking Opal. All that for a girl who may or may not have even loved him.

He pulls a bent cigarette from his pocket and lights it, a soft plume of smoke floating out into the night air. She watches it, her head back against the hard concrete, watches the smoke drift out into nothingness, break apart, disappear. There's something to it, some truth that she can almost grasp, and then it's gone again, evaporated, nothing.

Julie climbs to her feet. August looks at her with those dark eyes, his lips parted around the cigarette. She's jittery from the two cups of hotel room coffee she's had, the rest of the pot waiting for her downstairs. The words from Reba's diary are fresh in her mind, and August's face is the most *honest* thing she's seen in a long time. She lifts her hand, rests it against the warmth of his cheek, and he doesn't flinch. The line of his jaw beneath her palm makes her want to say something, to *do* something. She could kiss him, right now, she thinks, and maybe he wouldn't mind. The questions are there in his eyes: *What is this? What does this mean?* But she doesn't know the answers.

"Good night, August," she whispers, even though the night isn't over for her.

She has more reading to do.

66

Lying in a stupor on the floor of his gallery, Toby dreams of her, except it was real once. He knows it really happened, and now he's reliving it all in his sleep.

It was the week after Jules had caught Reba leaving his bedroom.

"Back again," he said when he looked up and saw Reba in his doorway. He was more surprised than he let on. He hadn't expected her to come back again, once Jules was on to her. He knew Jules well enough to know that if she'd confronted him, she'd have confronted Reba too. Bitch had never been one to keep things to herself. It was ballsy of Reba to come back there—during the day, no less. She locked his bedroom door behind her. Smart girl. He was painting, sitting on the floor and leaning into the wall with paint streaks on his arms and on his tank top. He'd just finished a line of coke, which he'd never have done if he'd known she was coming over. It made him focused but jittery, not what he needed with her around. Not to mention that he'd never done that around her before. Only marijuana, and not even much of that.

"You told her I smoke pot?" Reba asked, with raised eyebrows.

"Yeah."

"Why would you do that?"

"Fuck, Reba, I don't know. What did you want me to tell her? The truth?" He'd protected her, and he didn't want to think about why. *Because he didn't want things to end* was the easy answer. His body went crazy when she was around, even then, when she was over by the door like she might run at any moment. If she came closer, he'd have to touch her, wouldn't be able to hold back.

"I actually thought I could trust you," she said, looking pissed off, which pissed *him* off.

"Hey, *you're* the one who showed up here in the middle of the night with no warning, fucked me senseless, and slipped out with hardly a good-bye. Maybe if you'd *let me know* you were coming I could have been waiting for you, could have kept an eye out for your supposed best friend, who obviously isn't such a good friend anymore or you would be telling *her* your secrets in the first place."

"I don't need your help," she said.

"Don't you? You tell me. I had to tell her something. Would you rather her think you have something going on with pot...or something going on with me? Not to mention the other boy."

Her face was red, and there she went again, protecting her man and all that shit. He was sick of it, really. He hadn't asked her to come over, hadn't asked her over on Thanksgiving night either, for that matter, but he'd done the best he could to help her out—and did it even matter? She opened her mouth like she was about to give him a serious piece of her mind, but only one sentence came out.

"Don't you dare bring him into this."

Toby got to his feet and crossed the room to her so quickly that he knocked over a small jar of skin-colored paint. *Screw it.* He was standing in front of her, and she was looking at him with that angry, unsure pout and he said, "Why not, Rebecca? It's all about him, right? Or…is it?" He couldn't help it; he grabbed the back of her head with his paint-streaked hands and kissed her the way she liked it. God, did she like it. Her hands were all over him, against his arms, in his hair.

"This is over," she said as she tugged his shirt up over his chest.

"It's not. You belong to me," he panted, as he pulled her down to the bedroom floor.

"I don't," she whispered, but he could tell that even she didn't believe it anymore.

67

I DON'T KNOW WHAT I'M CAPABLE OF. I DON'T KNOW WHAT lines I won't cross, who I won't hurt. It has to stop.

If Toby doesn't touch me, I will be able to stay away. If I don't think of him, of not only the way his body feels against mine but other things, like the way he caresses the skin of my naked back, the soft kisses on my palms, then I'll be okay. Like the way he asks about my life sometimes, like he could actually care. But it doesn't matter. I'm done with him, have to be. I told him so. I haven't been to Toby in almost a week, not that he hasn't tried—showing up at my window, catching me as I come home from school. *That's fine. You'll come back. I know you will.* Both times I've gotten away before he could touch me, put his hand on my arm or neck or, God, anywhere. If he touches me, it will melt my self-control like an ice cube in the Mississippi sun, and it will all be over and I will want him again and again.

I watched him from my bedroom window. He was working

on his Firebird in the driveway, his jean-covered legs splayed and his upper body hidden beneath the car. I watched him crawl out and climb inside, a look of intense concentration on his face as he cranked the car and listened to the engine. He was beautiful like that—alone, with all of the attitude stripped away. I had to keep myself from raising the blinds, from opening the window so he could see me when he looked over. Because then he would see the longing, naked on my face.

This want, this desire—it's for Toby alone, for his lean body and the lines of his hip bones, his long hair and cocky smile, the way he calls me *Rebecca* in his rough Southern drawl like my name is the sexiest word anyone has ever spoken. I always thought that love and desire would come together, two ribbons around one pretty package. But I don't love Toby. I can't love Toby. It's August, isn't it, that I love, that I'm risking everything for?

I'm not so sure anymore.

68

Saying it was the worst night ever isn't enough. Can there be anything worse than worst? It was that. It was that kind of night.

I can't believe I let Jules talk me into Southern Saddle. I can't believe I let Jules talk me into anything at all.

We'd gone nearly three weeks without speaking, which was awful, and awkward, and all manner of unpleasant words that you would associate with not speaking to your best friend.

And then two days ago, there was a knock on my bedroom door, and when I opened it, Jules was standing on the other side. We stood there in the doorway, staring at one another for what seemed like a decade, before Jules finally spoke. "I'm sorry. I really am. I shouldn't have acted like that."

And just like that, we were friends again. And I was glad. Even with all of the secrets between us, being without Jules made me feel stranded on a raft in a lonely ocean. Friendship is like that, I guess. Comforting, even with its flaws.

"I'm sorry too."

"You know you can talk to me about anything, right?"

I nodded and looked away, because it wasn't true.

So last night, Jules insisted that we should do something fun, something adventurous. I could have told her no. I *should* have told her no, but I didn't, so we ended up at Southern Saddle, our summertime stomping ground.

Nothing much had changed in the months we'd been away—the wood-paneled walls, torn vinyl booths, wooden tables with the slick waxy coating on top. We claimed a booth and I mindlessly sank a fingernail into the tabletop, making a crescent shape there. A country cover band we'd never seen before was playing, and Jules started to tap her foot. What is it about a place like Southern Saddle that makes Jules come alive, when the same makes me want to hide away?

"I'll go get us some drinks?" Jules asked, and I nodded. I didn't offer to go with her. I could have been at home, feet tucked into a blanket and a book in my hands. I could have been with August at the river, though it has gotten harder to meet there now that the weather has finally turned cold.

I've started to feel anxious around August the same way I do around Jules. I never know, when I open my mouth, if my words will betray me and the truth will fall out, flat and sharp-edged, knifelike. Oddly, the only one who knows me anymore, all of me, is Toby. He knows everything: my dangerous affair with August, my dangerous affair with *him*, my problems with Jules, my dad's loss of the promotion, the fact that I am not *really* doing drugs. Maybe it was a mistake to keep him away, after all. He certainly knows my body more intimately than anyone else. Somehow, he had become an expert on me.

Maybe it all meant something.

Or maybe not.

I've heard people use the phrase *out of sight, out of mind*, and I wonder if a warped version of the opposite could be true as well. Not *out of mind, out of sight*, but *in mind, in sight*. Because when Jules came back to the table and set two plastic glasses down on the table, she had an annoyed expression on her face. "Well, this night has taken a turn for the worse. Guess who I ran into? *Toby*."

It was a natural response—my head turned automatically to look for him, and there he was, at the bar, talking to Bryant and absentmindedly running his fingers through the long, dark hair of the woman whose arm was wrapped around his waist.

My hands were shaking as I reached for my glass, and the liquid inside sloshed out onto my fingers. When I took a sip, I could tell that Jules had already added the alcohol. When I felt the sting on my tongue, I took a long, hurried gulp of the mixture and tried to keep the hurt I felt from flashing across my face like a stupid, too-bright neon sign.

"Ugh," Jules groaned. "Well, maybe we can at least talk him into giving us a ride home later, unless he ends up leaving with that *thing*."

"Who is she?" I managed to croak. I could feel my heart beating angrily in my chest. All the while, I tried to maintain an expression of calm, and I wondered how Jules could manage it, acting, because this pretending *hurt*.

The woman was older, clearly, and dressed in calf-high boots and a denim miniskirt. Her cleavage spilled defiantly over the cups of her tight halter top. *Isn't she cold?* my erratic mind wondered. Her hair was dark and straight, with choppy bangs invading the line of her forehead and lips smeared with orange-red lipstick. She was boldly, shamelessly *pretty*. They made a dark and sexy couple, Toby and this woman. Toby's blue-and-black flannel shirt hung open, exposing his white V-neck tee beneath. There was a silver necklace against his throat, and his hair was pulled back into a ponytail. I've seen his ragged, worn-in blue jeans before. I have unzipped them, watched them fall from his hips into a denim puddle.

I felt like I was going to be sick.

"Don't know," Jules said. "I've never seen her before. Seems like they just met tonight."

"She looks *disgusting*," I spat out, before I could help myself. I slapped a hand across my mouth to keep the rest of the words inside, the obscenities that fought to escape from my lips. I could feel my eyes widen in surprise.

"Wow. Say what you really think," Jules said, laughing uneasily. Because those kinds of words, in that tone, don't usually come from my mouth.

"Sorry," I said quietly, removing my hand and tearing the wrapper off my straw with much more aggression that was necessary. I took another long drink of what must be Coke and vodka, which sounds unpleasant but actually wasn't terrible at all; in fact, it was probably the only thing keeping me in the booth, functioning, and not running out of the bar in confused tears.

We watched them for several minutes. I drank and drank. I don't know why, but I have never imagined Toby with anyone else. It has never occurred to me, not when he looks at me the way he does, like he couldn't possibly ever want another person the way he wants me. The power I thought I had, before—I felt it stripped away from me suddenly. I was ordinary in my jeans and sweater; I was nothing special. Not compared to *that*.

"He's in love with you, you know."

"What?" I looked up, startled, from the paper wrapper I was tearing to shreds on the table.

"Bryant."

"Bryant?"

"Bryant. The bartender. He's checking you out right now."

I sighed, furious with myself for being disappointed. "Jules, you know it's *you* he's checking out, right?"

"No way."

"Yes. He told me. He likes you. He's always liked you."

I tried to work up a smile for my friend, my eyes darting over to see if Bryant was really looking our way. What I saw, instead, was the mysterious woman leading Toby to the back of Southern Saddle, past the restrooms and toward the employee exit. "You know what?" I said, after draining the rest of my drink. I could hardly form words. "I think I'm going to go to the restroom."

I stood up, realizing I was tipsy—more than tipsy—when the room swirled uncomfortably around me. At least I got far enough away from Jules before I started to stumble and had to slow down and focus. If Jules thought I was drunk, no way would I have the chance to follow Toby. The pair had already disappeared through the metal door in the back. As soon as I reached the hallway with the restrooms and the employee exit, I rested a hand lightly on the wall. Better.

I pressed my palms to the metal door and pushed softly, then harder when it didn't budge. I was at once desperate and terrified to see what Toby was doing with this woman, what he would do with someone who *wasn't* me.

He told me once that I belonged to him. But no matter what I'd allowed myself to believe, he never said anything about belonging to me.

The door groaned as I walked out in the darkness. It was a wasteland of asphalt and metal Dumpsters with trash spilling out of their wide mouths. The employee parking was poorly lit by dim, flickering streetlights. The music from inside the bar was muffled but audible, the beat relaxed and happy. I didn't see anyone outside, and I stood still for a moment, listening.

I heard him, his voice, a moan. I followed the line of the building and turned a corner, and there he was, leaning back against the stucco, eyes closed, a strand of hair having escaped his ponytail and settled against his cheek. And the woman, on her knees in front of him on the dirty asphalt, hands on his hips and her red-lipped mouth all over him.

"Mmm." The noise came from him, but he didn't touch her, didn't grip the back of her head or pull her closer, like he does with me. Instead, his hands were flat against the wall, as though holding himself in place.

I watched. The streetlights flickered on and off like a bug zapper on a summer night, and the whole scene felt like something from a haunted house, something from a nightmare.

I couldn't hold back my choked sob.

Toby's eyes snapped open, and his green eyes seemed darker when he looked at me. It felt like roots had grown out of my feet and through the parking lot, and I was shivering and burning up and I couldn't move for what felt like the longest moment of my entire life. All I could do was watch the grotesque scene shimmering and swirling in front of me.

His mouth opened like he might say something, but he didn't, and then my legs were working again and I was clumsily running back into the bar. Then the scene finally changed, and I was in the restroom at Southern Saddle, hunched over in a cramped stall, retching.

69

TOBY'S AWAKE AGAIN, AND THE BUZZ HE'D COUNTED ON TO carry him through the night is already wearing off. He hauls himself out the side door of the gallery and up the stairs to his apartment. The lock is a goddamned mystery—he can't even find the right key on his key chain—and why does he bother locking the door anyway? There's nothing but a staircase in between the gallery and his apartment, and if someone made it into the gallery to steal his paintings… well, then they might as well take everything.

He fumbles with key after key, and eventually, after a few hours or seconds—who fucking knows?—the door swings open. The loft is ancient, something a New Yorker like Jules would probably find trendy. But he just liked the convenience, and he'd gotten a discount on the loft when he rented the space underneath for his gallery. He owns them both now. The keys slip from his grasp and thud against the beat-up hardwoods. Big windows overlook the town of Opal. He can just barely see the lights from The Inn from here, maybe a mile out, and the glowing sign for Southern Saddle. He doesn't go there anymore, hasn't for a while. Not since the night when Reba caught him there with that woman.

He remembers Reba's face that night, remembers thinking, indignantly, that none of that shit was his fault. Hadn't Reba broken it off with him? Hadn't she told him it was over? Hadn't she run away any time he'd tried to talk to her? All the time he'd been with her, Toby hadn't even thought of another woman, even though he knew Reba still had the other boy. It was because she *consumed* him. How could he waste his attention on anyone else when there was the possibility of Reba?

But he could only hear her tell him no so many times.

It would have been no big deal, except that Reba had to be there to see him try to move on. He blamed Jules instantly, because he knew Reba well enough by then to know that she would never suggest going to Southern Saddle herself. She didn't belong there, in that sleazy, smoky hellhole. But hadn't he wanted her to see? He'd already spotted her when he let that woman lead him out back… What was her name anyway? Chloe? Carly? Hadn't he wanted Reba to feel it, that jealousy like poison? Hadn't he wanted her to feel what he felt?

He changed his mind, though, when he saw the horrified expression on her face.

He was already pulling away from the woman when he heard the metal door of the employee exit slam shut. How had Reba made it out there without him hearing? Well…he knew the answer to that. He zipped and buttoned his jeans. "Goddamn it," he muttered.

"What was that all about?" Chloe or Carly or whatever-her-name-was asked in her fake smoky voice. Everything about her was that way—carefully planned to make desperate men like him find her desirable. There was nothing special about her at all.

"Not your business," Toby said as she got to her feet. "Go back inside."

"Are you kidding?" she asked, attitude masking the hurt he could see in her eyes. But he didn't have it in him to care about Reba and Chloe/Carly both, and he didn't even know this chick.

"Go," he said, stepping away from her. He didn't feel bad about leaving her there in the shadows.

Jules met him in the hallway near the bathrooms, her eyes watery like she might cry. "Toby, you have to get us home," she said. She grabbed for his arm, and he instinctively snapped it back.

"I don't *have* to do anything," he said.

"It's Reba. She's sick. I've got to get her home. Please."

"Where is she?" he asked. Jules pointed to the women's restroom. Toby threw open the door, and there she was, in her pretty sweater and jeans, kneeling on the toilet paper–strewn floor and gasping for air.

"Reba," he said, reaching for her. What did he think he was going to do, scoop her up like some goddamned white knight and carry her out of there? She ignored him. "Reba," he said again, kneeling beside her and touching her elbow. She jerked away from him as though his hand were a hot poker. "*Rebecca*," he said finally. "Let me help you."

"Get away from me," she sobbed.

"No, I—"

"GET AWAY FROM ME!" Her scream filled the bathroom, and he staggered away from her as she wiped her mouth with a piece of toilet paper and stared at him with a look of pure hatred. Jules was in the room then, grabbing his arm, pulling him away.

"What did you do to her?" she asked, almost yelling herself.

"Nothing. I just wanted to help!"

"Don't help her," Jules hissed. "Don't touch her. Go get the car. I'll bring her out."

He stormed away. He wanted to fight, wanted to throw glass bottles against concrete walls, wanted to use his fists to make someone feel what he felt, which was helpless. He'd never felt so helpless in his whole life.

He had the car waiting in front of Southern Saddle when Jules walked Reba out, her arm around Reba's waist, helping her along. Before he even knew what the hell he was doing, he was out of the car and opening the passenger door of the Firebird so Jules could get Reba into the backseat.

"Reba, what happened?" Jules asked quietly, after several minutes of silence in the car. But she wouldn't answer. Toby watched her in the rearview mirror, her red-rimmed eyes, head lolling against the window. She looked defeated. Was it alcohol, or was this all because of him? Maybe a mixture of the two, but did he have that kind of power over her? He wouldn't have thought so.

"You can't take her home," Toby said casually. As if it was no real matter to him. As if he didn't want to pull the car over and make Reba look at him, make her listen as he explained. As if he didn't want to put his arms around her. "Not like that."

"No shit," Jules said. "We'll take her to Molly's. She can stay with me until she feels better."

"She ever gotten sick like this before, from drinking?"

"Never."

He couldn't stop staring at Reba as Jules maneuvered her out of the car and into the house, but Reba wouldn't let him help her, wouldn't let him touch him at all. She wouldn't even look him in the eye.

70

TOBY. GODDAMNED TOBY, JULIE THINKS. IT WAS HIM ALL ALONG, tearing Reba apart, making her want him…making her *love* him. It seems impossible that someone like Reba could ever have feelings for someone as vicious, as catastrophically screwed up as Toby. He took advantage of a young girl, took what was lovely and magical about Reba and perverted it.

And Reba loved it. Turns out that even before Toby, even before August, Reba was never as purely *good* as Julie wanted her to be.

She can't deny her anger at Reba, can't deny the betrayal she feels. For so long, Julie has thought of Reba as the star in some doomed love affair, with August as her costar. But in truth, it was Toby all along, Toby dragging Reba into darkness, and Reba begging for it.

You aren't who I thought you were, she told Reba once, in anger. Except now, Julie knows it was the truth.

Though she'd forgotten it until now, Julie has Toby to thank for finding out about Reba and August in the first place.

She'd just gotten home from a date. Cold weather was finally on its way, and she felt uneasy for some reason, like the chill in the air was carrying something else with it. Something grim.

"Call me," she'd told her date, with a smile on her face. But she hoped he wouldn't.

She didn't tiptoe, wasn't unusually quiet when she closed the front door. She knew Molly wasn't home, and only God himself knew where Toby was and what he was up to. They hadn't spoken much since the thing with Reba at Southern Saddle. He'd asked her the next day if Reba was all right—like he gave a damn. It was lucky he'd been there, though, to get them home so quickly. It was strange what had happened. Reba didn't usually drink enough to get sick. Stomach bug, maybe, she'd said.

Julie figured Toby would be out, but no, his music was blasting, shaking the walls of her bedroom. Toby liked metal and heavy alternative, songs that gave him an excuse to sing along, to roar. This time, the music was loud, but the song was slower. Nine Inch Nails, that one slow song. Still, she'd never get to sleep if he kept it up. She walked down the hall and banged her fist against his bedroom door for a full minute before turning the knob.

Toby sat cross-legged on the floor facing the wall, a bottle of whiskey beside him and a joint in an ashtray on the floor. His paints and brushes were laid out in a line in front of him.

"You could have it all… My empire of dirt…" he sang along, unaware of her. He was painting the girl again, had made it up to her shoulders, her smallish breasts. She was lovely.

"Turn the music down," Julie said, raising her voice and, when he still didn't turn around, turning the stereo volume down herself. Low.

"Jesus, Jules," Toby said, finishing a pull from the joint he'd picked up. He pushed his hair back from his forehead and looked at her as though he'd never seen her before. "Didn't I tell you to knock? You scared the shit out of me."

He didn't look scared, though. "I did knock," she said.

"Turn the music back up."

"It's too loud. You're not the only one who lives here."

He balanced the joint on the lip of the astray and stood up, shakily. "I'll listen to whatever I want, whenever I want."

She looked at him and glared. His eyes were red, and his speech was slurred. He wore a white tank with paint smeared all over it, like he'd been wiping his hands on it instead of on the rag lying on the floor.

"Are you ever going to grow up?" she asked quietly, calmly, trying for all the world not to lose her temper with him again.

He shrugged. "You don't know a thing about me. Don't know much about anything that goes on around here, actually. Right under your nose. I could tell you some stories, little girl."

"You're drunk, I know that much."

"Hey, at least I'm not whoring myself out all over Lawrence Mill. What, did you just get in?" His eyes moved, a compass, taking her in. She was still wearing her going-out clothes, boots and all. "'Cause those don't look like your pajamas."

She sighed, offended and exasperated.

"Oh, come here," he said, reaching to the floor for the whiskey bottle and flopping down on his bed. "Sit down, share with me." He offered her the bottle. She didn't know what was up with the sudden change of attitude, but she took the bottle and sat beside him on the bed. The whiskey was a hot fire in her stomach.

"Hey, I don't hold it against you," Toby said, shrugging again. "We all have our vices, right? Right? Maybe I'll say fuck it, and tell you all about mine. Bet she'd love that."

"Pretty sure I'm aware of your vices already," Julie said, eyeing the whiskey bottle, the joint.

"Those aren't vices. Those are hobbies." He chuckled, shook his head. "Her, though. *She's* my vice, my fucking downfall. Women."

"I have no idea what you're talking about."

"That's for damn sure." He laughed, bitterly. "She's out there with him now, I bet. Doing things to him, letting him do things to her. She *loves* him, I guess. Whatever that means."

"Yeah…anyways," Julie said, drinking more from the whiskey bottle and feeling the heat shoot through her again. She didn't want to have anything in common with Toby, least of all a shared inability to understand things like love. She passed the bottle back to him. She needed to get out of there. Toby was clearly wasted, or very high, or something, and he was making no sense at all.

"What's with you dirty girls, anyway? Those sweet, innocent faces, nothing but lies underneath." He looked her up and down again. "I mean, I expect it from you. But I didn't know you'd rub off on Reba the way you did." His hand rested on her shoulder, and it felt like an electric shock. He swayed back and forth on the bed.

"What?"

"Reba McLeod," he slurred in a singsong voice, so her first and last name ran together. "Who would have guessed? I mean you, you look the part at least, sex kitten and all that. Not her, though. So sweet. So fucking sweet."

"What are you talking about?" Julie felt suddenly nauseous. "Is this about the pot? She told me about that."

He laughed. "Lies, lies." Then he shook his head and looked up at her like he was just realizing she was there. "Never mind. Go to bed, Jules." He turned away from her, as though she'd already left.

"What are you talking about?" she asked again.

"Nothing." He took a long drink from the bottle, then began to mumble to himself. Only it was just loud enough for her to hear. "Little Julie can't see…doesn't know the things her friend does at night…"

"You're lying. She's not like that."

"It's all lies, baby. All lies."

"What do you know?" she asked, her voice rising, uncertain, borderline hysterical. *He's drunk*, she told herself. He didn't know what he was talking about, couldn't even complete a coherent sentence. She couldn't explain why she was listening at all, when everything in her said to disregard him completely.

"Little Julie, little Rebecca," he taunted. "Secrets, secrets, secrets."

"Tell me," she said. He was silent, drinking from the bottle again. "Tell me!" she shouted, grabbing the bottle from his mouth. It flew from her hands and fell on the carpet at the end of the bed.

"Goddamn it, Jules!" His arm flew back as if to hit her, but instead, he let it fall limply at his side. He stood and picked up the bottle, salvaging what little was left. Most of it had already seeped into the carpet, filling the room with the stale smell of bars and drunken kisses. "You want to know? Look out your window once in a while. Sneaking out, sex, lies. I bet she's with him right now."

"It's not true," Julie whispered. She stood, reached for anything, found the little square mirror on the dresser, the one she'd seen him use for coke. She threw it furiously across the room, and it shattered against the wall, pieces flying, a slash of a scar left behind, right across the chest of the painted girl on the wall.

Toby jumped back as though the shards had sliced him open, even though he was nowhere near them. His eyes were even redder, and watered suddenly. "No, it's not," he said. "It's not true. Jesus Christ, I didn't mean it."

His sobs followed her as she ran from his bedroom. "I didn't mean it, Jules. Wait! I didn't mean it."

But when she looked outside, she could see Reba's open window, white curtains swaying back and forth in the December wind. She ran from the house, slamming the front door behind her hard enough that it hit the doorjamb and flew open again. She didn't stop until she reached the street, and then she turned around, went back into the house to grab a flashlight from the junk drawer in the kitchen, and rushed out into the night.

71

THE GRASSES IN THE FIELDS WERE FLATTENED, BROWNISH IF she could see them in the darkness, but Julie didn't risk turning on the flashlight yet. They didn't whip against her legs but threatened, instead, to tangle her feet as she ran. *Not true not true not true*, she repeated to herself as she hurried into the night. She didn't know where Reba would go in secret; there was as good a chance as any that whomever she was seeing had picked her up in a car and they'd gone God-knows-where. She couldn't explain why she ran straight for the river, for the little bridge, how she knew to find Reba there.

Julie's long hair tossed and twisted around her back and shoulders as she moved, the cool wind blowing strands across her cheeks and eyes until she wasn't sure if she could see at all. Her boot heels sank into the ground with every hurried step. That night, the path seemed to be miles long. In the naked fields, before she entered the forest that guarded the riverbank, she ripped the boots off, first one and then the other, her socks next. She threw them all to the ground, abandoned, and moved forward, barefoot. She'd come back for them the next day. Rocks and cold dirt and gnarled tree roots scraped against the unprotected bottoms of her feet, but she could hardly feel them.

It was a lie. It had to be. Toby was wrong, and she was crazy for believing him, for thinking any of this. Probably if she turned around right now and went back to Reba's bedroom window, she would see Reba in there, sleeping peacefully. And then everything would be okay. She hadn't even thought to look in the window before starting this wild search. Maybe Reba had just wanted the window open while she slept. Maybe it was all so simple, and Reba wasn't hiding anything at all. Except…even if it wasn't too cold for open windows by then, it all made a perverse kind of sense, and Julie *did* believe Toby, even if she didn't know why.

Go back, she kept thinking. Her feet were cold and starting to sting from the rocks, and her heart was a tin drum beating fast and hollow in her chest. And she didn't want to know anymore, wanted to return to her room, to her life, which was sinful and meaningless, while Reba remained exalted.

Julie finally had to stop and catch her breath. She tried to prepare herself. For what, she didn't know. It wasn't going to happen. There was no one out there but her. When she could hear the river babbling ahead, she turned right, heading toward the old footbridge.

She heard them first, before she saw them. Her bare feet crunching the fallen leaves with each step must not have been as loud as she thought, because they obviously didn't know she was there. She heard Reba's voice, unmistakable, so soft that Julie wouldn't have caught it, had she not been listening so hard for that very thing. "Don't let me go." The small words swirled and burned in Julie's ears, in her throat, in her stomach. She could feel the heat of them all over her body, and it was so much worse than Toby's whiskey.

"I won't, I promise," a voice said. A deep, masculine voice. Julie heard a rustling of clothes (being removed or struggled back into, she couldn't tell), the wet animal sound of kisses.

"Let's leave here. Let's go away, away from everyone. Can we?"

"What? What would your dad think?"

Julie held her fist to her mouth to keep from screaming. She was hidden, stock-still against a tree but so close to them. She shouldn't be listening, but this shouldn't be happening. Her Reba. She felt betrayed, she felt forsaken, she felt *everything* shameful she'd ever done in a way she hadn't before. Clearer, like before then she'd seen her own life through a stained-glass window with roses on it, or orchids, or something religious. And now it was only a window, and everything was transparent and hard and ugly.

"I don't care. Let's run away, August. Together, you and me."

"I wish we could. I wish it so much."

"I'm serious. Let's do it. Why can't we?"

There was silence for a moment. "Reba, you know we can't. I wish things were different, I do. But I can't leave my family, and you can't leave yours, and graduation is right around the corner. We don't have any money, and it'd be crazy to leave now. Besides, when we graduate and you're in New York with Jules and I'm in Virginia, we can do whatever we want. It's not that far away."

"But…he'll kill you."

"What do you mean?"

"He'll kill you."

"Reba, I don't understand. Who'll kill me? Your dad? Does he know?"

Reba started to sob, leaves rustling around her. Julie thought of moving, of getting out of there, but her feet wouldn't budge.

"Tell me, please," he said, his voice cracking, rising. In anger or frustration, Julie couldn't tell.

Reba mumbled something, too soft, this time, for Julie to hear. For even the boy to hear, apparently.

"What?"

"I'm pregnant."

Julie gasped. The flashlight slipped from her grasp and tumbled to the forest floor. It snapped with the impact, illuminating Reba, frozen in the act of pulling the boy close. His dark hands on her shoulders.

"Jules," Reba whispered. Julie thought Reba might stand, but she sank, instead, to the ground. Her long, black skirt was tucked around her legs like sinister petals. In the harsh glow, with her head buried in her palms, she looked like some wild, wilted flower.

Julie took a step back, and another, and then she was running and couldn't stop. She kept going until she tripped in the field, fell down on the ground and clutched at the flattened grasses, tree limbs swaying around her in the winter breeze.

72

WHEN JULIE SNAPS THE BOOK CLOSED HOURS LATER, SUNLIGHT is trying to force its way in through the heavy curtains and she can feel her cheeks, hot with hatred. She's finished Reba's diary, read every single entry, and she can't think of a time when she's ever hated a person more than she hates Toby right now. There's anger at Reba too. She can't deny that, but it's futile, fruitless—there's no outlet for it. She changes into fresh clothes quickly and smears enough makeup on her face to cover the raccoon-like circles beneath her eyes, left behind from alcohol and tears.

This changes things.

She scribbles a note to August, then grabs her purse, her keys, and Reba's journal, taking an extra moment to tie the book closed, wrapping the silky ribbon into a delicate bow when what she wants to be doing with her fingers is wrapping them around a throat, wants to clutch a knife blade, a gun handle.

She wants blood.

She feels guilty leaving the book and the note outside August's door, and she hesitates there, trying to decide if she should leave the diary for him at all. It would be better for him if she destroyed it, if he never knew the truth about the girl he loved. So much better. But she thinks of Reba, and all of the lies, and knows that this one time *she* can give August the gift of the truth. It's a cruel, awful truth, and Julie doesn't like to think of him reading the book alone, but she knows it is right.

So she leaves them, the book and her note, on the carpeted floor outside August's hotel room for him to find at a more reasonable hour.

She walks as fast as she can through the lobby, even though it is barely six thirty a.m. and no one is around to see her. Still, she feels sneaky as she walks out into the empty Saturday morning streets. She knows August will feel betrayed when he wakes up and finds that she has gone.

But by then, she'll have already confronted Toby.

73

THE HAYWOOD STUDIO IS ON THE BOTTOM LEVEL OF AN OLD brick building in a long row of old brick buildings in downtown Opal. Close enough to The Inn that Julie had been able to walk, though it had taken her a while. She can't believe Toby has his own art studio, that success could really come to someone as scheming and awful as her cousin.

The morning sun is blinding, and the sidewalks are empty at this early hour. She doesn't even know if the studio is open yet, and she feels suddenly very stupid. *Of course* an art gallery or studio—or whatever the hell this place is—isn't open at seven in the morning. Her anger had overcome her logic, and she'd walked nearly a mile without a thought as to whether Toby would actually be here.

The studio has a wooden plaque beside the door, the word *Haywood* carved into it in gloomy, gothic script. Julie stares at the sign and fights the urge to tear it from the brick and smash it into the sidewalk. Through the glass pane of the door and the floor-to-ceiling windows, she can see huge art installations lining the exposed brick walls and imposing black-painted chandeliers hanging unlit from the ceiling. But there *is* a light glowing near the back of the studio, from a staircase maybe. Someone is here. She hasn't come all this way for nothing.

She presses the button by the door three, four, five times. The door trembles back and forth in its frame with the force of her fists pounding against it. He *will* hear her. Little birds teetering along on the sidewalk fly quickly away from the sound. She'd thought the walk would help calm her down before this confrontation, but she's just as livid as she was when she left the hotel. She stops, waits. A car drives past. When no one comes down the stairs, she resumes banging against the glass pane.

Finally, the sliver of light from the stairway spills into the gallery. And there he is. Toby, looking hungover as hell, but otherwise every bit the same as he did the day he let her out at the airport. *Good riddance*, he told her.

Looking at him as he walks out of that back room—with his long hair tied back and his V-neck T-shirt covered in flecks of paint so that he looks more like a ragged housepainter than an actual artist—Julie is the closest she's ever come to *wanting* someone dead. She can feel it, this rage, rising up through her body, and she might burst through this damned door if he doesn't open it soon.

He doesn't look as surprised as she wished he would, but for a moment, he does look scared. Maybe it's the murderous expression she knows she is wearing, or maybe it's the way she's still beating her fists against the door. He walks cautiously to the door and twists the lock.

"Goddamn it, Jules," he mutters, looking around like she might not have come alone. "You gonna knock the door down?"

He steps back as she swings the door open with one arm and bursts into the room, her fury in full, vivid bloom as she sees that face, that full mouth that has fed her probably a thousand lies.

"You goddamned liar!" she screams, rushing him before she has thought things through. She wants to tear him into pieces, wishes she was made for it. As it is, she can only pound her fists into his chest as he backs away from her with his eyes wide and his mouth open in shock. "You evil, disgusting liar!"

She has backed him into a wall, but still it seems like ages before Toby realizes that she is actually hitting him, before he grabs her wrists and holds them in the air, like a movie paused in the middle of the action.

"Jesus Christ, Jules!" he shouts. "Who the fuck do you think you are?"

She pulls her wrists from his grasp and finally steps back, breathless. "You lied to me," she says. "All this time, all these years." She looks around the gallery and then closes her eyes. It's too hard to look at them—all the paintings of Reba: Reba in her bedroom and in Toby's, Reba's eyes agonized and accusing as she stands out back behind Southern Saddle, Reba on the bridge, even a few of Julie and Reba together. God, she should have guessed when she saw Toby at his New York show—although, in her own defense, the works he featured then had been far less…obvious.

"I don't know what you're talking about," Toby says as he wipes the back of his palm across his mouth. But it's hard to lie when the evidence is larger than life and hanging on the walls in front of her.

She licks her lips, preparing to savor this moment, this bombshell, this uncovering. "Reba had a diary."

"No, she didn't." Toby's response is immediate and expected. He never knew about the diary, after all.

"She did. Pretty purple thing, tied with a satin ribbon. And guess what I found out when I read it?"

Toby looks defiant. "Who's lying now, Jules? She didn't have a diary. Why don't you tell me the real reason you're here."

"She had a diary. *You belong to me*, you told her. *When you want to go to him, come see me instead.* Sound familiar?"

"You don't know what you're talking about. You don't know a thing about it."

"Yeah? Then why don't you tell me? Why don't you tell me what really happened at the bridge? Did I really push her, or was it *you?*"

She expects him to yell, to shout, to scream. She does not expect him to fall apart on her. But that's what he does, sinking to the floor and folding in on himself, running his hands through his hair and causing it to come loose from its rubber band. "Fuck," he says, his voice cracking. He closes his eyes. "I didn't... I didn't. It wasn't like that. It was an accident. She just *fell.*"

She blinks and stares at him, there on the floor. "I didn't kill her," she says flatly.

He leans back and stares at the painting. "No. You really never figured that out?"

She hadn't dared to really think it. It doesn't take away the devastation of having lost Reba, but it takes away the weight of it. Believing Toby—believing that *she* pushed Reba from the bridge—changed her entire life. And it wasn't even true.

"Why?" she hisses at him, her fingers grasping the small counter behind her, gripping the ledge to keep from launching herself at him again, from tearing his hair out. "Why did you make me believe I did it? Do you hate me that much?"

He looks up at her, and she can see the tears pooling in the corners of his bloodshot eyes. He is probably playing her with the waterworks; he probably has another lie to feed her.

"I never *said* you killed her, Jules. That may be what you heard, but it isn't what I said. But you *were* there, drunk out of your mind, and Reba fell into the river, and you *stood there*. I yelled at you to get help, to do something, and you just stood there in some kind of fucking daze. You may not have killed her, but you sure didn't do anything to save her, either."

Julie stands there, stunned. She thinks back to that night at the river, to her fuzzy memory of the two people arguing on the bridge, how it always felt like she was watching the scene unfold instead of being a part of it. Because she *wasn't* part of it.

"You're *sick*," she says. "You hurt her, you tricked her, you used her. If you didn't push her off that bridge yourself—which I'm not even sure I believe—that still doesn't change the fact that there is blood on your hands. If she'd never gotten involved with you, she'd still be alive."

Toby laughs, a cold, cruel laugh. "Yeah, well, I think that could be said for all of us. You ask me, you're as much to blame as I am. As the boy is. She'd have been better off to stay away from the whole lot of us, wouldn't she?" He holds his arms out, palms facing up, and she can see, then, the long, thin scars on his wrists. "You think I don't wake up feeling guilty every goddamned day of my life? You have no idea what I feel."

Don't look at them, she thinks, trying to keep her eyes off those scars, trying not to feel sorry for him. *He doesn't deserve it.* "I know you were obsessed with her then," she says, looking around the room at all of the paintings of Reba. "And I know you still are."

He follows her eyes, looking around at this strange shrine to Reba. "It's not an *obsession*," he says fiercely. Then he laughs again, that same harsh laugh. "I *loved* her."

"Yeah, join the club. We all loved her, Toby." She thinks of the irony of it, that the three people who claimed to love her the most seemed to have all played a role in her demise. She suddenly feels that she has to escape from this poisonous space, escape from Toby having a breakdown before her eyes, escape from Reba's eyes staring out at her from a dozen paintings.

"I didn't mean... I didn't mean for things to happen the way they did. I thought I had some kind of power over her, but it was the other way around. I fell in love with her, and I thought she might...might have loved me too. I don't know how, and I don't know why, but there was something real between us. It was more than an obsession."

She *could* tell him that he is right, that Reba felt something for him too, but the words won't come. She can't bring herself to give him even an ounce of peace. Even if he had suffered. Even if he *is* suffering.

"She had something real with August too," Julie says quietly. It felt more thrilling than she'd ever admit to be able to add to the hurt.

"That wasn't his baby," Toby says, and she can tell that he truly believes it. "Reba's baby... That was *mine*. My baby...my family..." He trails off, and she can actually hear his sobs. And she knows that she doesn't have to do it, doesn't have to be as evil as he is, doesn't have to wound him the way he wounded her.

In the end, she can't resist.

"Toby," she says, her voice even, controlled. "There *was* no baby. There never was. Reba lied to you. She lied to all of us."

He looks up, stunned. "No," he says. "She wasn't like that. Reba wasn't like that."

Julie can feel her lips turning up in a hard little smile. "Well, then I guess she learned something from you after all." She turns to the door, prepared to leave him like this, reeling from a truth he can't bear to believe. It's poetic, she thinks. The brutal lie Toby let her believe ten years ago changed the course of her life. The same way that Reba's deception changed Toby's life, left him hungering for a family that didn't even exist.

"I want that diary, Jules," he says, reaching an arm out as though to grab her, but he is too far away. "Please…I need to see it."

He is a shell, a broken version of the cruel teenager she once knew, and she sees that she hadn't even needed to try to tear him to pieces—he's already in tattered shreds. And she hates it, hates him for being so vindictive in the past and now so vulnerable.

She looks into those hard green eyes one final time. "Fuck you, Toby," she says, before she walks out of the gallery and leaves her cousin behind forever.

74

I MISS JULES. IF SHE WERE HERE, IF SHE'D NEVER STUMBLED UPON August and me that night in the woods, then we would be watching old Christmas movies in our pajamas on my living room floor, spinning our stories about the future, about spending our winters together in New York City.

That's how it's supposed to be. When we were kids, my mama would buy us matching flannel pajamas with reindeer or Christmas trees or snowflakes. Jules would have Christmas dinner with Molly and Toby, and then she'd come over to my house and we'd put on our matching pj's. We'd find whatever movie was on TV—*Miracle on 34th Street, It's a Wonderful Life*—and lie in the floor with pillows beneath our heads. Sometimes Mama or even Daddy would sit on the sofa and watch along with us. The lights from the tree in the corner would flash onto the TV screen, adding bright, brilliant colors to the black-and-white films.

It isn't like that this year. Instead, I sat through an uncomfortable Christmas dinner with my parents, mostly quiet except for the clanking of silverware against the china and my daddy's occasional small talk. He was in a strangely pleasant mood, and I don't know whether it was because of the holidays, or if he has finally gotten over losing the stupid promotion.

"You know, the truck has been making a funny noise," he said casually. "I saw Toby out in the yard yesterday, and he said he'd take a look at it for me, once the holidays are over. The boy knows a little something about cars, apparently."

I felt sick at the mention of his name. Toby was nice to my daddy? Toby was nice to *anyone*?

"Oh, really?" It was the most I could get out.

"He's a good kid," Daddy mused. "Wish he didn't have that long hair, but I guess I was a bit of a rebel in my time too. He'll keep me from having to take the truck in to the shop, maybe save me a few bucks."

I would have laughed, but I was in complete shock. Toby—a good kid? A *kid* at all? I fought to keep a blank expression on my face because I could feel an entire universe of emotions threatening to break free.

And now I am alone in my room on Christmas night, and the soft noise of my radio playing isn't enough to distract my thoughts from the biggest lie I've ever told.

I'm not pregnant.

I'd considered the possibility, after Southern Saddle. Surely seeing Toby with someone else couldn't have affected me so much, so viscerally that I'd been *physically* ill? And for a few terrifying days, I considered buying a test. But then I started my period, so apparently Toby *could* affect me that way. Toby, and one very strong drink.

It isn't easy and it isn't simple, the kind of agony I feel. Which is why I let myself cling to August, sweet August who *cares* about me. Which is why I made the crazy suggestion that we go away together. Except once I said it, in that moment, it seemed like the perfect idea. I could love August again, the way I am sure he loves me, if I could only get away from Toby. August and I could go away together, and Toby would disappear. The only thing left would be the sweet perfection I'd felt with August before I stumbled upon Toby in my bedroom.

Except…*was* it perfection? What we had was *nice*. A sweet, genuine boy falling in love with a sweet, genuine girl. But I'm not that girl anymore. Now that I know about darker things, darker *feelings*, I wonder if being with August could ever be right again.

But then August said he wouldn't go away with me, and I felt angry and betrayed. The same way Toby made me feel that night at Southern Saddle. And I felt vicious suddenly, vengeful. I wanted one of these boys to feel the way they made me feel.

The lie tumbled out of my mouth like a grenade. Explosive.

Bad enough that I said it to begin with. But I was immediately punished for it (by God, or the universe, or whatever), because Jules was there, saw me with August, and heard my fake confession. And now I can't take it back, can't admit that I could lie about something so sacred.

I haven't spoken to Jules since that night by the river. What would I say to her, anyway, when I can't lie and I can't tell the truth?

75

It was Nell who finally set Julie straight all those years ago about love and friendship and everything else. Nell gave her exactly what she needed, only a little too late.

In the cold, empty week between Christmas and New Year's, Julie visited the flower shop, entering through the front door like a stranger and not through the back like she was used to. She was worried that Reba might be there, but she didn't see her when she looked in through the front windows.

"Just a minute!" Nell called from the back, when Julie walked in.

"It's me," Julie said.

"Hey, Jules," Nell said with a smile. "How was your holiday?"

"Okay, I guess." When Julie didn't say more, Nell's expression immediately turned to one of concern.

"Everything okay, sweetie?"

At which point Julie burst into confused, selfish tears. But when Nell started toward her, Julie took a step back. She so desperately needed to talk to someone, but could she trust Nell with Reba's secret? Could she trust anyone at all?

"I'm sorry," Julie said, wiping at her tears. "It's Reba. Have you... have you noticed anything going on with her?"

Nell sighed. "Noticed *something's* going on, that's for sure." She sat down slowly on the stool behind the counter. "What do you know?"

Julie's eyes darted around the shop and finally settled on a crack in the old hardwood floors. She is a traitor. She is everything she has always despised in a friend. "There's a boy..."

"Uh-huh..."

She looked up at Nell. "You already know, don't you?"

"Know what?" Nell asked.

"About the boy?"

Nell nodded.

"How did you know? Have you talked to her? Why didn't you stop it? Do her parents know?"

"Jules, honey, slow down." Nell sighed again. "I see a lot. I've seen him around here, with her. Figured it was a romance. But some things aren't my business to tell." She looked at Julie, hard. "Not your business to tell either, you know."

"Nell, this is bad! This is like, like Penny and James all over again, except worse, because it's...because it's *Reba*. How could she do it? It isn't her."

"Come over here and sit down." Nell patted the empty stool beside her. "Listen," she continued when Julie took a seat. "You're better than this. Don't you dare turn into one of these ignorant, racist fools. You love who you love. I'm willing to bet that our Reba didn't plan to be running around with the son of her daddy's new boss—"

"*What?*"

"Oh hell," she said. "You didn't know that part?"

"No. How did you?"

"Like I said, I see a lot. I hear a lot. I know a lot about this town."
Julie was silent.

"Reba doesn't have to live up to *your* expectations of her. She's not
doing any of this to hurt you, you know."

Jules was still, thinking. "She's pregnant," she finally blurted out.

For the first time, she managed to surprise Nell. "Honey, please
tell me you're joking."

"Not."

Nell shook her head. "Our girl's got some trouble coming her way.
Her daddy's likely to kill that boy."

Toby interrupted them then, a bewildered expression on his face
as he came in to pick up the day's deliveries.

76

I COULD *FEEL* HIM IN THE DARKNESS OF MY BEDROOM LAST night, even though I couldn't see him. I didn't know what noise he'd made to wake me, but I knew he was there.

"Toby?" I whispered. My hazy mind imagined him sliding into bed next to me, curling his arm around my waist like it isn't all about sex between us.

Like he loves me, maybe.

"Rebecca," he said. He was sitting in the chair by the window; I could see his silhouette once my eyes adjusted. "I hear you've got a new secret."

I sat upright in the bed, glad he couldn't see my eyes widen. Or the look of shame I knew I was wearing. "Did someone send out a memo?" I whispered, all traces of the hope I'd been too groggy to keep from my voice suddenly gone. I didn't think Jules would tell anyone, didn't think she would betray me like that, even in anger.

"What can I say? I hear things."

I crossed my arms, feeling silly in my tank top and flannel pajama bottoms. I was struck again by how different I am from the woman Toby was with in the parking lot of Southern Saddle. Thinking of that night made me tremble, the hurt and anger I'd tried to bury blooming inside me all over again.

"What do you want?" I asked.

"It's not mine," he said. "Is it?"

"Go home, Toby."

Then he was sitting beside me on the bed, his hands clenched on my shoulders. "Tell me the truth, damn it. Is it mine?" His voice sounded ragged, and I couldn't tell what he wanted to hear. Not the real truth; I had too much pride for that. I thought of which answer would hurt him the most. Didn't I want to hurt him, the way he'd tortured me?

I looked into his eyes. He once told me that he owned me, told me that I *belonged* to him.

"Yes," I said quietly, and then his hands were pushing my hair from my face, and he was kissing me and holding me so tightly that I felt like I would shatter into a million jagged shards like some ugly, breakable *thing*. "I mean…no," I gasped, pulling away from his kisses. He stared at me. "I mean…I don't… Toby, I don't know." I'll never get used to lying. It was especially hard to lie to him. The whole thing felt wrong, and he was looking at me like he wanted to kill me, his green eyes boring into mine. I knew that any minute he would see through this terrible charade, and then what? If anyone would see the truth on my face, it would be him.

But his expression softened, and he touched my cheek with the rough pad of his thumb. "It's okay," he whispered. "I get it. I'm not *him*, Reba. But you can trust me. You're not alone."

Even though Toby had left the window cracked in my bedroom and the crisp air was slipping into the room like wisps of smoke, I felt too warm. I felt like laughing, but I was in too deep. Toby, suddenly caring about me, about our potential child? What would he do, support the baby with drug money?

I had to remind myself that there was no child, that it was as false as Toby telling me that I could trust him. But the novelty of his arms around me in an embrace that was something other than sexual lulled me into the strangest sense of safety, and I was soon sinking into sleep while his fingers combed through the thick waves of my hair.

When I woke up, it was morning and I was alone, and I wondered if I'd dreamed the whole thing.

77

OH, REBA, JULIE THINKS AS SHE WALKS BACK TO THE INN. She wishes she could talk to her now, wishes she could yell at her, could put some of this blame on her. Would Julie have been a different wife, a different mother, a completely different *person*, if not for all of this guilt? Unbidden, the memories of those first precious months with Evan spring to her mind—the only time since Lawrence Mill that she felt truly weightless, like maybe things would be okay. Like maybe she could become someone new, someone without secrets. Someone less damaged.

First, it was only the days when she and Evan had class together (Tuesdays, Thursdays) that they ended up stretched, blissfully, lazily, in Evan's bed once class ended, the sunlight blazing through bare, curtainless windows. Then there were other days, missed classes, nights together.

Evan would play Zero 7 and Miles Davis and other strange,

sensual music that Julie had never heard before, and they would lie tangled together, one of her legs stretched across both of his, her head on his stomach, looking up at him. They would talk about music and acting and the things they wanted, and the things they dreamed about.

Evan was auditioning for real plays, nothing very glamorous yet, off-off Broadway productions and low-budget projects. She couldn't believe he was so confident.

They'd known each other less than six months, maybe less than five. The sun was floating in through the windows when she opened her eyes and found him watching her. His eyes were bright and sleepy, his hair a mess.

"Good morning," he whispered, leaning over to her, brushing her long hair with his fingers. He smiled that seductive almost-smile, and she traced his lips with her thumb.

"What should we do today?" she asked, sleepy and happy. His sheets were woven around them, and their legs and thighs were pressed together and she could feel him against her and it was all *so* wonderful.

He kissed her. "I have an idea. But you're going to think I'm crazy."

She looked at him, her eyebrows raised, curious.

"Sometimes it feels like as long as I have you, nothing else matters all that much," he said. "Do you feel that way?"

"Definitely," she said, rubbing her eyes. She smiled lazily and kissed him. He was always a philosopher in the mornings.

"If I ask you a question, do you promise not to say no?"

She always thought that if she pulled herself tightly enough against him, the line between the two of them would blur and she would see all of his secrets and he would see hers. They would never have to speak the words, because they would know each other so intimately. She would never have to tell him about Reba. "Mmm," she mumbled then, pressing her lips against his ear.

"Julie," Evan murmured. He was looking at her and she felt winded, even before she knew what was coming. "Julie, let's get married."

There was a dress. Not several, not a whole gaggle of dresses, not the way she'd always thought, dreadfully, of weddings. No dresses for bridesmaids or mothers or guests. Just the one, chosen by Evan at a boutique on the way to the courthouse. It was almost summertime, and the dress was light and creamy as milk—the only time, Evan joked, that he remembered Julie wearing white. It was long but casual, swooshing around her legs as she walked. It felt tropical, as though they were going to walk along the beach, not to be married.

She laughed at Evan because of course you couldn't just go to the courthouse and get married. There were licenses and paperwork and things; there must have been. But no. They were there, at the courthouse, and Evan had somehow convinced the clerk to waive the twenty-four-hour wait period, and Julie wore a flower in her hair, and they were saying the words. And then they kissed, too passionately for the courthouse, and she was a wife. She smiled in a way that didn't make her face ache—a genuine smile, a smile that slid onto her face almost without her realizing it. Amazing, how easy things can be sometimes.

The memories are snippets from a film, from a life that is no longer hers. She remembers the feelings: the happiness, that newness.

She remembers thinking that she understood, finally, the meaning of the word *bliss*. And she believed, stupidly, that Evan could make her forget all of the things that had come before.

She was wrong, of course. She could see now that she'd attached herself to Evan, hoping for some kind of anchor, something to keep her from drifting away in her own private sadness. It's hard for her to regret it, though, when she thinks of Beck. Even if not for their daughter, she'd never wish it away. But if it hadn't been for Reba's death, would their marriage have happened at all?

78

JULES TOLD. THERE'S NO OTHER POSSIBILITY. TOBY WOULDN'T have known if Jules hadn't told.

It was the first day back to school after the holidays, and I waited at the end of my driveway for her. At first, Jules looked cautiously happy, like she thought we were about to have a reunion or something. I could see her expression change as she got closer to me, and maybe she could see how angry I was. I hoped she could.

"Reba," she said brightly, with a hesitant smile.

"You told."

"I didn't!" She reached out to touch my arm, but I jerked it away.

"You're lying. You had no right." My blond hair was piled up, a messy ponytail on top of my head, a skinny blue headband holding back tendrils. I hadn't bothered with makeup, not even lip gloss, and I knew there were circles under my eyes. I was tired, sleepless, and Jules looked at me with a concerned expression on her face.

She couldn't help a retort, though. "Speaking of lies. You should have told me…well, everything. I thought we were friends."

"Right," I said, rolling my eyes. "I wanted to tell you. I tried."

"No, you didn't."

"About August? Of course I did. I tried to tell you when I first met him, back in the summer. But you didn't want to hear it. Don't you remember?"

"No, I don't," Jules said. But she was lying. I could tell. "That isn't the point, Reba. This is serious. Forget all of that stuff. Let me help you."

"I don't need *your* help," I snapped. "I need you to keep your mouth shut."

"I will… I am! I didn't tell, Reba!"

"You aren't who I thought you were," I told her, before walking away.

"Yeah, well, you certainly aren't either!" Jules shouted after me.

How simple, and how *satisfying* it would be to tell Jules the truth about everything. To watch her jaw drop as I describe those nights with August and the things I've done with Toby, and how much I like it all. That I am more like her than either of us ever imagined. How there is no baby, that it is one big lie fabricated to hurt those men who made me fall for them. That I am ruthless. That I am calculating.

So why didn't I tell her when I had the chance?

I guess even after everything, I still care what Jules thinks of me. And to know that I would deceive everyone, intentionally, with no purpose other than revenge? To know that I was with Toby, even while I was seeing August, and that I want Toby, still? It would be enough, I know, to destroy the friendship that has already become so fragile.

Because I can't stand the thought of the way that she would look at me.

Still, I can't keep up this awful charade. Sooner or later, it's going to be obvious that I'm not pregnant. I've got to come clean, wash all of this dirt and sin, all of these ugly lies, from my hands. Too late to be pure again, but maybe there is some hope for me still.

79

Julie takes her time getting back to the hotel. She wanders down the streets of Opal, replaying her visit with Toby, letting it all sink in. The sunlight is warm and bright, but she can see dark clouds gathering lazily on the horizon. By the time she arrives at The Inn, she feels ragged, drained.

But she didn't push Reba from the bridge. She did not kill her best friend.

Julie doesn't know what to expect of August. Surely, he has read the diary by now. She can't imagine *his* pain, now that he knows the truth of it all. It's funny, in a way that isn't, that their lives have been molded by this one girl—this one girl who was everything to them—and not one of them really knew her.

And she betrayed them all.

The girl at the counter is a teenager, and Maggie Harris is nowhere to be seen when Julie makes her way through the hotel lobby. She goes straight to August's room. The journal and her note are gone, but when she knocks on the door, there is no answer. She traces her fingers along the metal door numbers, waiting, thinking that maybe he is trying to avoid her. But after five minutes of knocking, pausing, knocking again, there is still no answer. He could have gone anywhere, could have gone back to the airport and left her here. She feels panicked by the thought of it.

She takes the elevator back down and is heading to Southern Saddle when she sees it through a side door—the hotel pool, twinkling in the sunlight. She can't explain her sudden thirst. It doesn't come from her mouth or her throat. It's bigger. It's her entire body that pulls her to the water. Maybe it's the burst of unexpected sunshine when she knows that a storm is on its way. It must be eighty degrees, when only a few days ago she arrived in Opal wearing a coat. She'd forgotten about Southern weather, how it will be cold and cold and then, without any warning at all, summer will arrive. No springtime or autumn, no in-betweens. There are the signs, the signals of those seasons—flowers blooming, leaves falling. But *cool* is a rarity. Mostly, there is only hot and cold.

The gate swings open easily, no padlocks, not even this early in the year. Despite the heat, the pool is deserted. It's probably snowing in New York right now. She can't ignore her strange yearning, as the pool sits shining and empty, the lounge chairs unattended. Brighton has recently acquired a membership to some elite swim club in Manhattan and has promised to take her and Beck as guests, when summer finally rolls around in New York. But she can't think of the last time she's taken a swim.

Of course, Julie has been in *this* pool before, as a teenager, with the young banker whose name she can't remember, the one who was in town doing business with the lumberyard.

Maybe it's the tendency toward recklessness, the urge to rebel that rises up within her just from being back here. Because she doesn't have a suit. Naturally, the idea of swimming, of any type of leisure, didn't creep into her mind while she was packing for this trip. But she chose black underwear this morning, hipster briefs and a matching bra with scalloped edges and no fancy adornments. The kind of underwear to be worn beneath clingy clothing. The kind of underwear that could *almost* pass for a swimsuit.

She can't recall the last time she's done something so ridiculous. In broad daylight too. She drops her purse on an empty lounger, tugs her jeans from her hips and lets them crumple at her feet before stepping out of them and pulling her shirt over her head. It catches on one earring, and she has to untangle herself before proceeding.

And then she is in the water, moving cautiously, one foot at a time on the underwater steps. The icy water is a shock to her senses and she gasps, but she doesn't stop her descent. In the shallow end, she falls to her knees and lets the water surround her, light and cool. She grasps the rough concrete edge of the pool, and she feels as though she is kneeling at an altar, though of course she has never done that. Evan is the lapsed Catholic. Southern Baptists don't bow down in servitude. They reach their hands upward, as if they could drag God down from the sky. Not that she ever really *was* Southern Baptist. Religion, if she ever believed in such a thing, was in the things she touched, the way she felt, the people she loved. But no matter; that reverence abandoned her long ago.

She thinks of Reba, of those summer days back at the Millworkers Association when they were barely teenagers, of painting each other's fingernails pink or baby blue or violet, listening to the radio on Julie's neon-yellow boom box. Country music because that's all the anten-nae would pick up, but any music was good on a gorgeous day. Reba's light hair turned green from all the chlorine. They couldn't see the changes in store for them, but it was probably better that way.

Julie sinks, lets her head fall under the water, pushes off from the pool's edge, and begins to swim, gliding along under the surface, hair slicked back against her scalp like a bath cap. The water is blue-green and a little murky, cloudy with new chemicals. Her eyes burn, but she keeps them open, sweeping her arms back and forth like a bird in flight. Her legs are still, indifferent. She carries herself along this way until her lungs feel as though they will burst like two fragile soap bubbles. And then she rises to the surface, gasping, and finds the edge she has been swimming toward.

80

August feels like a fool. Here he is, at the end of his journey, having achieved everything he set out to do: find Jules, find the diary. He just wasn't counting on finding this ugly new reality.

He'd loved Reba without question, without hesitation, without a single suspicion that the love he felt might not have been reciprocated. He'd loved her the way you can only love someone once, that first time, before you know better. Before you don't have it in you anymore.

He should get the hell out of this godforsaken place, pretend that he hasn't spent a decade of his life chasing a ghost, a figment. His version of Reba and the reality of her are so drastically different that it is sobering. The perfection... He'd made it up, and the diary was proof.

Jules would understand if he left. And if she didn't, did it even matter? Wasn't Jules just a means to an end, a way to get at these answers? It hardly matters that he likes her, enjoys her company, finds her smart and stunning.

But thinking about Jules makes him wonder if she's okay. Reading the diary wouldn't have been easy for her, either, since she'd created her own pristine version of Reba. She's been gone for a while, and he's had plenty of time to finish the diary, to learn the truth.

And the truth is that he was nothing. He was meaningless, a fling, a fleeting moment. He isn't some tragic hero, spending his life mourning his lost love. The girl he's been mourning doesn't even exist.

She was a liar. For so long, he'd wondered what it might have been like if he and Reba could have made a life together, what it would have been like to be a family. If he would have been a good father.

How she died doesn't even matter to him anymore. It has hardly a thing to do with him. But he can't ignore the pain he feels, as though this all happened yesterday and not ten years ago. He doesn't know how to make it go away, but he figures he can try his best down at the bar, if they'll serve him this early in the day.

He drinks enough Bloody Marys at Southern Saddle to count as breakfast and to make him feel numb, at least for a while. He's abandoned the bar and is walking down the hallway back to the hotel when he sees someone swimming, alone, in the hotel pool. He recognizes the black purse slung over the arm of a lounge chair even before he sees Jules bursting, breathless, from beneath the water's surface.

81

Julie is neck-deep in the hotel pool in her underwear when she spots August. Funny how they gravitate toward the same places, how they like to be alone in the same ways. He has a plastic cup in one hand, and she can tell by his relaxed posture and his untucked shirt that he has been drinking already, and she doesn't blame him. His eyes meet hers. She can feel herself bobbing, shoulders up and down in the water, her muscles tensing, breath coming in shallow gasps that have little to do with her underwater swim. He nods, a wordless hello.

She watches him, water droplets streaming down her face.

"Going for a swim?" she asks in a voice that is meant to be light but comes out choked.

"Not so much. I didn't expect to see you here…back here, I mean." He sits in one of the lounge chairs and sinks his head down into one palm. "I read it. The whole damned book."

She doesn't respond, doesn't know what to say.

"I loved her," he says quietly. "But she didn't love me. I was barely a footnote. It wasn't me, not ever. It was never me."

82

I DON'T KNOW IF I HAVE BEEN AVOIDING AUGUST ONLY BECAUSE I feel *so guilty* for lying to him, or if the magic of being with him was lost the second Jules stumbled upon us in the woods. But I haven't been to the river, haven't met his eyes in class or in the hallways.

Still, it took him a few weeks to approach me. And then yesterday, I looked up, and he was standing at my locker.

"August," I whispered to him, my eyes darting around the crowded hallway. It was in between classes, and students were everywhere. But no one seemed to notice August peering over the metal door of my locker. "What are you *doing?*"

"We should talk."

I was silent.

He reached out to touch a strand of hair that had fallen into my face, but pulled back when he saw what must have been a horrified expression on my face. I forced myself to look into his eyes. He was perfect, but I knew, without a doubt, that he wasn't mine.

"Talk to me," he said.

"It's over," I whispered finally. "This is over."

"No, it's not," he replied quickly, too quickly. "It's not. You're... We're..."

"I was selfish to start this with you," I said quietly. "I... It was wrong. From the beginning. It's too dangerous, and it has to stop." I desperately wanted to avoid telling him the truth.

"Dangerous?" he said. "Reba, we're well past dangerous. You can't shut me out. We have to talk about this, about what we're going to do."

"You don't need to worry about it." I looked down at the floor, couldn't possibly keep lying while looking him in the eyes.

"Of *course* I need to worry about it." His voice was louder now, and he had attracted the attention of at least a few students moving down the hall.

"Okay," I said. "Okay." I was quiet for a moment. "Meet me by the river, then. Tomorrow night, after the play. The journal... You should read it. It will explain. I'll bring it to you. And...and we'll talk, okay?" It was the last thing I wanted, but it would end things, without question.

He nodded. "You'll really be there?"

"Yes."

"Okay. Tomorrow, then."

"Tomorrow."

83

THE AIR IS WARM AND HUMID, THE THICK CLOUDS ABOVE SO filled with rain that they could burst at any moment. Julie pulls herself up over the pool's edge, water dripping from her body as she stands, shakes out her hair. She tries not to feel self-conscious standing before August, but she can feel his eyes on her body.

"A towel would be nice."

He disappears into the lobby, briefly, and returns with a white hotel towel. She wraps it around herself, and though it only reaches to her thighs, she feels less exposed as she sits down on the lounge chair beside him.

"I thought of destroying it," she says quietly. "The diary. I thought of getting rid of it so you would never have to know the truth. Do you wish I had?"

He looks at her thoughtfully, and it feels like his large, dark eyes really *see* her. "No," he says. "It's hard, you know. I thought I was important. I thought I meant something to her—"

"You did," she interrupts.

"Yeah, I meant *something* to her. But I wasn't…the one she loved."

"I'm sorry."

"All these years, I thought she jumped off that bridge because of me. And she didn't…I guess. I guess it didn't have much to do with me at all."

"Toby said that she fell." Julie looks down at her feet, at the dark puddle of water on the concrete. "That it was an accident."

"And you believe him?"

"I don't know. I mean, if he cared about her, why would he kill her? And, say he *did* do it—say he pushed her. What can we do about it? It was a decade ago, and it was declared a suicide. It's not like there's justice to be had."

They'd come to Lawrence Mill with a mission, to learn the truth about Reba…but Reba was the lie all along. It feels like mistaken identity, like the diary was written by an impostor. But Julie knows it wasn't. She sighs. "When he told me about it…it felt right, you know?"

"So…" August says, looking at her, his gaze hopeful and sad all at once. "You and I… Neither one of us was as important as we thought?"

She looks away from him. "Toby said I was there. That I didn't push her, but I *was* there. That I was drunk, that I stood there and watched, even though he yelled for me to help. If I'd gone for help…"

"Stop," August says. "Stop putting yourself through this. *You* are not responsible for this. Reba made bad decisions. Reba lied. Her death is *not* your fault."

Julie tries to believe it, that it was all inevitable, somehow.

"How did it end," he asks suddenly, "with you and your husband?"

She's caught off guard by the sudden change of topic, and she laughs, a bitter laugh, and pulls the small towel around her tighter. "The way that things end. I was…crazy. I was wrong. There are women out there who would do anything to catch Evan Huntley, and I messed it all up."

"Wait. *Evan Huntley* is your husband?"

She nods. "Well, ex-husband."

"Evan Huntley the actor?"

"I didn't know you followed theater."

"I don't, but my mother does. She and my dad go up to the city pretty regularly to catch different shows. She's a big fan. And he's your husband?"

"Ex-husband."

"He's kind of famous, Jules."

"I know." She doesn't tell him how degrading it is to rely on Evan's money to live, to care for Beck. How Julie uses as little of it as possible—a city apartment, a nanny for Beck, food—and puts the rest away for Beck's college.

"So what happened? Why'd he leave?"

She sighs, letting herself imagine what it might be like now, if she hadn't let it all slip away.

"The at-home test was right. You're pregnant," the doctor said. He was smiling.

"But…I'm on birth control."

"Doesn't always work," he said. "Congratulations."

Julie walked around for hours, even though the doctor's office was only blocks from Evan's apartment, where they both lived now. His place was small, but she didn't have many things.

Reba's voice echoed in Julie's head in a way that it hadn't in the year that she'd been with Evan. They'd only been married six months. *Pregnant*, the voice whispered, and it sounded desperate, like Reba's had that night by the river.

Julie was afraid to go home, didn't want to tell Evan, to make it real. When she finally did get back to their building, she sat on the front steps staring out at nothing at all, thinking of Reba, everything rushing back with the force of a river's current. Evan found her there on his way home from a play practice. "My Julie," he said, always dramatic. "What are you doing out here in the dark?"

When she looked up at him, his smile turned. "Oh no," he said. He helped her up and led her to the tiny apartment. He sat beside her on the small sofa and took her hands in his. His hands were warm. "What is it, Julie? What's happened?"

And she told him.

He was surprised. He looked her up and down, and then he laughed.

"You're happy?" she asked, uncertain.

"I love you, Julie," he said softly. "Why wouldn't I be happy?" He kissed her cheeks, her eyelids. "Don't cry. It's perfect."

"But we're poor!" she said. "And I don't know how to...to *mother*." She sniffled. She was exaggerating, because they weren't poor, not exactly. Evan had gotten the lead role in an off-Broadway play, and she had a part-time job. But her point about being a mother was true. She couldn't even remember her own mother, and it wasn't like Aunt Molly had been a great role model.

"Shh," he said, holding her. "We'll be fine. Don't worry about a thing. Everything will be fine."

For the first time, she didn't believe him.

It's nearly unthinkable now, how quickly she lost it all. The child growing inside her forged a link back to Reba, at least in Julie's mind, forced her to think of things she had managed to avoid in her fairy-tale year. While Evan slept at night, or while he was at play practice during the day, she tried to piece it all together again in her mind. Julie was a monster. She'd killed her best friend *and* her friend's unborn baby, and yet, she was pregnant with a child of her own? It didn't seem fair. She stayed up nights, in a corner of the room with only one dim lamp burning, and let the shadows dance around her. Evan would find her in the mornings, asleep in the corner.

As the days wore on, she began to feel an unexplained rage toward him. Sometimes, when he looked at her, her love and hate mixed together and she wanted to kiss or slap him, each with equal intensity. Press lips to lips, or send her hand sailing against his face with a loud smack, fingertips grazing the light sandpapery stubble there.

It was new, the anger. He'd done nothing different, changed in no perceptible way. But she'd trusted him, believed he would somehow bring her peace, and he'd failed her, because that peace hadn't lasted.

"Julie, what's happening to you?" he asked one night. And she told him little pieces, little things about Reba. But the whole story, the intricate details… Those she kept for herself.

At first, she couldn't imagine quitting school, didn't see any reason to. It wasn't common, but she also wasn't the only pregnant woman she saw in her classes. But then, she couldn't summon the energy to go. She spent her days under the thick solace of the comforter, her head buried beneath a pillow, keeping the world away.

Evan was exasperated. Sometimes, he would come home overly cheerful, as though he hoped it might rub off. He would wear a sly smile and hold his hand against her stomach and call her amazing. It didn't help.

They argued loudly. She was terrified of everything, and Evan was terrified of her. And obviously worried. She could see herself shattering the fragile things she loved. But she couldn't stop it.

She was eight months pregnant the night he finally gave up on her. They had fought again, her words heated and heartless. He came home quietly, his face soft, ready for peace.

He sat beside her. "I brought you something," he said and presented her with the gift.

She ran her hands over the heavy, hard-backed book. It was brown with a pattern of gold etching. There was no title on the front, and she was confused, turned it sideways to see the spine. *Romeo and Juliet* was written in ink that sank, a golden wound, into the deep brown. The book fell to her lap, dropped so quickly that it might have seared her skin.

"You told me once that you were Juliet in high school," he said cautiously. "But I looked around, and you don't have the book. So, I found this in the used-book store. It's really old. I thought you might like to have it."

She was silent as she stood slowly, gripping the book as though it were a thorn against her hand. She felt blood rushing into her face.

"Why would you do this?" she whispered.

Evan stood up. "I thought you would like it. I just want us to be okay." He stepped backward at the look on her face. "Is it...bad?"

He didn't know. She'd never told him that Reba died the night of the play. But she blamed him anyway. Lights seemed to flash before her eyes, stage lights, blinking on, off, on. She saw Reba in the crowd, saw Reba falling down into the river. And she couldn't make it stop.

She hurled the book across the room, flinging it away as hard as she could, as if making the book go away might change the truth. She heard the shatter too, afterward, and was appalled at what she had done, though she couldn't admit it. She heard the loud thud of the book as it hit the fire escapes below, as she stared in horror at the jagged hole she'd made in the window.

Evan looked at her like she was a monster, someone he'd never seen before and would never want to again.

"Evan," she whispered. She wanted to explain; she really did. But he was backing away to the dresser, grabbing clothes, stuffing them into a bag.

"I can't do this," he said, his eyes sad. He stared at her, and she opened her mouth to say something, to tell him about Reba. But she was speechless, and he walked out the door. The cold air blew in from the window. She waited to feel something. But her body had been invaded and her mind consumed, and she couldn't feel anything else at all.

Evan took their daughter because Julie begged him to, just after they settled the baby in her arms for the first time and the name had come so easily from her mouth. Rebecca. And he kept Beck for more than a month after, while Julie huddled, restless, in the bed that she had once shared with him. She couldn't be a mother. She was convinced she'd never be able to. And then one day there was Brighton, pounding on the door to the apartment. She waited for him to leave, but he didn't, only waited outside, knocking, until she couldn't stand it any longer and let him in.

She'd been on antidepressants for two weeks when Evan brought the baby back, swaddled, alien. *Play touring the Southeast,* he said. *You've got to grow up, Julie.* Something cold. She'd hurt him, and things had shifted between them. She held the baby awkwardly there, in the doorway, watching Evan walk away and wondering what to do with an infant.

84

"So...that's what happened," Julie says, rubbing her fingers against the rough terry cloth of the hotel towel.

"I'm sorry," August says. He's on a lounge chair next to her, legs splayed, looking up at the clouds.

She nods. "Me too. That stupid play. Can you believe I made preparing for that play my entire world? If not for that, I might have noticed the changes with Reba. Maybe things wouldn't have been any different, but at least I could have *tried*."

She thinks back to the night of the play, to Ms. Madrie sighing dramatically and saying *The show must go on!* when Julie tried to tell her that she couldn't go through with it. The truth was, Julie no longer had any interest. Juliet and her sordid saga were nothing compared to the very real situation with Reba.

"Just nerves, dear, just nerves," Ms. Madrie said, her face aglow with excitement. She patted Julie's shoulder and moved on. But Julie had never been nervous about the stage.

So she couldn't get out of it, and there she was, in full Shakespearean garb on that January night, a reluctant Capulet.

"Ready?" Brandon Lomax asked, in full costume himself, without glasses, strands of wavy hair falling into his face. He pushed it back nervously, but the strands fell again, undaunted. He made a surprisingly handsome Romeo, and Julie thought back to the crush Reba had on him once.

"Of course," Julie said with an insincere smile, but he didn't notice.

The Lawrence High School Drama Spectacular always brought a crowd, not just from Lawrence Mill but from Opal and Woodbrooke too. Mostly because there wasn't anything better to do. It was no surprise when people began streaming into the old auditorium almost an hour before the play was scheduled to start. Julie watched the crowd from behind the thick, musty-smelling purple velvet curtain, surprised when Jake came in with a much younger girl. Sister, maybe? She spotted Nell too.

Before the lights dimmed, Julie caught sight of Reba. She was hardly more than an apparition in the back of the crowded auditorium. Even more surprising was Toby, only a few seats down. She couldn't think of why Toby would come out to watch the play. He wasn't exactly a proud relative. Toby and Reba were both alone, but watching them, Julie could see that they were aware of each other. She could sense a strange sort of current running between them, sparking, flaring at both ends. The whole thing was off somehow, and it made Julie feel unsettled.

Then the play began. Her lines were flawless, her movements fluid, but she couldn't shake the weirdness of Toby and Reba, almost together. Brandon's acting, which had never been exceptional, was startlingly accurate. He didn't hesitate, never missed a single line, and he grew more attractive as the night went on. But she was Juliet, and he was forbidden.

The show passed by in a blur. The only things of interest were the kisses, the times when, helplessly, she threw herself into Brandon-as-Romeo's arms and kissed him, *really* kissed him and he looked startled. She told herself that it was the madness of the play, but it was a release and she knew it. All the tension, all of the worry, she tried to pass on to the poor boy through the pressure of her lips on his. Or maybe it was vengeance, but she knew Reba didn't care. Brandon was nothing to her, not anymore. Not ever, really.

Only Nell came to the stage to congratulate her after the show, with a huge bouquet. Jake didn't stay, but Julie didn't care. Maybe those kisses had seemed too real to him. She didn't see Toby or Reba anywhere, though she looked for them after.

Brandon didn't mention the kisses, only smiled shyly at her when she was packing up to go home. So she must have been the one who initiated it, the make-out session out back, behind the auditorium when everyone else had gone, when they were out of costume but still in stage makeup. He didn't ask for an explanation, and she was grateful. It didn't go any further, and afterward, he drove her to Aunt Molly's house and told her she was a wonderful actress.

It was after midnight when she made it up to her room that night, the house completely dark until she switched on her bedroom light. A storm was creeping up outside—she could hear the low growl of thunder in the distance. She fell onto her bed, tired but restless after the performance. There was a bottle of whiskey hidden in her closet, and she dug beneath shoes and piles of clothes until she found it. The coppery liquid seemed to glow, but maybe it was only her relief at finding it—something to settle her frantic mind.

She poured the whiskey into the cap to take shots, hadn't mastered drinking straight from the bottle like Toby. The heat of the alcohol was soothing, and she felt herself finally beginning to unwind. She was on her second shot when she heard the groan of a car cranking. She pulled herself, curious, from the hard mattress to her window and pulled aside the blinds. When her own reflection glared back at her, she snapped off the overhead light so she could see out into the darkness. It was Mr. McLeod's black truck, headlights off, backing slowly out of the garage next door.

What would Mr. McLeod be doing out so late? She pressed her face to the window, imagining dozens of dramatic scenarios. Mr. McLeod having an affair. Attending a secret poker game. The worst: Reba taking her daddy's truck out to meet the boy. Surely she hadn't grown that desperate. In the bed of the truck, Julie could see a plastic gasoline container sliding around, dull red under the streetlights as the truck drove away.

She didn't move from the window, and she wasn't sure why. Waiting for Mr. McLeod's return, she guessed, or for some clue as to where he'd gone. Nothing happened for more than an hour. She sipped shot after shot of the whiskey until more than half the bottle was gone, flipped through magazines, doodled strange designs on sheets of notebook paper. But she didn't leave the window. She couldn't begin to explain what she was doing, why she was sitting there in the dark, watching, riveted. An observer. A spy. She was tired and her muscles felt so relaxed. Her eyes were closing, yet she couldn't convince herself to move to the bed, to sleep. *Wait*, a lonely, persistent voice in her head kept saying, and she couldn't drown it out with alcohol. *Wait.*

But it wasn't Mr. McLeod she saw. Instead, there was movement in Reba's room. A light went on, then off again, and suddenly, there she was, her light-colored oversize sweater too visible against the dark shrubbery as she slipped out the window. A jagged shard of lightning illuminated the sky. Reba held something flat—a book maybe—to her chest as she walked quickly away from the house, sticking to the shadows. And then she disappeared completely into the night.

It was the strangest thing, but moments after she watched Reba go, Julie heard the door to Toby's bedroom click open, heard his footsteps in the hall and on the stairs, and then the sound of the front door opening and closing.

85

"Jules came here," Toby says, his cell phone jammed against his ear. He's pacing back and forth across the gallery. He hasn't bothered opening up shop today. He doesn't feel like it. Fuck it. "She said Reba had a diary. Did you know Reba had a diary?"

He can hear Nell sigh on the other end of the phone. "Yeah, I knew. Jules got it from me."

The room keeps wanting to spin around him, won't come to a goddamned standstill long enough for anything to make any kind of sense. "Why didn't you tell me? All these years… You know how I felt about her… Why didn't you tell me?"

"I should have just tossed out the damned thing," Nell says. "It wasn't good stuff, not for you, and not for Jules, and not for August. I never should have given her that book, but I saw right quick that she wasn't leaving without it."

"Why?" His eyes are wet. "How could you keep it from me?"

"Toby…Toby, listen to me. You're better off without it. If you asked Julie right now…I bet she'd tell you that she was better off without it."

"Was there ever a baby?" His voice is rising; he can't seem to help it. "Was she ever really pregnant?"

Nell's silence tells him everything he needs to know. He hangs up the phone. He can't remember ever hanging up on Nell before. She betrayed him, he thinks. So did Reba. Maybe. He can't even tell anymore what's betrayal and what's loyalty. He doesn't have a clue who knows best, only that he sure as hell doesn't.

The night Reba died. If he hadn't been such a fool, such an idiot, so impatient, then things might have been different. He should never have followed her. He'd have been pissed, really pissed, to know that she lied about the kid…but it wouldn't have changed the way he felt about her.

But that night, the night she died, he'd decided he wasn't putting up with it anymore. He wasn't going to stand by while she went out to meet the boy again. He'd offered her his help, and she'd seemed grateful, seemed almost as though she *liked* him, not just the things he did to her. That night in her bedroom, his arms around her… Well, things had seemed different. Like they were a real couple or something.

He'd turned completely soft. Why else would he have followed her to the play? He'd wanted to sit next to her, but he knew she'd get pissed. Maybe he'd been imagining it, but he would swear he could feel the heat radiating off her, even from two seats away. She'd known he was there, and he could *feel* her wanting him. And it didn't matter whether that was his kid or not—he wanted her too, and it had been all he could do to sit there in the dark theater and not move closer, not put his hands on her. After the play, she'd walked past him and let her hand brush against his. She had been close enough that he could smell her shampoo, and he'd almost lost it then, almost grabbed her up in his arms and kissed her and let everyone know that this was *real*, damn it.

But he hadn't. He'd lost his nerve, hadn't wanted to upset her. Hadn't wanted to push her away again. So he'd gone home, done a line of coke because he thought he would work on his paintings, but instead he sat in front of his window and watched hers for what felt like hours. He wanted to go to her, climb through her bedroom window, and make love to her between those white sheets. He saw her old man's truck leave the driveway, and that was weird. Not his business, though. Reba was his business, and he couldn't believe it when he saw her climbing out the window. For a moment, he expected to hear her knocking at *his* door, but no—she headed off toward the woods, and he felt like punching something.

He had no idea what she really felt for the other boy, for August, but it wasn't the same as what she felt for him. The thing between them was stronger, was different from anything Toby had ever felt in his entire life. After the other night, the way she'd drifted to sleep in his arms, he'd been stupid enough to think that she would get rid of the boy. What was the point of being with August, anyway? The kid wasn't brave enough to stand up and say he might be the father of Reba's baby, and Reba sure as hell wasn't going to drag him into it.

But there she went, off into the night to meet him again. No more, Toby thought, as he jumped up and pulled on his shoes and rushed out the door.

He shakes his head, trying to bring himself back to the present. He'd thought he was going to make her choose, issue some kind of ultimatum. He can't stand to think of it now. Frustrated, he hurls his cell across the gallery. Damned phone doesn't even give him the satisfaction of smashing properly; only the battery and battery cover drop out from the back. He stands there staring at the useless thing, in pieces.

86

I FEEL A CERTAIN SENSE OF FINALITY. NO MATTER WHAT, THIS IS the last time I will meet August in the dark.

This book is the only way to give him the truest truth, to give him words I'll never be able to say. Everything is here, from the beginning, when things were still soft and sweet. How everything started with Toby. How I became this villain. The intricate web of lies, with me at the center like a sadistic spider. Worst of all, that the baby is no more than a deception made on a whim, woven into existence in my own imagination.

He'll never speak to me again. Why would he? And though I don't like the idea of him hating me, don't want to sully those lovely memories of the two of us together before things grew so complicated, I also feel an overwhelming sense of relief. Giving August this diary feels right in a way that nothing has in the longest time. He will hate me, but he will be safe—safe from my daddy's rage, safe from my own rampant dishonesty.

So, August, when you read this, I hope that maybe you'll under-stand, even if only a little bit. You're more than this, and you deserve better than some silly Southern girl making a mess of your heart. And because of that, it feels good to let you go.

87

August listens to Julie, talking about the play, talking about what happened after...

But he remembers his own side of things. Sitting in his room, waiting. Remembers the light—not too bright, hardly more than the flicker of a candle's flame, but it was enough to see him clearly, if his mother or father or sister had walked in. What would he have said? He thought, then, that maybe Reba had been right and they should run, and he thought of packing a bag and taking her away. They could go to Virginia. He had family there.

He regretted waiting so long to talk to Reba about the baby, but when she told him that night at the river, he'd been terrified. And then with Jules finding out about them at that moment... Well, he could have handled the whole thing differently.

He thought of Reba's family and wondered if her father would kill him after all, when he found out.

The trophies on his dresser from his football days caught his eye, shining as they were in the soft light. Trophies used to mean something. He hadn't wanted things to turn out this way with Reba. He hated that he was the one to put her in this position. It was his fault, really. From the beginning, it was all his fault. It was too much to think about, so instead, he imagined her smiling, the way she had when they first met.

He was sliding into his jacket when the phone rang, shattering the silence in the house. Surely Reba wouldn't call him at home, not unless there was some kind of emergency. It occurred to him that she might not even know his phone number. He didn't have a phone in his bedroom, and he moved quickly to the bedroom door in an attempt to reach the living room phone before the noise woke the entire house. But he was too late—his father stood in the dark living room, phone in his hand.

"The house," his father said when he hung up. He was in his nightclothes, a white tee and boxer shorts, but he didn't ask why August was fully dressed and wide awake. "The new house. It's on fire. They're saying arson."

August and his sister rode in the backseat to the new neighborhood, Megan asking sleepy, curious questions about who would want to burn down their new house. Rain sprinkled onto the windshield, and loud claps of thunder shook the car as August watched the odometer up front, thought of how each mile took him farther from the river, where he was supposed to be meeting Reba. Already it was one a.m. Already he was late.

They could see the grayish smoke rising up from blocks away, and instead of the new house, which had been nearly finished, they saw remnants of the fire, small orange flames still flickering, even in the drizzle, and the blackened skeleton of a house. Three fire trucks crowded around the destruction, and two firefighters in full gear sprayed water onto the charred debris. There were policemen waiting to talk to August's parents.

One of them introduced himself. "Mr. Elliott," he asked, "can you think of anyone who would do this intentionally?" August could, but he kept his mouth closed tightly. He thought of Mr. McLeod, of the things Reba had warned him of. He couldn't imagine that Mr. McLeod had found out about his connection to Reba, though, and figured this must be his way of finally getting revenge on August's dad for the promotion. He should have told, he knew it, should have done what was best for his family. But he couldn't, kept seeing Reba's face and knew the pain it would cause her. Because he would have had to explain how he knew.

When no flames lingered and only puffy clouds of smoke billowed into the night air, it was after two a.m. The policeman was asking August's family to come to the station to file a report, and then they were climbing into the car to follow the police cruiser, all of them rain-drenched and exhausted. His mother started to cry. August touched her shoulder and mumbled something he hoped was soothing, but he felt panicked himself. He needed to get to Reba, but if Mr. McLeod would do this to August's father because of a workplace grudge, what would he do to August when he found out that Reba was pregnant, and that the baby was his?

He couldn't shake the thought of Reba waiting for him in the rain. Even now, after reading the diary, it's a mental image he can't completely extinguish.

88

JULIE WOULDN'T HAVE FOLLOWED REBA, THAT NIGHT, IF NOT for all of the questions in her mind and the whiskey making her bold. Was Reba meeting August? What if August had changed his mind about running away, and they were leaving town? And if they were, why would Toby try to stop them? He'd left too soon after Reba for it to be a coincidence.

But maybe it was. Julie didn't know anything anymore. She shoved shoes on her feet and ran from the room. She shouldn't go after Reba again, she knew it, but if Reba was planning to leave, she had to find a way to stop her. And if she wasn't, then Julie still needed to make amends. She needed Reba in her life, needed her best friend back.

The air was cool and lightning flashed, a sharp, bright warning in the sky, but Julie ignored it, the same way she ignored the fat raindrops splashing into her hair. She was clammy, nervous, determined as she stumbled through the fields. The trees, naked without their leaves, passed in a blur. What would she do when she found Reba? What if she interrupted her with August again? Reba would be furious to know that Julie had followed her a second time.

What if they really were running away, and Julie was too late?

When she saw Reba, Julie stopped, digging her heels into the ground. Reba was walking back and forth across the little bridge. She seemed to be talking to herself, waving a tiny flashlight around as she moved, but Julie couldn't make out the words over the rushing noise of the river and the angry slapping of the water against the craggy river rocks.

89

REBA

THE DETAILS HARDLY MATTER, ONCE YOUR STORY IS COMPLETE. All those memories turn blurry at the edges, and that anger and panic and guilt wears away to something softer. That's how it happened for me, at least.

Here's what I remember about that night:

Where is August? I thought. My clothes were soaked, and if he didn't show soon, I knew I would lose my courage. I waited on the riverbank, and then, when my nerves got the better of me, I started pacing the bridge, careful to stop before I reached the vicinity of the seventh plank. The bridge was a safe place; it reminded me of walking home from the flower shop with Jules, of hopping over the seventh plank as kids.

I held my journal beneath my jacket in an effort to keep it protected from the storm. Giving the book to August wouldn't do any good if it was too damaged to read.

There were footsteps in the forest, but when I turned, it wasn't August I saw.

It was Toby.

"Rebecca," he said in a voice that sounded more like a growl. Thunder roared in the sky as he grabbed me by the arm, and my flashlight clattered onto the bridge and rolled to the bank, and I let him pull me into his wet embrace. His mouth on mine was hungry and primal as rain splashed our faces. The journal was crushed between us, but Toby didn't notice. It took a breathless moment for me to remember that August should be there any second. It would be difficult enough to pass along the journal and let him read the truth; to let him *see* the truth with his own eyes would be cruel and vicious, and I didn't want to hurt him more than I had to.

I pushed Toby away, or tried to, but he held me against him. "I told you," he said into my ear. "You're mine."

Which was the whole point. "Yes," I said, struggling to take a step back. The bridge creaked beneath us, the boards slippery in the storm. "Yes, but, Toby, you shouldn't be here now. Later...we'll talk later."

"After you've been with the other boy again? I don't think so." I could feel the heat of his breath on my ear, and I shivered in the darkness. "You know that baby is mine," he said. "You *know* it. He's not touching you, not anymore. Not with my baby inside you."

I could hear the rush of the water below and the pouring of the rain and the naked tree branches bending and scraping against one another. "Toby," I gasped, "it's not what you think..."

"Why?" he said. "What makes him so special, Reba? Why is he so much better than me?"

He kissed me again, hard, possessive.

"Toby, stop!" I said, finally pushing him away and scrambling back. "Stop it!"

"Say it," he said. "You think he's better."

"He *is* better," I said. "He's better than this, than you and me and this…this whole dirty thing."

He was unusually quiet for a moment, and the sounds of the storm pounded against my ears. His voice was low, hurt, when he spoke again. "Dirty thing, Rebecca? Is that what our kid is to you?"

"No," I said. I knew I should tell him the truth, but I couldn't, not yet. "No… I should go… I should…" I backed up, thinking that I was going to run then, run home and avoid it all, at least for the moment. But he caught my arm, and I pulled away, wild, like a frightened animal.

I jerked my arm free and slipped backward, stumbling on the wet bridge. I knew I must have stepped on the seventh plank when I heard the sound of the wood snapping under my feet and saw the horrified look on Toby's face. I knew then that no matter what games we'd played, Toby loved me. It was written on his face, etched in with the fear.

Toby loves me, still. It's possible that he loves me *more* now, when I'm beyond his reach. I don't know why that is.

I reached my hand to the lone rail to keep from falling, but with my weight against it, the old wood groaned, swayed. Broke.

I wanted to tell Toby that I loved him too—and it was the truth—but I was falling, the journal sailing from my hand. It lodged in brush on the riverbank and was still in one piece, wet but not destroyed, when Nell picked it up later. I watched her do it, even though she couldn't see me anymore.

I thought of my family as I went, of Mama's eyes and her good intentions. Daddy and his stupid, stupid beliefs. I thought of Jules as a child, crawling from the backseat of a car with a frightened look on her face. Jules and me with our toes in the cool river water, chasing each other through the field. I fell so fast, but it felt like forever.

The most enduring memory I have, now, is of Toby: lovely, broken, lit up in a flash of lightning, his face the last thing I saw before my head smashed against the side of the bridge and I went tumbling down, the river waiting to swallow me up. Water rushed all around me, and things turned dark.

The fall was horrific. But when I woke up again—if that's what you want to call it—everything was okay, and nothing mattered all that much.

I was perfect and lonely and beautiful.

90

Toby starts a pot of coffee in the loft and tries to pretend he can do anything besides think of her. But it's completely futile. He takes his mug and goes back down to the gallery, flopping into a chair and staring at the paintings. The coffee helps his hangover, but not his mood. The painting that draws his attention this time is the one of Reba on the bridge. It's the hardest one he's ever painted, trying to capture that gut-wrenching moment when she hovered on the edge, her mouth an O of surprise.

She'd been in his arms one second, and the next she was fucking *falling*—and all he could do was watch as her head cracked the side of the bridge and then she splashed into the water.

"No!" he shouted when he could find his voice. "*No!*" He didn't know how his eyes caught Jules when the sky lit up again, but he saw her, hiding behind a tree and still as a statue. "Help!" he shouted to her. "Jules, get some help!" But she just stood there, and Toby wondered if he was imagining her because he *needed* someone to help him.

He scrambled off the slick bridge and down the slippery bank, screaming the whole way. His feet slid out from under him and he tumbled down the riverbank and he was soaking wet and covered in mud and it didn't matter. He just had to get to Reba because she was down there somewhere alone in the river, and he was her only chance.

"Reba!" he shouted as he waded into the river, the water up to his knees. His boots and jeans were soaked but he didn't care. He couldn't see her, couldn't feel her beneath the surface. He followed the current away from the bridge, shouting for her the whole time.

"Help!" he yelled again, hoping that Jules had come to her senses up there and had gone for someone, if she was real at all. The water was dark and moving fast, and he could only see anything when the lightning flashed overhead—and where the hell was Reba? How would he find her?

He thought of their crazy relationship, how he'd almost blackmailed her, how he'd waited in her room. But he'd never forced her, even if things were messed up, and he adored her. Damn it, he *adored* her and he would take it all back if it meant that she would be safe and sound in her bed and not floating down a goddamned river.

Probably those weren't even tears pouring down his face; probably it was just river water and rain.

He followed the river for what felt like hours, and maybe it *was* hours, because the sky was growing lighter, even though the storm hadn't let up. He must have been a mile from the bridge, at least, when he saw it, a soaked tangle of golden hair, and there she was, facedown in the water.

His Reba. His whole damned life.

"Reba," he said, flipping her over and shaking her. "Reba!" Her blue eyes were open but blank, and he knew she couldn't see him. "Reba, please...please..." He pulled her to the bank and carried her out of the water, her drenched clothes heavy and sagging, her limp feet still grazing the river. "Reba, Reba...Rebecca..." He settled her on the ground and smoothed her hair. One hand came away blood-stained, and he thought of the awful sight of her head smashing against the bridge, and how he couldn't even hear the sound of it over the storm and the rushing water. And her eyes, looking at him, except not looking at him, just open.

Molly had made him take a CPR class once, and he hadn't wanted to do it. He'd done nothing but bitch about it, and now he racked his brain to remember, and then he was going through all of the motions, so systematic...and still, nothing but those watery eyes and no pulse when he put his fingers to her neck—but there had to be, and he just couldn't find it because he was freaking the fuck out, but it had to be there because Reba wasn't *dead*. She wasn't.

It was evil, it was wrong—the way a person could be *there* one moment and be completely absent the next. How life could go so easily. How existence was so fucking fragile.

He could see the gray light of the sun tucked into the clouds in the forest, and still she was lying there and he couldn't wake her up and he couldn't make her breathe so he clutched her to him, wrapped his arms around her, and held her the way he'd held her in her bedroom that night, the way he'd always wanted to hold her. They were soaked and it was cold and the dirt from the riverbank was clinging to them, and he didn't care.

Without her, there was nothing to care about.

He stumbled into the flower shop as Nell was flipping on lights to start the day. She jumped when he walked through the door and then she stared, dumbly, at Toby, who was dirty and soaking wet, and holding on to the frame of the door like he might fall over if he didn't, while rain drizzled down behind him and thunder rumbled in the dark morning sky.

"Toby, what is it?" Nell asked, her voice wary.

Water pooled at his feet and it seemed natural to sink to his knees, so that's what he did. He could feel the rough metal bottom of the doorframe scratching his legs through the torn denim of his blue jeans, and the pain felt good. "Reba," he croaked, and then he was gasping for air. "Call…call someone for help…" and he would have told her more except that he couldn't fucking breathe.

"Toby!" she shouted, moving toward him and shaking his shoulders as he sobbed. "What happened? Where is Reba?"

He looked up at her and the words were in his throat, but he couldn't say them because to say them would make them real and it wasn't *real*.

"Tell me," Nell said, holding him by the arms and staring at him. She looked scared and angry and concerned all at the same time, and why wasn't she calling for help, when he'd already told her that someone should come and help? "Tell me what's wrong."

"Dead." The word choked him, and he was gasping again because he'd said it and made it real. "She's dead… Oh God, she's dead." And then he was shaking and holding on to Nell, sobbing on her shoulder because she was there and he didn't know what else to do.

"Toby," Nell said. "Toby! Where is she?"

"River," he sputtered.

"Okay," she said quietly. "Okay." And then she pulled away from him and he was still there on the floor in her doorway and she was finally calling 911 and telling them something and then she ran out the back door and he was in the empty shop and the rain splattered against the windows and then he knew, really knew that it wasn't a nightmare or a bad trip. He got to his feet and stumbled out the door.

It was all real, and Reba was dead.

91

JULIE REMEMBERS THAT NIGHT ALL THOSE YEARS AGO, remembers waking up curled into a tight ball, shivering. She didn't know where she was, only that the ceiling was made of tree limbs with sharp light stabbing through the branches. Her clothes were wet, and her head rested against the gnarled roots of a tree. She could hear the rush of the river, full from last night's rain.

She was in the forest, but she didn't know why. She sat up. Her head pounded, her hands were dirty from the wet ground, and pine needles clung to her jeans. And somewhere, she could hear voices. Julie crawled along the ground, pushing aside bushes and vines that she dimly hoped weren't poison ivy.

When she made it to the riverbank, she saw them, though they were farther down and on the opposite bank. Paramedics, police. Nell, orange hair unmistakable, her face in her hands.

Little pieces started coming back to Julie then. Nighttime. An argument. Running through the woods. Running *away*.

Whatever bad thing that was happening on the other bank was her fault.

She ran to Molly's house, flew through the front door. Molly, sound asleep on the sofa, didn't stir as Julie ran past her, up the stairs to her room, ripped off her dirty clothes. Something was wrong, terribly wrong, but she didn't *want* to know what.

Just as soon as she'd cleaned her face and pulled on sweatpants and a tank top, someone knocked on the front door. She stumbled into the hallway, made it to the top of the stairs in time to see Mr. McLeod standing in the living room, red-faced but unusually quiet. Molly, wide awake now, looked up at Julie with an expression closer to pity than any she'd ever seen her wear. "It's Reba."

Julie doesn't remember falling down the stairs.

Nothing broken, they said when she woke up in the sterile white of the hospital. Shock, or something. Two policemen were waiting to talk to her, but all she could do was stare at them blankly, until they finally shook their heads and walked away.

She slept, and when she woke, Toby was there in her hospital room, the newspaper in his hand.

"Stop faking," he snarled, the moment she opened her eyes. "I said, stop faking. I know you're not 'in shock.' I told the police that you were at home all night after the play, if that's what you're worried about."

"What?" she said, her voice hoarse from sleep.

"I know you were there," he said.

"What?" She couldn't look him in the eye.

"You're shitting me, right?"

"What happened, Toby?"

"You really don't remember?" he said. "You don't remember what you did?" She shook her head, silent.

"It's your fault," he said, and there was a cruel and frightening edge in his voice. "You were there. You could have done something. You as good as pushed her."

Surely she'd heard him wrong. "I-I *pushed* her?"

He tilted his head to the side and studied her. After a moment he spoke. "You're lucky I don't tell everyone what really happened."

Oh God. She hadn't… She couldn't have pushed her best friend off the bridge, could she? She remembered two people arguing on the bridge, though it felt more like she was *watching* it all happen, and everything was dark and stormy, and she couldn't hear the words. "How do you know?"

"You told me. You woke up earlier, and you told me."

"Oh God," she said. "You should tell. *I* should tell. They'll know… They'll come for me…and oh God, everyone will know about Reba and August, and the baby…"

Toby tossed the newspaper onto her lap. "They don't. You don't tell them anything about Reba, not about the boy, the drugs, nothing. And I won't tell them what you did."

She looked at the paper.

"Do you hear me, Jules? Do you fucking hear me?"

"I hear you," she whispered.

His boots made scuffing noises against the hospital room floor as he walked out the open door.

Her horrified tears fell onto the newspaper as she read the headline. "Mysterious Death of Lawrence Mill Teen under Investigation." The paper described Reba's death as a puzzling tragedy with too many unanswered questions, namely, what was a seventeen-year-old girl doing at the bridge alone in the middle of the night? Apparently, police found no evidence that anyone was with her that night, though the police chief admitted that the rain turning the riverbanks to mud would have washed away any footprints. No sign of foul play. The reporter didn't come right out and say it, but the whole article suggested suicide, even going so far as to say that classmates interviewed described Reba as a quiet girl, someone who always kept to herself. Depressed, maybe. A girl no one really knew. A ghost.

Julie wished then that she *had* talked to the police when they'd come to question her, instead of sitting there with that useless stare. She couldn't believe there was no evidence to link her to the crime. Surely police would find *something?* The paper said that drowning was the official cause of death, but autopsy reports were pending. Once they cut Reba open (Julie shuddered at the thought), they would discover that she was pregnant, and then it would be the town's biggest scandal. And then police would start to look for the father. They'd come back to Julie with questions. Would she confess, say that she'd killed Reba? Would she tell the truth about it all? She didn't know.

The worst part was Reba's smiling face staring up at her from the black-and-white photo on the page. Accusing her. Asking her why.

"Oh God!" Julie screamed. She felt like a killer. She tore the newspaper into shreds, screaming and crying, until a nurse came rushing in with a sedative.

"You poor thing," she heard the nurse say, before she tumbled back into sleep.

92

Toby hated Jules so, so much after that night. If she hadn't been so drunk, so stupid… If she'd gone for help instead of standing there in the woods staring like a fool, then Reba might have still been alive. And she didn't even *remember*, didn't have to see that last expression on Reba's face every time she closed her eyes, and it wasn't fair.

He'd needed someone else to *feel* it, and when Jules had misheard him in the hospital, he'd just gone with it. Let her wonder what she did, let her feel wrong, and bad, and guilty.

Like he did.

When he opened the door to his bedroom, the painting of Reba was staring back at him from the wall, the slash from the mirror repaired and every bit of it finished now with the waterfall behind her. Why the hell had he painted her like that, there? Almost like he'd known it would end this way. Almost like he'd seen how the whole thing would unfold.

He grabbed his paint jars and unscrewed them, then hurled

them one by one against her painting, so that odd, awful colors splattered against the ivory of her skin, covered the soft bends of her fingers, marred the perfect pink of her lips. The mess of paint seeped down onto the carpet and pooled there, and he didn't care.

He needed to sleep, needed to close his eyes and forget it all for a while. He tore through his drug stash, little bags flying to the floor as his hands dug deeper. Pills, surely there were pills in there somewhere.

If he could get to sleep, maybe it would stop. Maybe she would be alive when he woke up. Maybe she'd be alive in his dreams.

Nell's shop was dark, and she was locking the door when he cleared his throat behind her. "You didn't tell anyone I was there," he said. She turned to look at him, her orange hair glowing like a flame in the evening light. "You protected me. Why?"

He had the uneasy feeling that she could see right through all the bullshit. "I protected *her*, Toby. As best I could at this point, anyway." She was quiet for a moment, and then asked, "Did you do it? Did you kill her?"

He swallowed. "No. I tried... I tried to save her."

"She meant something to you," Nell said as though it was the simplest, most obvious thing in the world. She had a tote bag over one shoulder, and he could see the corner of a book sticking out, something with a purple cover. Vaguely familiar.

He nodded, and he was fucking pathetic, because he couldn't keep from looking down, from sucking in a deep breath.

"What happened at the bridge, Toby?" When he didn't respond, she asked again. "I covered for you, you know. Told the police that I was the one to find her, the one to pull her out. Even helped put this crazy suicide idea in everyone's heads. Figured it was best no one went digging too deep. Don't you think the least you can do is tell me the truth? *Your* truth, at least?"

"You knew," he said. "The baby. I forgot that you knew." Nell shook her head and opened her mouth to speak, a hand held up as though she might argue with him, but she closed her mouth again when he said, "That was decent of you, to lie. To help."

"Tell me what happened." And she was there, and he owed her, and there was no one else to tell. No one else would ever know that any of it had happened. So they sat down on the porch in the fading sun, and he told her everything. And she listened, and she didn't judge him. They'd never been close before, but from then on, it seemed like she was looking out for him. Got to where he trusted Nell more than just about anyone else he knew.

He's got to admit, diary or no diary, he still does.

93

August read about it in the paper. *The paper.* It still stings to think of finding out that way. He hadn't met Reba at the bridge like he'd said he would, and she was dead. Did she think he'd deserted her, that he'd left her to face things alone? He'd gotten her into this terrible mess, when all he wanted to do was love her. She'd killed herself, and it was all because of him.

After the fire, his father's boss approved an immediate transfer back to Virginia for the safety of their family. August would go back to his old high school that he'd hated leaving, and Lawrence Mill would be a wonderful and terrible dream—a place where he'd found his would-be future and it had jumped off a bridge and disappeared forever.

He didn't care, then, if he ever came back.

94

BACK THEN, JULIE COULD HARDLY BRING HERSELF TO VISIT Reba's grave. It was a special kind of torture, but she made herself do it. It seemed like the sun was shining cruelly each time she visited. How could the sun shine when Reba was gone? If only it would rain, and she could feel it on her hair and her skin, as real and wet and stinging as tears.

The sun exposed her for the killer that she was. If she hadn't been such a coward, if she hadn't been desperate to leave Lawrence Mill, then she would have marched herself down to the police station and told them the truth. They would have locked her up, in the prison thirty miles outside of town, and she would have become an urban legend, and then people would have forgotten about her completely. She didn't know what was worse—being held responsible for it or getting away with it.

Drowning, the police said. That Reba jumped off the bridge in the middle of the storm, hit her head on the way down, drowned in the raging waters.

The stone wasn't up yet, but Julie knew where to find Reba—the fresh patch of earth, not even grass-covered yet. Just dark-brown Mississippi soil. When she sat there, she tried to pretend she was on the soft carpet of Reba's bedroom floor and that Reba was beside her and that the noise of the wind in the trees was a song on the radio.

But Reba wasn't beside her. Reba wasn't anywhere at all.

"I'm sorry," Julie whispered into the ground. "I'm so, so sorry."

Things went back to normal, or as normal as they could be when Reba was gone.

Mr. McLeod was arrested for arson, but the police were kind enough to wait until after the funeral to arrest him. And then they let him go, because, for all of his talk, there was a convenient lack of evidence to tie him to the fire at August's house. Or, if there was evidence, it had gone missing. It helped that Mr. McLeod was friends with the police chief, and that the Elliotts left town suddenly and wouldn't come back to testify.

Reba's autopsy results were manipulated—at least, Julie was convinced of it then. She didn't know how, but maybe the police chief helped there too. Maybe he told the McLeods about Reba's pregnancy in private, or maybe he hid the information and never told anyone at all. Julie waited and waited for the results to be released, but the autopsy only confirmed drowning as the cause of death. Nothing more was ever mentioned. Julie went to Nell the day she read it in the paper, and Nell didn't seem surprised. She just shook her head and said something about not looking a gift horse in the mouth. Julie wanted to confess, at least to Nell. But in the end, she was too afraid.

And then August left, and there was no one else to know the story, and there was no one else to suspect that Julie could be cruel enough to kill the only person in the world who cared about her. And the baby—if she'd killed Reba, she'd killed the baby too. Julie was all alone, and it was all her fault.

The doctor had given her little white pills to take home with her, and she walked, sedated, through the halls at school, alone. People stared at her; people talked. But she didn't care.

She knew, even then, that nothing would ever be the same.

95

"You left, right after everything happened," Julie says, her knees tucked against her chest, the towel falling loosely from her body. The clouds have turned the afternoon sky so dark that it feels like night, and still they haven't moved from their lounge chairs.

"Yeah. Dad demanded his old job back, and after he told the corporate office what happened and what he suspected, they moved us back up to Richmond. I've been there ever since."

"Have you ever told anyone?"

"I've never even come close."

"So...what happens now?"

"I don't know."

Impulsively, she moves from her lounge chair to sit next to him. "I don't know how to move past all this," she says.

"Jules, here's what I think. We were kids, all of us. I want to hate her for all of the lies, for making me think...that I was *special* to her. But she was a kid too, caught up in things that she didn't know how to handle. We all made mistakes. I'm starting to think that maybe we shouldn't hate ourselves for it."

She can feel the words taking tentative hold in her mind, can feel herself toying with the idea of letting them stay.

His kiss is unexpected but soft, almost familiar. The wind shakes the trees along the fence, and his chest is muscular beneath her palms. Their bodies press together warily, and the lounge chair groans beneath their combined weight.

And then it starts to rain, and he pulls her closer.

She pushes him away, gently, after a few moments. "I'm not her," she says, and he nods, trailing hesitant kisses along the line of her shoulder.

"I know," he whispers, and she can feel his warm breath and the cool raindrops along her skin. "God, Jules, I know."

Part of her can't believe this is happening, that she is following August to his hotel room, letting him slowly peel the soaked underwear from her skin, that she is undoing the buttons on his shirt, all in silence. His skin is hot against hers and she clings to him as he lifts her up in his arms and settles her onto the bed. Rain beats against the window-panes, and it's the only sound besides the tender noise of their kisses. It's different, with him, or maybe she is the one who is different. She's still too filled with emotions from the past few days to hide much, to wear the mask she has worn with so many others. She can't pretend it's only about sex when it isn't about sex at all, not when she *needs* to cling to someone. No, not someone—it has to be him.

She spends the rest of the day with him, in his hotel room, with the curtains pulled open to the storm outside. She can't decide if it's wrong. Any other day before today, she wouldn't have dreamed of touching him, couldn't have imagined taking something that had been so completely *Reba's*. But now she knows that he wasn't, hadn't been.

"Jules," he murmurs against her skin, and she wonders why the name doesn't feel so wrong when he says it.

When she finally falls asleep in his arms, the clouds have moved away and late-evening sunlight filters through the window and into the shadowy room. She knows that he is awake later, in the middle of the night when she slips from his bed and back into her clothes, but he doesn't stop her from leaving. She can feel his eyes on her as she tiptoes out.

❦

"So…" he says to her the next morning, at the small table in the break-fast area of the lobby.

"So…"

"There's something I'd like to do today, before we leave," he says.

"Me too, actually."

After they are packed and the bags are loaded into the small Honda, she drives the car back to Nell's, to the recreation center behind the flower shop. They walk to the little footbridge in the hazy morning light. August climbs carefully down the riverbank, finally crouching when he reaches the river's edge. He opens the clasp on the large manila envelope he's been clutching and pulls out a small stack of photos. When she makes it down the bank herself, Julie looks over his shoulder and gasps. Such beautiful photos of Reba, some up close, some far away, some from outside Nell's shop with Reba's hand shading her eyes from the hot summer sun. She can't help but be reminded of Toby's gallery, of the paintings. She thinks of the similar ways that the two men have memorialized Reba, thinks of Toby in his studio, still painting her, while one at a time, August slides his photos into the river, and they watch as her face sinks into the water and is carried away by the slow-moving current. "Good-bye," Julie hears him whisper.

They make one final detour, and then Lawrence Mill and the town of Opal are fading in the rearview mirror. Julie has a feeling she'll never be back.

At the airport, August hugs her, his arms warm around her waist. And then he is gone to catch his flight back to Virginia, and she is boarding a plane to New York, and she is surprised at how much she misses him already.

She knows more than she ever wanted to, and it aches, this knowledge, but it also feels like freedom.

96

Toby almost misses the envelope propped against the door when he steps out to check the mail. The yellow of it catches his eye, though, and he leans down and picks it up. It's got his name scrawled on the front, and when he tears it open, a faded, water-stained purple book falls into his hands.

97

The taxi careens through the streets of New York City, carrying Julie home from the airport.

She knows that Brighton will be waiting for her when she gets home. Loyal Brighton, who came so quickly when she called him all those years ago, when Evan left a crying baby Beck in her arms and she had no idea what to do with her. In the first weeks, months, she felt wrecked. Brighton found her many nights curled up in the bathtub, in her closet, on the kitchen floor, pathetic.

Beck never knew. By the time she was old enough to hold on to her memories, something had changed. It was Brighton who made Julie believe that she could do it, that she could be someone's mother. He never tried to make her feel bad for needing some time to warm up to it all. She loves him for it.

Sure enough, he is waiting on the steps of her building when the taxi pulls up to the curb.

"Welcome home," he says, embracing her as though she has been gone for years. He looks at her, hugs her again, reaches for her bag. "How was the trip? I wondered if it would do you some good. Did it?"

"It was... Wow, I guess it was enlightening," she says finally.

"Well, come on," he says. "Fill me in." Julie pays the driver and follows Brighton up the steps into the building's lobby and up to her apartment.

The lights are out, and the apartment is chilly. But she is home. Brighton moves to the kitchen and pours two glasses of white wine from a bottle in the fridge.

She takes a sip of the wine and sets it down. She's thinking maybe she'll stop drinking for a while. After a deep breath, she starts to talk. About how she thought she'd killed Reba, how thinking of herself as a potential killer shaped *everything*, how she found so many little ways to punish herself, how she drove Evan away because of her own guilt.

"I know how you feel about Evan," she says. "But it was never his fault. You should know that. It was always me, pushing him away."

"What does that have to do with your trip to Lawrence Mill?" Brighton asks.

She takes a deep breath. "It wasn't true. I didn't kill her. She...fell, I guess." And then she tells him everything else—about the diary and what it exposed, and how it proved wrong all of the things she thought she knew about Reba.

"Wow," Brighton says, when she is finished. "That sounds like one screwed-up story." She looks at him and nods. "So, *Jules*," he says, and hearing her name that way, from someone other than August, doesn't bother her the way it would have only a few days ago. "What happens now?"

But she doesn't really have an answer.

❦

Julie opens the door to her apartment, and Evan and Beck cross the threshold. "Mom!" Beck says. Julie reaches down to hug her and Beck squeals with delight, and Julie feels an almost painful kind of pleasure.

"Did you have a good time?" Julie asks, smiling and drinking her in.

"Yes! I had a very good time. Daddy took me to see a concert at Central Park."

"He did?" Julie looks up at Evan, and he smiles. "That sounds like a lot of fun. Hey, why don't you go put your suitcase away and let me talk to your dad for a second?"

"Okay. And then will you tell me about your trip?"

Julie nods, and Beck tugs her little suitcase into her bedroom and disappears.

Evan. He's unshaven, his blue eyes vivid against his skin, against the soft pink of his boyish lips. She thinks of how simple it might be to search Evan's eyes for a flicker of something she used to see there. He's so precious and so familiar to her, and the reasons she thought that she didn't deserve him are gone, aren't they? How easy it should be to love him now, to say so…except that she doesn't know if it would be the truth anymore.

Instead, she reaches her hand out. It lands on his elbow. His sleeves are pushed up, and her hand touches bare skin. He flinches but doesn't pull away.

"Evan," she says.

"Julie, I…" He trails off. He steps back, and his boot toe catches the rough fringe of the ragged rug beneath his feet. He looks down and shakes his foot to free the threads. "You should really get rid of this rug," he says.

"I hurt you," she says. They have never discussed it, how things ended. "I hurt you back then, but I didn't mean to, not ever. I was wrong, and I'm sorry."

"Really. This rug is terrible."

"Evan," she says again. She studies his brown boots, his jeans. Then she cautiously looks up at his face, his strong cheekbones. The flutter of his eyelashes as he blinks, when he finally looks at her again.

"I know, Julie. Of course I know."

Beck steps out of her room, sees the two of them together, Julie's hand on Evan's arm, his hand covering hers. Beck's eyes are wide— she's never seen them this close together, never imagined her parents as people who might have loved each other. It's a gift Julie wishes she could give her daughter, but looking into the light, lovely blue of Beck's eyes, it feels as if she can almost, finally see things clearly.

Julie holds Beck's hand as they walk through Central Park. The sun peeks shyly from behind a cloud, and the trees are yellow green with new leaves. It is warm, and she and Beck have happily shed their winter coats and boots. The park is crowded with bikers, runners, couples walking, mothers pushing strollers. Picnic blankets.

It is beautiful, and she wishes that Reba could be there with her. The real Reba, and not some impossibly perfect idea. She wishes Reba had told her the truth all those years ago. She would have gotten angry like teenagers do, and they would have gotten past it, like good friends get past lies, even big ones. It's a version of a fantasy she's had a hundred times, probably, since finding out the truth, but now she sighs and lets it finally drift away. She can't change any of it.

It only took a few days for her anger to fade once she returned to New York, and she was glad, then, that she'd left the diary in the sealed envelope outside Toby's gallery. Julie *isn't* the same as Toby, isn't vindictive like him, not really. She couldn't keep Reba's words from him, no matter that he held the truth from her for so many years. Toby's pain isn't the same as hers, she knows, but that doesn't mean that his wounds aren't real. She knows it was the right thing when she remembers the long scars along his wrists and how he'd crumbled to the floor at the mention of Reba's name. Those paintings. And Julie had felt lighter once the journal was out her hands, out of her possession. Now it is gone, to Toby, where it will heal him or hurt him, she isn't sure which.

"Where are we meeting Daddy?" Beck asks.

"On the bridge."

Beck laughs. "But which one?"

"This one." Julie watches the pigeons, gray-blue and shiny, pecking at the sidewalk. When she looks up, she sees Evan in the distance, walking toward them. These two beautiful, charming people—one of them is hers, and the other *could* be, maybe.

He raises his hand in greeting, and Beck waves back frantically. Julie falters as they cross the bridge, though the wood is sturdy enough beneath her weight. When they reach him, his hands on hers feel crisp and dry as long-dead petals. And he isn't enough.

Evan takes Beck's hand, and Julie kisses her good-bye. It's a Friday afternoon, the start of Beck's weekend with her father. Julie doesn't watch them walk away, only turns back and crosses the bridge, one steady step at a time. A street vendor has a small kiosk set up near the bridge. "Flower, miss?" he asks as she approaches. He holds one out to her and she looks at it, the fragile droop of the bloom, the petals stained carmine. And she should know, as she pulls a few bills from her wallet and takes the flower on a whim, that something is about to change. But she walks alone, past the bridge and the water that is trickling along, unsure, but moving still.

98

August hasn't been able to stop thinking about Jules since Lawrence Mill, can't get her out of his head no matter how hard he tries. It's brought him back here to New York, and now he's standing outside her door. Same old song and dance. He doesn't know what to expect, how she'll react. Maybe it was over for her after Lawrence Mill. Maybe that strange night was more about closure for her than anything else, any kind of spark.

Either way, whether she wants him or not, there's still one last thing he hasn't shared with her. One last confession he needs to make. And she's not going to like it.

Meeting Reba was never an accident. August had come to Lawrence Mill angry at his parents for pulling him out of his school in Richmond, where he was popular and well-liked. There was a girlfriend he'd left behind. It was the end of the world for him, being dragged to some godforsaken hick town in the middle of nowhere.

He'd been bitter about the whole thing. For that first week, he wouldn't even speak to his parents, just took his camera out and disappeared for hours. And then his dad had gotten grief from some asshole at work. August overheard his parents talking about it, and all at once, he had a new and narrow focus for his anger.

Even before the Internet, finding someone was easy enough. When he knew the guy's name, he'd gotten hold of the local Yellow Pages to find his home address. The plan for revenge was only half formed—eggs and toilet paper, maybe, some kind of property destruction. But when he went to scope out the house, he saw her. He knew her face. It was the girl from outside that rickety shack of a store, where he'd been snapping photos for a few days. When his flash had gone off, she'd stood up and stared right out at him. He hadn't even known she was there.

Gorgeous, young, sweet, and probably the apple of her racist father's eye.

And so his plans changed.

He'd read in the paper about the whole debacle with Penny Decker and James Whoever. He knew what he was doing. He *wanted* to start something. He was dying to.

It was easy enough to make sure that she saw him the next time he was out with his camera, to pretend that he was running away from her. To let her chase him.

He'd wanted to make Reba fall for him, wanted her daddy to catch them together, wanted the whole damned town to know about it. Wanted to get his adolescent revenge. Mr. McLeod was the symbol of everything that had messed up his teenaged life, and he could *do* something about it. All he had to do was manipulate one pretty girl.

He never thought he'd actually fall for Reba. He scrapped his entire plan after that afternoon in the flower shop, when he'd shown her his photographs and she'd talked about those lilies. Once he cared about her, it was impossible to take his revenge at her expense.

But still. He'd gone looking for Reba, gone out with a mission—to use her for his own purposes. When he and Jules were back in Lawrence Mill together, she kept looking at him like he was some kind of saint, like he was the only honest thing in a river of lies. But he wasn't, isn't, and she needs to know.

Julie holds the lily to her nose as she walks home, breathing in the powerful fragrance, spinning the stem in her palm. The scent is so strong that, in the elevator up to her floor, she feels almost light-headed. Like being in Nell's Flower Shop all over again, except now the aroma doesn't invoke panic but something else, something heavy and sensual. She feels the strangest sense of anticipation that she doesn't understand, until the elevator doors open again and she sees August standing outside her door. August, who should be in Virginia right now, back to his life, and not here in New York, pacing back and forth outside her door, a bouquet of flowers in his hands.

"Jules," he says, his smile uncertain. His face is familiar and not, alluring and accepting, and she knows, as surely as she'd known since the night she arrived home from Lawrence Mill, though she hadn't breathed a word of it, how much she's missed him. How badly she wants to know him.

"Yes," she whispers, as the lily falls, forgotten, from her fingers to the carpeted floor of the hallway.

He can't risk it, not now, with her looking at him like no one has in such a long time. Not with that smile on her face.

Her embrace is warm and comforting and almost perfect. It probably doesn't even matter that he can't come clean.

READING
GROUP GUIDE

1. How does Reba's diary serve as a narrative device within the story?

2. What do you think is Julie's central motivation for agreeing to return to Lawrence Mill?

3. Who, if anyone, do you think is responsible for Reba's death?

4. How is the relationship between Julie and Evan similar to the relationship between Reba and August? How are the two relationships different?

5. Why do you think Nell never told anyone (not even Toby) about Reba's diary?

6. How do you think Toby will react to Reba's diary once he reads it? Will it change anything for him?

7. Racism is an ugly stain on the town of Lawrence Mill. How would things have been different if Reba's parents—and the town—had been more accepting of an interracial couple?

8. Do you think Reba and Toby really loved each other, or was their relationship purely physical?

9. Why is Reba's innocence so important to Julie? Do you think people hold their friends to higher standards than the ones they set for themselves?

10. In what ways is the decaying old mill a metaphor for the relationships in Julie's life?

A CONVERSATION
WITH THE AUTHOR

Where did you get the idea for *Secrets of Southern Girls*?

I've always been interested in how a person's past shapes and informs who they become in the present. I'm also fascinated by identity and self-awareness—how we see ourselves versus how other people see us. I knew I wanted to take those big concepts, add two teenage friends, and drop it all into a small town and see what happened. Things took off from there.

Of all the relationships in the book, which one do you think is the most important?

The friendship between Julie and Reba, definitely. Despite the romantic involvements, it's the friendship between these two girls that really drives the story forward: what they each want out of their friendship, what they expect from each other, the secrets that drive them apart. Julie puts no store in romantic entanglements (until Evan, at least), but she carries the weight of this broken friendship with her for a decade.

Why did you choose to make Reba and Julie's friendship so pivotal to this story?

I had a very clear picture in my mind of these two friends: one of them a free spirit who was quite intellectually and emotionally mature for her age and yet very innocent at the same time, and the other who had a certain level of sexual maturity but lacked that emotional knowledge. I was enamored by their friendship, and I wondered what kinds of trouble they'd get themselves into, both together and on their own.

What was your inspiration for the town of Lawrence Mill?

I grew up in a small town in the south, which gave me some logistical inspiration (mainly, the mill itself). But I wanted to create a town where not everything is friendly and charming and happy. I wanted to create a town that had some ugly to it, that had a dark side. The racism in Lawrence Mill isn't exactly a secret. I think that, unfortunately, that's not too far removed from reality for some small towns in the south, even today. It's something that I was afraid to write about, and that's how I knew it was something I *needed* to write about.

Which character from *Secrets of Southern Girls* was your favorite to write?

Believe it or not, Toby was my favorite. He's a complete mess, but I was so invested in his journey. Throughout the writing process, his voice was the one that came to me the clearest.

There's music in the background in many of the pivotal moments in *Secrets of Southern Girls*. Why did you choose to make music so prominent?

A few reasons. One is that I love nineties alternative music, and I was excited for a chance to make it part of this story. The other is that

I think there is a special relationship we have with music when we're growing up, where a song can have a powerful, lasting effect. I don't think we are quite as susceptible to that power as adults. It made sense to me that in those very intense moments between Reba and Toby, not only would there be music playing, but they would *notice* it.

How long have you been writing?

For as long as I can remember. My grandpa had this shiny electric typewriter when I was a kid, and I remember the first time he let me use it. I fell in love. I would sit there for as long as he'd let me, typing story after story. Luckily, the stories have evolved (somewhat) since then.

Where do you find inspiration for your writing?

Everywhere. Mostly, by trying to pay attention to everyday life. I find that the ideas I take the farthest are based on one very mundane kernel of truth, turned around and around until something that began as commonplace ends up as something else, something twisted and complicated.

ACKNOWLEDGMENTS

I would like to thank the following people for helping bring this book to life, and for being simply wonderful humans in general.

Hugs and kisses for my mom, for instilling in me a radical notion that I could do and be anything. I believed you. To Papa, for bringing me back down to earth—as only a dad can—when I let that radical notion get out of hand. You're the best in a crisis. Thank you for your advice and love.

To Mike, my dad (some of us get two), for never saying no to five-year-old me when I showed up at your recliner with a stack of children's books and the demand that you READ.

My grandparents, for all the stories. I hope you never read this book but are proud of me anyway.

To my wonderful team at New Leaf Literary & Media. All of the glitter and confetti for Suzie Townsend, the best agent a girl could ask for. I can't thank you enough for all of your hard work to make my dream a reality. Sara Stricker, you are a ray of sunshine. Thank you to Hilary Pecheone, Kathleen Ortiz, Mia Roman, Pouya Shahbazian, and Chris McEwen. I'd be nowhere without you.

To the wonderful folks at Sourcebooks. Shana Drehs, you are an incomparable editor. Your insight has made this book so much better, and being on this journey with you has been so much fun! Thank you for making my debut experience fantastic. Thanks to Liz Kelsch,

Heather Hall, Adrienne Krogh, Danielle McNaughton, Heather Morris, Valerie Pierce, and Heidi Weiland. I'm so grateful to have you all in my corner.

To Philip Lee Williams: literary mastermind, mentor, and, most importantly—friend. Your guidance, support, and wisdom have brought me back every time I thought about walking away from the writing life.

To Whitney Hoffman: reader, editor, and sweet friend. And Jason Lemper, Man of Honor for life. I could fill a book with our antics.

To Jess Dallow, who first plucked my little story from obscurity. I'm so grateful to call you my friend.

To Quentin and Barkley, my two furry babies, for all of the love and snuggles. You've both made my life so much better.

To my 17 Scribes debut group: I've learned so much from all of you, and I'm grateful to have had such a wonderful support system during this year.

To Brenda Drake, fairy godmother of the writing world. Thank you for all you do.

To my coworkers at my day job. Thanks for making every day fun!

Finally, to Patrick. For keeping our house from falling down around us while I chase my dream. For being my moral compass. For making me smarter. For everything you do, and everything you are. I love you.

ABOUT THE AUTHOR

Haley Harrigan lives in Athens, Georgia, with her husband and their adorably quirky Yorkshire Terrier. She holds degrees in creative writing and public relations from the University of Georgia. This is her debut.

Photo credit: Anne Yarbrough
of Anne Yarbrough Photography